CREAM TEASE

'Six shillings?' he answered in apparent disbelief.

'Well . . . maybe a crown then . . . four?'

'Six,' Sapphie insisted.

For a moment Mr Sumner said nothing, his face growing gradually redder as he looked from one girl to the other. 'You really mean it, don't you?'

'Yes,' Sapphie answered.

His expression changed slowly, to a dirty smirk. Again he spoke.

'Down here then, by the sluice, where we're out of view, but I don't know about six shillings. Two and six is the going rate in Bristol, and that's for the works.'

'One crown.'

'Done, but for that I'll want those bubbies out.' Without a word, Hazel began to unfasten her dress.

CREAM TEASE

Aishling Morgan

This book is a work of fiction.
In real life, make sure you practise safe, sane and
consensual sex.

First published in 2003 by
Nexus
Thames Wharf Studios
Rainville Road
London W6 9HA

www.nexus-books.co.uk

Typeset by TW Typesetting, Plymouth, Devon

Printed and bound by
Clays Ltd, St Ives PLC

ISBN 0 352 33811 3

Contents

1

Steeple Ashwood, Somerset – September 1938

'Are you sure he's like that?' Holly asked.

'Absolutely certain,' Sapphie answered her.

'Certain sure,' Hazel agreed. 'The way he stares at us, how could he not be? I still don't see why it should be me who does it.'

'Because,' Sapphie stated, 'you are the housekeeper's daughter, and we are ladies. Besides, you have done it before. We wouldn't even begin to know how to go about it.'

'But it's your dress,' Hazel answered, her pretty face setting briefly into a sulky pout, only to brighten again as she noticed a cluster of particularly fine blackberries in the hedge. Reaching up, she selected the largest of the fruit and popped it into her mouth. Sapphie turned to her.

'What do you think you are doing?'

'Eating blackberries. Want one?'

'You'll get juice all over your face and hands, stupid! You look a fine little baggage as it is, without having a dirty face.'

Hazel stopped, her expression growing more sulky than ever as she stepped down from the hedge to the hard earth of the lane. Sapphie ignored her, walking forwards faster than before. Holly spoke.

'You can have as many as you like on the way back.'

Hazel didn't answer, but began to walk more slowly, meandering back and forth across the lane. Finally Sapphie lost patience.

'Do come on, Hazel! You know what will happen if you don't hurry, don't you?'

Immediately Hazel's expression changed to alarm. She hurried forward. Holly spoke again.

'But what shall we say?'

'I shall speak to him,' Sapphie said confidently. 'It's called the Solitary Vice, I've seen it in a book.'

'What book?'

'The Solitary Vice, stupid. It's on the top shelf, right in one corner.'

'Oh.'

For a moment none of them spoke, Sapphie walking purposefully on, Holly following, Hazel taking a moment to pop a surreptitious blackberry into her mouth. The lane came to an abrupt halt, the hedges giving way to a view across the flat, open fields of the Somerset Levels. Some two hundred yards away a man stood beside a sluice, clipboard in hand as he made a careful note of something. He was middle-aged, stocky, dressed in a cheaply cut suit of charcoal grey cloth starkly at odds with the rural surroundings. Sapphie gave a satisfied nod.

'There we are. I said he'd be here.'

'Yes, he is, but . . .' Holly began, only to stop, and then continue in a nervous babble. 'You're not really going to ask him, are you, Sapphie? I mean, how will you address him? You can't call him Mr Peeper, he'll be dreadfully insulted, and besides, solitary vice sounds silly, because Hazel will be doing it, won't she, so it won't be solitary . . .'

She broke off at a hard look from Sapphie. Behind them, Hazel had paused to eat more blackberries, her fingers and lips already stained purple.

'What shall I call it then?' Sapphie demanded.

Hazel paused to swallow her mouthful before answering.

'The boys in the village call it "making the little bald man sick".'

'I don't think that's very polite,' Holly protested.

'It's not a polite thing to do, Holly,' Sapphie pointed out, 'and do stop that, Hazel, you look a complete frouste.'

'I do not! And if I do, why don't you do it then?'

'Hazel Mullins!'

Hazel opened her mouth to reply, but shut it abruptly. As she glanced across the field to the man from the Water Authority her sulky pout returned, stronger than ever.

'I think "Pearl Fishing" is a nice way to say it,' Holly said thoughtfully.

'That's for girls, stupid,' Sapphie answered her.

'Well, it ought to be something nice,' Holly insisted. 'Something romantic. I don't like to use nasty words.'

'Romantic?' Sapphie echoed in disbelief. 'She's going to offer to pull on Mr Peeper's John Willy, Holly. I hardly think that is romantic.'

'Well it should be. Perhaps if she says she'll play with him?'

'He'll think I mean blind man's buff or something,' Hazel objected.

'No, he won't, not Mr Peeper,' Sapphie said with conviction. 'Now do come on!'

Sapphie set off across the field, walking fast, a picture of grace and confidence with her pale blue summer dress floating around her legs and her long, pale hair hanging loose down her back. The others followed, Holly looking nervous and twisting a strand of rich brown hair around one finger as she went, Hazel dragging her feet at the back. The man looked up as they approached, his ruddy features working into a guilty leer as he saw who it was.

'Good afternoon,' Sapphie addressed him confidently.

'Good afternoon, girls,' he rasped, his tiny eyes flicking between them at the level of their chests. You're Miss Yates, aren't you, from the hall?'

'I am,' Sapphie answered and gestured to the others. 'May I introduce my friend, Miss Holly Bomefield-Mullins, and Hazel Mullins, who is a maid.'

He nodded to each, now grinning openly. Sapphie went on.

'I am afraid we do not have the pleasure of your acquaintance.'

'Mr Sumner,' he answered. 'Surveyor. Been blackberrying? Nice day for it.'

'How d'you do, Mr Sumner,' Sapphie went on. 'Now, my friend Hazel has something to say to you. Go on, Hazel.'

As she spoke she had pushed Hazel forwards. Immediately Mr Sumner's eyes fixed on Hazel's chest, where her brown curls lay over the full swell of her breasts, the cheap material of her dress doing little to hide their shape, or the twin points of her nipples. She looked back, her expression growing more sulky than ever as she took in the reddened lump of his nose, his bristling moustache and the roll of sunburned fat where his collar met his neck. He looked at her in expectation. She said nothing.

'Go on,' Sapphie urged.

Hazel threw Holly a pleading look, then one of reproach to Sapphie. Both were ignored. At last she spoke.

'I've got to offer to . . . to do you in my hand . . . to beat your tom tom for you. For six shillings.'

'Six shillings?' he answered in apparent disbelief.

'Well . . . maybe a crown then . . . four?'

'Six,' Sapphie insisted.

For a moment Mr Sumner said nothing, his face growing gradually redder as he looked from one girl to

4

the other. When he did speak there was anger in his voice.

'You're having me on, aren't you? Why you wicked little –'

'No,' Sapphie interrupted, even as Holly had begun to back away. 'Our offer is entirely genuine, rest assured, for Hazel to play with you for six shillings.'

He looked at her, his gaze shifty, doubtful, as if searching her face for signs of deceit or amusement. She remained serene, although Holly's stomach was fluttering and Hazel looked as if she was going to be sick. Finally he spoke.

'You really mean it, don't you?'

'Yes,' Sapphie answered.

His expression changed slowly, to a dirty smirk. Again he spoke.

'Down here then, by the sluice, where we're out of view, but I don't know about six shillings. Two and six is the going rate in Bristol, and that's for the works.'

'The works?' Holly queried.

'A good, hard fuck,' Mr Sumner answered, clicking his tongue on the final syllable and then chuckling as all three girls went abruptly red.

'Well, all right, two and six,' Hazel said doubtfully.

'No,' Sapphie broke in. 'A half crown may buy what you say in Bristol, Mr Sumner, but we are not in Bristol, while I am quite certain that Hazel is of a beauty rarely encountered . . .'

She paused. Mr Sumner was nodding, his eyes fixed to Hazel's ample chest, which she had pushed out to make the best of her figure. He swallowed.

'Four shillings.'

'One crown.'

'Done, but for that I'll want those bubbies out.'

Without a word, Hazel began to unfasten her dress.

'Down here, love, down here,' Mr Sumner urged. 'You'll get us seen.'

5

Hazel stepped forwards, still fiddling with the fastenings of her dress. He scrambled down beside the sluice to stand on the narrow concrete ledge beside the water. As he reached a hand up, she took it, her dress falling open as she climbed down to reveal her bare shoulders and the full swell of her bosom.

'No brassière?' he queried, licking his lips.

'Hardly,' Sapphie remarked, Holly making a nervous adjustment to her own garment.

'You should,' Mr Sumner rasped, 'shows 'em off better, not that yours need much more showing off . . . My, you do have a big pair, don't you?'

He had finished as Hazel's breasts came bare, two plump pillows of pale girl-flesh topped by stiff, rose pink nipples. Mr Sumner stood transfixed, spittle running down his chin as he admired them. When he finally spoke it was in a hoarse croak.

'My but you are lovely. May I touch them?'

'If you must,' Hazel sighed.

He immediately wiped his hands on his trousers, then reached out, to take one fat pink globe in each hand. His tongue flicked out to lick up the spittle from his chin as he began to fondle them, squeezing and running his thumbs over her nipples, and all the while muttering endearments while his eyes seemed about to pop out. Only when he tried to put his mouth to a nipple did Hazel start back.

'Mr Sumner!'

He growled something unintelligible and released her breasts. His hands went straight to his fly, to fumble the buttons open with shaking fingers. Holly watched, unable to take her eyes away despite her butterflies and the hard lump in her throat, wondering how a man's cock would look in the flesh. She swallowed hard as he delved into his underwear, and took hold of Sapphie's arm.

Mr Sumner pulled out a thick, dirty brown penis, already swollen, but with the bulbous head still well concealed within an unpleasantly meaty foreskin, the slit at the end showing a tiny bead of fluid. Holly's mouth came wide at her first sight of a man's cock, in wonder, at how something so ugly could at once be so compelling. The thought of touching it made her feel sick, yet there was no denying the horrible, and scarcely resistible, urge to do exactly that.

Hazel showed no such anxiety, reaching down to take hold of the hideous thing and starting to tug in a casual manner. There was something resentful in her manner, and a little disgust, but no more than when she was made to muck out the horses or any other task she considered inappropriate to her position.

Already Mr Sumner's cock was starting to stiffen, his foreskin rolling back with each tug of Hazel's hand to reveal ever more of the wet, red knob within. He went back to pawing her breasts and she didn't try to stop him, just tugging faster at his rapidly growing cock. Soon the head was out, red and shiny in the September sunlight, bulbous with pressure, the neck caked with a pasty white substance. For the first time in her life Holly caught the scent of cock, setting her gagging even as her nipples came to attention in the confines of her bra and her quim gave an all too familiar tingle.

Sumner had begun to grunt, and Hazel tugged faster still, steadying herself against the concrete wall of the sluice as she masturbated him with a frenzied jerking motion. His cock was now fully erect, the great turgid head glossy with pressure, the shaft taut in Hazel's hand. Her bare boobs were bouncing to the motions, the plump, soft flesh quivering in his hands as he groped, her nipples rock hard, two firm, fleshy points the size of the largest of the blackberries she had been eating. His hand went to her wrist, suddenly, to halt her frantic wanking in mid-stroke.

'Suck me,' he groaned, 'go on, love, take it in that pretty mouth.'

7

'Why, you dirty –' Hazel began, only to be cut off by Sapphie.

'Six shillings, Mr Sumner.'

He grunted, 'Bitch!'

'Six shillings, Mr Sumner,' Sapphie repeated, her tone revealing no more than the slightest catch.

He hesitated. Hazel went back to masturbating him, now slowly, running her thumb over the fleshy excess of foreskin beneath his shaft. He moaned.

'Yes . . . like that . . . only with your tongue. I'll pay.'

Hazel gave a long sigh of resignation, but went down on one knee. Mr Sumner placed a hand on top of her abundant brown curls, to guide her towards his cock. She turned one last glance towards Sapphie, of deep reproach, then took the thick, dirty brown erection into her mouth. Her cheeks sucked in, her full lips pushed out, and she was sucking. Holly continued to watch, in mingled fascination and disgust, sick to her stomach, but wondering how it would feel, and taste, to suck on a man's penis. She bit her lips, imagining going down on her knees, her mouth coming wide, the big, ugly, smelly cock thrust at her face, then in her mouth . . .

She shook herself, trying to push away the disturbing thoughts and the desire to take Hazel's place at Mr Sumner's feet. It was impossible, disgusting, that she should be made to do anything of the sort, yet she knew full well that, had it not been for Hazel, that was exactly what she would have been doing. Closing her eyes, she tried to imagine herself responding to the polite attentions of some well-bred young man. It didn't work. At a particularly wet sound she opened them again, to stare in rapt attention at the thick brown shaft moving wetly in and out between Hazel's lips.

Mr Sumner was getting urgent, his face red, beads of sweat running down over his forehead, his hand clutching in Hazel's curls. Suddenly he had grabbed what little of his cock protruded from her mouth, making a ring of his fingers to tug frantically at the shaft, fast, faster, and stop. Hazel's eyes went wide, her cheeks blew out, something white and sticky looking erupted from around her mouth. Immediately she pulled back, her face setting in utter revulsion.

'He's done his business in my mouth!' she exclaimed. 'I never . . .'

She trailed off, to spit a great, thick gobbet of sperm from her mouth on to the concrete wall, where it began to run down, the creamy white colour marked here and there with the purple of blackberry juice. Mr Sumner was oblivious, still milking the last of his come from his cock. Some went on to her breasts, to draw out a fresh exclamation of disgust from Hazel. Holly put her hand to her stomach, fighting down the urge to be sick.

'I trust that was to your satisfaction, Mr Sumner?' Sapphie asked.

'Very fine, thank you, Miss,' he answered as he tucked his cock back into his trousers.

Hazel stood, a trickle of lilac coloured spunk running down her chin, her eyes downcast as she began to fasten her dress.

'Six shillings, I think we agreed,' Sapphie stated casually.

Mr Sumner didn't answer immediately, buttoning his fly before digging into his jacket pocket. He brought out a handful of change, which he began to count.

'Don't you have a crown?' Sapphie asked.

He shook his head, still counting. Hazel had covered herself, although her straining nipples still made two very obvious bumps beneath the fabric of her dress. Holly turned her face away as the two big breasts were covered. Despite a sense of relief that it was over, she found it impossible not to feel a touch of disappointment at how brief the act had been, and a thrill at having watched. Finally Mr Sumner spoke.

'Four and threepence ha'penny.'

'Four shillings, three pence and a half-penny?' Sapphie responded.

'I'm sorry, my dear,' Mr Sumner said. 'I thought I'd more. Seems I haven't.'

'Mr Sumner –' Sapphie began angrily, only to be interrupted by Hazel.

'That's plenty enough, let's just take it.'

She had held out her cupped hands as she spoke, and Mr Sumner poured the money into them. Sapphie spoke again, irritably.

'We had agreed on six shillings, Mr Sumner.'

'No cause to be disagreeable, my dear,' he answered. 'Call round for it later. My lodgings are above the White Lion.'

'I hardly think it would be suitable for us to come to the lodgings of a single gentleman,' Sapphie pointed out. 'Never mind if they are above a public house.'

He shrugged.

'You must pay us the balance of what you owe next time you see us,' she went on, 'and –'

'I'm off to Bristol tomorrow,' he cut in. 'If you want your money, come to the White Lion.'

'That, as you well know, is out of the question,' Sapphie snapped. 'You must –'

'Not to mind,' Hazel broke in. 'We'll take what we have, but if that should happen again, Mister, you are to do your business in your hand.'

'I prefer it in the mouth,' he answered.

Hazel was going to reply, but shut up at an angry gesture from Sapphie. Instead she climbed up from the dyke. He chuckled as they set off back across the field, Sapphie still chiding Hazel.

'Now we shall have to use a cheaper pattern, or forego the lace. Really, I said we should make him pay first.'

'He'd still only have had four and threepence ha'penny,' Hazel pointed out, 'and that only leaves us

. . . eight pence ha'penny short of what you needed anyways.'

Holly stayed quiet, thinking of how it would have felt if it was her who had been made to suck on the big, ugly cock until it erupted its fluid into her mouth.

2

London – October 1938

Alexander Gorringe turned into the Haymarket to find the bulky form of his friend Herbert Maray coming the other way. They linked arms by old habit, turning to the north as Alexander spoke.

'How was Devon?'

'Wet, muddy. I'm just back.'

'And the relict?'

'Cousin Genevieve? Completely dotty, absolutely raving. We shipped her off to a sort of genteel bin in Exeter. Best place for her.'

'I dare say. So that makes you Squire of Kerslake, does it?'

'I imagine it does, not that I can sell just yet, otherwise I would. It's too remote for me, even as a country place. How about here?'

'Pretty grim. Chamberlain's gone over to Germany again, but it won't make a blind damn of difference. They'll invade and we won't do a ruddy thing about it.'

'Well, so long as there's peace.'

'Not a chance. Hitler's spoiling for a fight. After the Sudetenland it'll be somewhere else, Alsace and Lorraine probably. There'll be war, no question about it.'

'Do you really think so? And we'll be drawn into it?'

'Realistically, yes.'

'Hell. So what can we expect, bombing raids I suppose, and gas . . .'

'That and more.'

'Hmm, perhaps Devon's not such a bad idea after all.'

'I wouldn't bother. They'll call you up anyway.'

'Do you think so?'

'Sure to, a man of your age, although they'll want a few stones off you.'

Alexander prodded Herbert's bulging torso, his finger sinking well into the fat despite the thick tweed jacket in the way. Herbert ignored it and continued to speak.

'I must say you seem pretty sanguine. You'll be in the thick of it, of course.'

'Damned if I will!'

'No? How do you expect to avoid it? Damn it man, you're a fighter pilot!'

'Oh, I dare say I can persuade Uncle Reggie that I'd be of most use in some cushy billet. After all, he practically runs the Ministry, and Mater will give him hell if doesn't make sure I'm out of trouble. Papa's not above pulling a few strings either, so long as it's nothing too obvious.'

'Well, yes, I suppose you're right. Don't suppose I could get in on the act, do you, old man?'

'Well, perhaps, if you were able to make some useful contribution. Better to volunteer than to wait until you get called up in any case. That way you get a much better chance of dodging the bullets.'

'Well, there's my place in Devon. Now they've packed old Genevieve off to the bin I can do as I please.'

'That's a thought. Let me work on it. I was going to speak to Reggie this afternoon, as it goes, after a quick whore. Join me?'

'For a whore or at the Ministry?'

'For a whore, you fool ... No, on second thoughts, both. I have an idea.'

'Oh, yes?'

'Yes indeed. Don't worry about a thing. I'll explain presently. Meanwhile, there really is nothing like a good whore to stimulate the mind.'

As he finished, Alexander made a dash across the road, neatly inserting himself between a bus and a delivery van. Herbert followed more slowly, holding on to his hat as he threaded his way through the traffic to the safety of the opposite pavement. By the time they had reached the far side of Shaftesbury Avenue Herbert was red faced, prompting Alexander to use his friend's school nickname as they came together on the pavement.

'You want to lay off the starchy foods, Puffer, or at least cut down.'

'I am on a strict regime,' Herbert answered in an offended tone. 'I can take meat only –'

'Look, there's that oily little pimp, Bob Tweedie,' Alexander interrupted hastily. 'D'you suppose he's any new girls in?'

'Couldn't say. Let's ask.'

They approached Tweedie, a small, neatly dressed man with his hair slicked back, the impression of the expense and cut of his clothes given the lie only by his bearing. He recognised them immediately and turned into a side street without speaking. After a quick glance up and down the road, Alexander followed, Herbert loitering nervously behind.

'Afternoon, Mr Alexander,' Tweedie greeted him, 'and what can I do for your good self, sir?'

'Anything new, Tweedie?' Alexander demanded.

'New? Yes, a beauty, gorgeous, a real pin-up. Irish girl, red hair. Molly's the name. Ten shillings an hour.'

'Ten shillings an hour! Good God, man, what are you, a pimp or a ruddy bandit?'

'There's no need for bad language, Mr Alexander. Seven, then, and you can have your money back if you ain't satisfied.'

'Do you really expect me to believe that? No, don't answer that. Very well, seven shillings for an hour, but she had better be good.'

14

'Oh, she is, Mr Alexander, sir, she is. What about your friend, or will you be sharing?'

'No, he'll have one too. Something exotic, plenty of meat.'

Herbert nodded enthusiastically.

'Got just the thing,' Tweedie answered. 'Yankee girl, name of Cora, black as your hat, tits like footballs.'

'That will do nicely,' Herbert put in.

'I'll do her for seven and all,' Tweedie went on. 'Normal, like, I'd want ten, but seeing as you're . . .'

'Ten shillings the pair,' Alexander cut in, extracting a single red-brown note from his billfold.

'Ten the pair?' Tweedie answered in exaggerated shock. 'Have a heart, Mr Alexander, sir. I got to clothe 'em and feed 'em, and they don't come cheap, not good girls like . . .'

Alexander made to return the note to his billfold, only to have it snatched from his hand.

'Ten it is then, sir,' Tweedie said quickly, 'but you're robbing me.'

'Which hotel?' Alexander demanded.

'No hotel, sir, no, not for you, sir. I got Molly set up in a flat in Whitfield Street, halfway up, near enough, above the tobacconist's. I'll get Cora round there too. Give me half an hour?'

'Very well, but this had better be good, Tweedie.'

'Have I ever let you down, Mr Alexander?'

Alexander answered with a sceptical grunt. Tweedie melted into the crowd moving along Shaftesbury Avenue.

'Can we trust him?' Herbert asked.

'Absolutely,' Alexander replied. 'He's no fly-by-night, and he's hardly going to risk losing my custom for ten shillings.'

'Oh, right. Whitfield Street, then.'

They set off, walking slowly across Soho and up into Fitzrovia, to arrive at the house just as Tweedie did. On the pimp's arm was a black girl, her cheap dress stretched taut across an ample bosom and hinting at an equally well-padded bottom. She was young, considerably younger than Alexander had expected, with a bold and impudent look to her face. As Tweedie slid a key into the lock, Alexander was already considering demanding that Herbert take the Irish girl and leave him the black.

'Cora,' Tweedie announced as the two men approached, jerking his thumb over his shoulder to indicate the girl. 'Say hello, Cora.'

Cora's response was a knowing smile, revealing white teeth between her thick, sensuous lips. Alexander smiled back and gave his moustache a tug, wondering just how long she had been a prostitute to retain so much fire.

'Pleased to meet you, my dear,' he greeted her, letting his eyes wander over her breasts and down, to admire the tight curve of her waist and the swell of her hips. Behind him, Herbert managed a gurgled greeting.

The door swung open and Tweedie ushered them inside, one corner of his mouth twitching as his eyes flicked up and down the street. Alexander made a polite gesture, indicating that Cora should go in first. She put her hand to her mouth, giving a muted giggle as she went in. Alexander followed, his eyes fixed to her sweetly rotating rump as they climbed up first one flight of steep, uncarpeted stairs and then another. Her bottom was, if anything, more appealing than her breasts, round and full and firm, well worth his attention.

Tweedie had gone, although Alexander knew he would not be far away. On the second floor, Cora knocked at a door with peeling brown paint and a broken B hanging sideways from a single screw. The door swung open. Cora pushed inside and Alexander followed, into a room overlooking the street. The floor was bare, paint-smeared boards, a single battered table stood to one side, a chair pushed in beneath it. The smells of boiled cabbage, dust and general staleness assaulted his nose, only to be pushed from his mind as he focussed on the girl who had opened the door.

She was tiny, the top of her brilliant ginger hair barely reaching his chin, despite being piled up in a fashionable style. She was also young, perhaps even younger than Cora, with a face that radiated innocence and vulnerability, with ash-pale skin, freckles and great, pale green eyes. Her body was no less appealing, neat, compact, slim, but with enough flesh in the right places to set his cock stiffening in his trousers. Most of it was on show too, her sole garment a set of old-fashioned combinations cut short at the legs.

'Splendid,' he remarked, reaching out to take a pinch of her cheek, 'old Tweedie wasn't exaggerating for once. Well, Molly, my pretty, is there somewhere a little more comfortable in this fine residence?'

Her answer was a nervous smile and a bob curtsey, taking the hem of her combinations between thumbs and forefingers as if they were a dress. Alexander chuckled at the sight, marvelling at her pert innocence, and marvelling anew as she turned to walk across the flat, revealing her rear view, with two of the most sweetly formed bottom cheeks he had ever seen peeping out from beneath the hem of her combinations.

He followed, Herbert and Cora coming behind, already arm in arm, into a very different room, as overdone as the other had been sparse. Cheap, colourful hangings obscured the walls, save for where a huge and ancient bed stood. A thick but worn carpet hid the floor. There were several armchairs, a dresser strewn with Molly's things, a wardrobe with the door open to reveal tawdry finery within. The smell of cabbage had been replaced by that of cheap perfume.

'Well, I must say, Tweedie does you proud,' Alexander remarked, selecting the most comfortable looking of the armchairs.

'He says I'm his best girl, sir,' Molly answered, her voice barely more than a whisper, but showing a pride that astonished Alexander. 'He says I'm just for the bettermost folk, sir, the gentlemen.'

'I should think so too, my dear,' he answered, hiding his astonishment at her naivety. 'Now, why don't you come and sit yourself down on my lap?'

He reached out, to pat her delectable bottom on the bare cheek where it stuck out beneath the tattered fringe of her garment. Her flesh felt cool, firm and ivory smooth, sending a new pulse of blood to his rapidly swelling cock. She gave the smallest of giggles and obeyed, allowing him to steer her down on to his lap. He let out a sigh of appreciation as the softness of her bottom settled on his thigh. More flesh had bulged out around the hem of her combinations, and he took hold of it, kneading gently as he let himself relax.

Across the room, Herbert and Cora had wasted no time. She had taken charge, opening the front of her dress to spill out two huge breasts the colour of dark chocolate within a chemise hopelessly inadequate to the task of holding them in. Herbert just stared, entranced, as she opened the garment to pull them out, fat and round and firm, each crowned with a wide nipple, the flesh so dark as to be close to true black. The teats were erect, twin bulges the size of small corks, with which she began to play. Herbert put a hand to his cock.

Alexander sat back, casually fondling Molly's bottom as Cora leaned forwards to help Herbert. Molly gave an encouraging wiggle and a shy glance from the corner of one beautiful eye. Alexander turned his full attention to her, drawing her in to see if she would allow herself to be kissed. To his surprise, she gave no resistance, opening her mouth to his as if she had been a lover and not a paid tart. He made the best of it, enjoying a long kiss as his fingers slipped beneath the hem of her combinations and into the soft crease between her buttocks, and down.

18

Briefly, he allowed his fingers to loiter on her anus, stroking the little fleshy bumps around the tiny central hole and pushing briefly in, to send a shiver of reaction through her body. Lower, her quim was moist and puffy, the outer lips plump and soft around the wet, fleshy folds of the inner, her mound well grown with silky hair. He cupped her sex, masturbating her with his fingers as his thumb probed the hole of her vagina. It went in easily, her passage creamy and open, making him wonder if she was genuinely aroused by him, or had simply been recently fucked.

In either case her reaction seemed genuine, her kisses growing more passionate as he manipulated her sex, her arms tight around his neck and shoulders. He took hold of a breast, feeling the small but rounded globe of flesh through the cotton of her combinations before delving into them to pull it out. She grew more passionate still, wriggling against him and rubbing her quim on his hand.

His cock needed attention, urgently, but he had no intention of wasting the hour for which he had paid. Gently pulling Molly back, he released her sex and took hold of her waist, easing her down. She understood, her huge green eyes darting a nervous glance into his as she went to kneel between his open legs.

Across the room, Cora had pulled her dress off, to leave her in the open chemise and a pair of voluminous knickers which, despite their size and loose cut, were absolutely bulging with plump, female flesh. She was sat on the bed, playing with her huge breasts even as she tugged at the stout pink erection protruding from Herbert's trousers.

Alexander extracted a cigar from his pocket humidor as Molly worked on his fly, pausing to watch her tiny delicate fingers as one button after another popped open. As he went through the familiar operation of lighting up, she burrowed into his long-johns, her hand

19

closing quickly on his cock. As she struggled to get it out she gave a giggle of what he was sure was genuine pleasure and perhaps surprise. He was close to erect, and he had to help her, reaching down to stretch his fly apart and pull out the full mass of his genitals.

Molly gave a delighted squeak as his cock sprang free into her hand, and his last doubts that her pleasure was a pretence dissolved. Her eyes were bright as she admired his cock, stroking at the smooth white flesh with every evidence of pleasure, to bring him up to full, straining erection within moments. He drew on his cigar as she took him into her mouth, and blew out a cloud of fragrant smoke as she began to suck.

Cora seemed no less keen than Molly. She had taken Herbert's short, thick cock between her breasts and was jiggling them up and down, to make her flesh bounce and slap on his. He was wide-eyed in rapture as he watched, his face red, his cock looking fit to explode.

Reaching down, Alexander took a firm hold of Molly's hair. Her red curls pulled free, tumbling around her pretty face as he pulled her head back. For one moment she looked surprised, and she was going to speak, until he pressed her lips to his scrotum. Immediately she gaped, her mouth stretching as wide as it would go to take him in, like an over-eager puppy trying to cope with an impossibly large ball. She took his cock in hand, tugging at the thick, wet shaft as she sucked on his balls.

Herbert was going to fuck Cora, and Alexander settled down to watch, smoking as Molly attended to his cock and balls. The black girl had turned on the bed, kneeling to present Herbert with an ample bottom made to seem all the larger by comparison with her trim waist, her tummy no more than a little, soft bulge hanging beneath her. Herbert climbed on the bed, his trousers now down, his cock sticking up from his long-johns, the flesh wet with Cora's saliva. Resting his ample stomach on the girl's upturned bottom, he slid his cock into her.

She took it with a sigh, apparently of contentment, and was starting to moan as her fucking began. Herbert took hold of her hips, his fingers sinking into the soft brown flesh, to jam himself deeper in to her body and set her huge breasts quivering beneath her. Each push also sent a shiver through the flesh of her bottom, as if she was being spanked.

Alexander gave a low chuckle at the thought, and wondered if taking Molly across his knee and smacking her fleshy little behind up to a glowing red would make her more or less eager. She had done nothing to deserve it, but that made no difference, only the balance between the urgency of his cock and his desire to get the most for his money. With her rolling his balls across her tongue and stroking his cock, it was impossible to think of stopping her. He decided to forego or at least postpone the pleasure, and to come in the hope of managing a second before Tweedie grew importunate.

With a conscious effort of will, he detached Molly's head from his balls. She came up, smiling, her face smeared with lipstick, saliva running out from over her lower lip. Her beautiful green eyes were brighter than ever, her face flushed with excitement. Alexander felt the urge to turn her across his knee and spank her grow sharply stronger.

'Well, my darling,' he said, 'time you were put on my cock, but first, I think I'll warm that pert little arse for you. Over my lap.'

Molly's expression immediately gave way to fear. She began to babble.

'No, please, sir, don't spank me, not that ... I hate that!'

Alexander chuckled, the desire to see her squirm and hear her squeals of pain as her bottom danced growing stronger still with her words. She was begging, her hands clasped before her, her beautiful eyes bright with tears.

'Yes,' he said. 'I shall spank you. I shall spank you hard. Maybe I shall spank you until you start to blubber.'

'Please, sir, no!' she pleaded. 'Please, anything but that. I can't stand pain, I can't!'

His cock twinged, and he realised that if he did spank her he was certain to come as her flesh wriggled against his erection. The spanking could wait; his cock couldn't. Clasping his cigar firmly between his teeth, he reached down to take her under her arms and lift her. Molly shrieked, but she came up, not resisting physically, but still babbling for mercy.

He swung her up high, to leave her pert bottom hovering over his cock, the cheeks spilling from either side of the lacy rear of her combinations, which had pulled up into her crease. She gave a moan of relief as she realised she was going to be fucked and not spanked, mumbling her thanks over and over.

She was fumbling for the buttons at her crotch as he took his cock in hand. They came open, the flap of her combinations falling away to expose her underside, her quim swollen and ready, the twin lips pink with blood, the hole wet and fleshy. Alexander reached out, to tuck up her tails and expose the full glory of her bottom. She pushed it out obligingly, making a full, pale moon of her cheeks, with the valley between well open to show off the pale pink dimple of her anus.

The little hole looked tight and inviting, the centre a touch puffy from the attentions of his finger. Briefly he considered buggering her, only to decide to leave the treat for another day as her tiny white hand came back to enfold his cock and pull it to her sex. She sat, his cock sliding up into her sex as she came back, to leave her perched on his lap, nude and penetrated.

He went back to smoking his cigar as she began to move, lifting herself up and down on his cock. She was eager, her breasts in her hands as she fucked herself on his erection, her head thrown back with her glorious red hair a tangle of curls on her back. He could see the thick shaft moving in her hole and glimpse the tempting rosebud of her anus as her cheeks spread. She moved suddenly, cocking one leg over his, then the other, to spread her sex wide in front. Her hands went down, and he saw that she was masturbating. He let her do it, trying to resist the urge to take a last few hard pumps in her body and come as she bucked and wriggled on his erection.

Herbert had no such reserve. His face was crimson as he pounded into the black girl's bottom, his hands locked hard in the soft flesh of her hips, his great belly slapping and bouncing on her upturned rump. Both were grunting, in time. Cora had her eyes shut and her mouth wide, drool running from her big lips as she was fucked. Herbert stopped, moved back and his cock came free. For an instant it stood proud over her bottom, white with juice, before he had snatched it, to tug with furious energy for a moment before thick white spunk erupted over the black girl's bottom and back.

As Herbert subsided with a satisfied grunt, to collapse puffing on the bed, Alexander took his hands from Molly's waist long enough to applaud his friend's performance. His own cock was rock hard, and he knew he could come at any moment. Still he held back, until Molly's fucking motions took on a new urgency. As she began to gasp he felt her pussy contract on his cock and he was pushing for all he was worth. She screamed, writhing her bottom into his crotch with desperate urgency as she went into climax. He held on, keeping her hard down on his erection as it jerked in orgasm, to fill her hole with his own sperm.

She was still coming, and he let her, watching her pretty bottom wiggle and shake as she went through her convulsions, finally stopping to lie back against his body and snuggle into his chest. He let her, surprised at the

23

display of emotion, saying nothing, but stroking her back and hair as he returned his main attention to his cigar.

'Well,' he remarked as Herbert finally stopped puffing, 'Tweedie certainly lived up to his promise. That would have been a bargain at twice the price, and we've not spent over the half-hour yet.'

Herbert nodded his agreement, apparently too exhausted to reply. Alexander went on, addressing Molly.

'So, my dear, how long have you been at this game?'

Molly began to play with a lock of her hair before replying.

'Two weeks this Friday, sir.'

'Two weeks, eh? Good heavens, no wonder you fuck more like a housemaid than a tart. Hmm, I don't suppose you've any wine in the house, brandy perhaps?'

'I've gin,' Molly offered, easing herself up from his lap.

'Revolting stuff, no doubt,' he said. 'Fetch it anyway, there's a girl.'

He sent her on her way with a back-handed smack to her bottom, making her squeak and setting the little cheeks quivering as she hurried for the door. Wet noises sounded briefly as she douched before returning with a bottle and glasses. Alexander accepted one, finding the gin every bit as vile as he had expected, but drinking it anyway. Molly came back to sit on his lap with her own glass, again curling up against him.

With an unaccustomed touch of sympathy, Alexander decided that she was probably lonely, and postponed both the spanking and the buggering he had intended to give her for a future date. It made sense anyway, as he was sure to get better service if he befriended her. Not just that, but her shock and dismay when he finally did give her a beating or introduce his cock to her anus would be all the more delightful. She spoke again, her voice little more than a whisper.

'I was to be in service. That is why I came over, from Coleraine. Only when I went to the house I . . . I . . .'

'There, there,' Alexander broke in, worried that she was about to burst into tears, 'that's no way to behave. Here, have some more gin.'

He took her hand, to lift her glass to her lips. She drank, gulping the liquid down until the glass was empty.

'My, but you know how to put that back,' Alexander remarked. 'So, time for another bout, I dare say.'

'Not me,' Herbert answered him. 'I'm pegged out. Perhaps before the end.'

'No?' Alexander queried. 'Well then, Cora, my girl, come over and join little Molly and we'll see how long it takes the two of you to put me back in action.'

Cora came without hesitation, to kneel at his feet. She was now nude save for her stockings. As Molly stood she peeled off her combinations, putting herself into the same near naked condition. She went down, pushing in beside Cora, who had already begun to kiss at Alexander's cock and balls. He slid his body forwards a little to make it easier for them, and smiled as he looked down. Each had a pink tongue extended to lick at the meaty sac of his scrotum, their skin otherwise contrasting black and white, as sharp as the idea forming in his mind.

3

Steeple Ashwood, Somerset – March 1939

Sapphie Yates took a step back to admire her handiwork.

Hazel Mullins lay across a heavy wooden nursing stool, her position awkward and shameful in the extreme. For one thing the stool was small and had no padding, leaving the top pressed hard to her stomach. For another her wrists were strapped tight into the small of her back with the strings of her apron. This in turn made it impossible for her to protect her bottom, which was bare, with her skirts tucked up beneath her bound wrists and her big drawers in a tangle of cloth at the level of her knees. A thick leather belt secured her in place, kneeling, with two slimmer belts preventing her from moving her legs. Her thighs were considerably longer than the legs of the stool, which left her bottom the highest part of her body, and open. The plump, hairy bulge of quim stuck out from between her thighs at the back and her anus showed. She was also gagged, one of her own stockings balled up in her mouth and the other used to tie it in place. As a final humiliation, a long peacock father had been inserted into the wrinkly brown dimple of her bottom hole.

'Now,' Sapphie stated, pulling a snap-tipped riding whip from an ancient elephant's-foot umbrella stand, 'your lesson. When you bring me tea, you will not say "I've your tea, Sapphie", "Tea's up", or any other such vulgar phrase. Least of all, you will not say, "Teatime, Swallowtail". Do you understand?'

Hazel began to nod frantically. Sapphie brought the thick leather sting down on the helpless girl's bottom with a loud crack, to set the broad white buttocks quivering and leave an angular red mark. Hazel kicked out at the sudden pain, nearly upsetting the stool, but managed no more than a muffled squeal. Sapphie went on.

'When you bring me my tea, you are to say, "Your tea, Miss Sappho", or possibly, "Good afternoon, Miss Sappho", given that the presence of the tea tray is evidence enough of what you are doing. Now, what do you say?'

Hazel managed a string of muffled grunts in response. Sapphie bent the stem of the whip back as far as it would go, over Hazel's unprotected bottom. Holding it with just one finger, she looked into Hazel's eyes, her pleasure rising at the fear and consternation showing in them.

'What do you say?' she repeated.

Again Hazel struggled to answer, but produced only indistinct mumbles and grunts. Sapphie released the whip. Hazel's body jerked as the thick leather sting cracked down on her skin. Her eyes had shut in her pain, and stayed shut as the new welt turned from white to an angry red. Sapphie waited until the waving of the peacock feather in the girl's anus had died to a gentle quivering.

'What do you say?' Sapphie demanded, struggling to keep the laughter out of her voice as she bent the whip back once more.

Hazel's reply was frantic, an indistinct gabble of sound, but obviously a plea for mercy rather than any attempt to repeat the sentence. Sapphie sighed and once more released the whip. It hit, Hazel's bottom bounced and there came the muffled squeal of pain. Sapphie laughed, and set to work on Hazel's bottom, smacking the wicked little whip in again and again, on both buttocks, until her victim was wriggling frantically in her bonds and producing a desperate, agonised squeaking through her gag. Only when both full globes of Hazel's bottom had turned a rich red and the skin was beginning to prickle with sweat did Sapphie stop.

Hazel had placed the tea tray on a low table after being ordered to bend for punishment. Sapphie went to it, to pour herself a cup as she considered whether or not to inflict further torture on the unfortunate maid and, if so, what it should be. Hazel was looking at her, big, brown eyes wide and pleading, brown curls disarranged into an unruly mop, boobs shivering in her fright.

Still considering what to do, Sapphie reached for the single slice of lemon laid neatly on a plate. An idea came to her as she squeezed a little into her tea. Turning thought to action, she walked back to the helpless Hazel, whose eyes followed her every step. She reached for the peacock feather, to ease it from her victim's anus, leaving the tiny hole open for one moment before squeezing slowly shut.

Sapphie chuckled, and again pushed the peacock feather to the maid's tight anal orifice. Hazel gave a sob of misery even as the little brown hole relaxed. The feather went in, deeper than before. Sapphie began to probe, pushing the stem of the feather deeper in each time, faster and faster, watching the muscular ring work, until at last Hazel began to make noises in her throat. Sapphie was smiling as she poised the lemon over the cleft of Hazel's bottom. The feather came out. Hazel's anus pouted, open just for an instant, long enough, as Sapphie squeezed hard on the lemon, to spray juice directly into the open hole, and also on Hazel's quim.

For a moment nothing happened, only for Hazel's muscles to go suddenly tight. Lemon juice squirted from the maid's anus as it went into spasm, to trickle straight into the already well-stimulated hole of her quim. Sapphie pushed the peacock feather firmly back up Hazel's bottom. She laughed, out loud this time, as the maid went into a sort of fit, wriggling and squirming her bottom and kicking her feet on the floor in a desperate, futile effort to cut out the pain. Muffled sobs accompanied the ludicrous, panic-stricken movements, and as Sapphie went back to her tea she saw that the girl's eyes were squeezed tight shut, with the first tears welling up in each corner.

Sapphie sipped her tea, considering what to do, and whether she should answer the urgent tingling in her sex. It would be the work of moments to squat down, pull up her dress, pull down her knickers and press her quim to the maid's miserable, tear-stained face. Hazel would lick, perhaps with a little more encouragement, but she would lick . . .

The door swung open, something completely unexpected, which set Sapphie's heart hammering in expectation of discovery by Hazel's mother. It was Holly, and Sapphie's rush of fear was replaced by irritation. Holly looked down at the bound, gagged and red-bottomed Hazel.

'Whatever are you up too, Sapphie?'

'Nothing really,' Sapphie answered. 'I was bored.'

'Well, I do think you might have asked me to play too. Anyway, never mind all that. There's a letter for you. It looks frightfully important.'

'A letter?'

'From the Air Ministry.'

'Whatever could they want?'

'I don't know. Come and read it.'

'I shall.'

Sapphie swallowed another mouthful of tea and put the cup down to follow Holly from the old nursery where she had been tormenting Hazel. The bound girl's last, pleading look was ignored completely and she was left, the peacock feather trembling above her upturned buttocks in a new and more urgent wave of panic. Holly continued as Sapphie caught up with her.

'Kitty is terrified it will be something to do with war preparations, but your Mater say's they'll never call women up, and certainly not at your age.'

'I wouldn't think so.'

They ran quickly downstairs to the hall, where Hazel's mother, Kitty, and Sapphie's mother, Cicely, were standing. Sapphie took the letter, pulling the envelope quickly open without troubling to use the paperknife. Inside was a neatly typed letter on official paper. The name of the man who had sent it was given as Mr R Thann, along with a long and important sounding title.

'Who's Mr Thann?' Sapphie demanded, scanning the letter.

'Reginald Thann?' her mother queried.

'Maybe, something beginning with R. Must be . . . yes, he's signed it. Who is he?'

'A . . . ah . . . friend of Lady Cary.'

'My mother?' Holly asked. 'What . . .?'

'Read the letter, Sapphie dear,' Cicely Yates cut in.

'I shall,' Sapphie answered promptly. 'It says, Mr R Thann MP . . . rhubarb, rhubarb, rhubarb . . .

Dear Miss Yates,

I trust you will forgive my presumption in sending this letter, and wish you to know that I do so in a spirit of forgiveness and Christian charity. It can scarcely have escaped your attention, or at least that of your mother, that our great country is upon the brink of war. This may seem distant, unimportant even, in rural Somerset, but let me assure you that the threat is both real and imminent. In order to meet this challenge, it is possible that our resources will be stretched to the limit.

It is one of the benefits of high office that I am privileged to information not commonly available, including the details of those emergency measures that may need to be imposed in the event of war. Among these measures is conscription for women, and it is with regard to this that I wish to offer what you should consider friendly advice from one older and wiser in the ways of the world than yourself.

Bearing in mind your unorthodox upbringing, and despite your not ignoble parentage, it is unlikely that you will be offered a position commensurate with your family background. Indeed, in some quarters it is being suggested that no special considerations should be given to those of higher birth, a disgrace in my personal view. Therefore, I advise that you take up a position in the Women's Auxiliary Air Force without delay, upon which you may be assured of treatment befitting your status.

Should you choose to accept my advice, please . . .

. . . rhubarb . . . rhubarb . . . Yours, rhubarb . . . Well?'

'The pompous ass!' Cicely snapped.

'So who is this Thann?'

'As I said, a friend of Lottie's, well, an admirer really. He was no friend of mine, certainly. He used to say . . . no, never mind that. He was as dull as ditch water, and desperately earnest, nasty too. There was always something about him that made my skin crawl. I can't imagine why he would want to help me, let alone you, unless out of guilt.'

'Guilt?' Sapphie queried.

'He was pretty beastly around the time you were born. They all were.'

'He does say "forgiveness",' Holly pointed out.

'Yes,' Cicely replied, 'as if he has something to forgive. As a matter of fact, I wouldn't be at all surprised if he does think that. He always was a

31

moralising little prig. I suppose it would be the Christian thing to do, to come to the aid of the fallen sinner, at least now that he doesn't have to worry so much about his precious career.'

'His advice seems genuine enough, in any case,' Sapphie remarked thoughtfully.

'No doubt,' Cicely agreed. 'I don't suppose he has the imagination to lie, or at least, not about this sort of thing. He's the most dreadful snob as well, so I suppose it's possible he may simply have sent this letter to all and sundry, or at least, all and sundry not of "ignoble parentage".'

'Perhaps. But if it's sound advice ... I mean, I wouldn't like to end up working in a factory, or something dreadful like that. Do you suppose that's what he's getting at? I mean, women worked in factories in the Great War, didn't they?'

'Yes,' Cicely admitted.

'Then I shall consider his advice,' Sapphie answered. 'You'll want to come too, won't you, Holly? Hazel must also.'

'Have you seen my Hazel, Miss?' Kitty asked, speaking for the first time.

'Hazel? No, not at all,' Sapphie answered quickly. 'Holly, we must think about this, come upstairs.'

She made for the staircase, paused briefly at the top to ensure that she was not being followed, and walked briskly down the corridor to the old nursery. Hazel lay where she had been left. The peacock feather was still waving gently above her well-smacked bottom, only now there was a broad, yellow pool of urine on the floor beneath her, with drips still hanging from the sodden hair of her pubic bush.

4

Kerslake Manor, Devon – September 1939

'Not bad, not bad at all,' Squadron Leader Alexander Gorringe remarked as he looked up at the façade of Kerslake Manor. 'It always amazes me how much effort people put into architecture in out-of-the-way places. I mean to say, it's not as if anyone who matters is going to see it.'

'As it happens,' Flying Officer Herbert Maray answered him, 'when my grandfather had the estate the then Prince of Wales visited, twice.'

'Still, just what we need, eh?' Alexander answered, ignoring the comment. 'Well out of Jerry's way, and comfortable enough, by the look of things.'

'Very,' Herbert answered. 'Cousin Jervis and old Genevieve did themselves proud. I've put you in the South Room, there's a fine bay –'

'The South Room? Not the master bedroom then?'

'Well, no, that's mine, naturally . . .'

'I happen to be your commanding officer, Puffer! I have to maintain my prestige, surely you can see that. You can have the South Room.'

'Well, yes, but . . . I mean to say!'

'Not another word! Move your things out, pronto.'

'But . . .'

'Puffer!'

'Yes, Alexander.'

'That's "yes, sir". At least, in front of the girls. We have to keep up appearances, you know.'

He turned to the dull green Austin 10 in which he had driven down. A pretty young WAAF girl with a wisp of strikingly red hair escaping from beneath her uniform cap sat at the wheel. She gave him a shy smile.

'Take her around the back, Molly . . . I mean Leading Aircraftwoman MacCallion. I take it there's a stable or something, Herbert?'

'Yes, I've had the old carriage house cleared out to make a garage,' Herbert answered him, 'and all the equipment is installed in the outhouses. I've barely had to touch the house itself.'

'Good.'

'There's some peculiar gear, I'll show you. It looks like Jervis and Genevieve used to spend their time giving each other enemas.'

'Really? Not much else to do around here, I don't suppose.'

'They had a thing called a clysopomp, weird sort of device, French. The really peculiar stuff is in a shed to the rear, a whole line of the things, six in all.'

'Highly eccentric, splendid. What did Cora make of them?'

'She thinks it's some sort of agricultural machinery.'

'Well, it is. How about other essentials? If they bring this rationing business into force there'll be all sorts of trouble, and imported goods will be the first to go. How are we for wine?'

'The cellar's well stocked. Jervis was a Champagne man, really, but there's a decent amount of claret and port, some brandy, not a great deal in the way of hock or Burgundy. Still, once ours are down we should have a good balance, and enough to stay the distance.'

'Hopefully, yes,' Alexander answered, tucking his swagger stick beneath his arm as they started towards

34

the door. 'It may last longer than they're saying. I mean to say, what was it last time – "It'll all be over by Christmas", and look what happened, four ruddy years of it. I'm damned if I'm going without a decent tipple for that long. I'll look it over later, but for now, show me these infernal devices of yours.'

'Upstairs then, the clysopomp is in the bathroom.'

'I should think so too, if half of what you say is to be believed.'

'It's no rumour, Alexander, just ask Charlie Truscott. He was there.'

'Oh, I don't doubt it for a minute. Damn peculiar chap, your cousin. Persuasive though, I'll give him that.'

They mounted the staircase, Herbert leading the way to a bathroom, a good part of which was occupied by the clysopomp. Alexander stood back to admire the device, astonished by the complexity of it and the effort that had so clearly gone into its creation. It was clearly old, and just as clearly well used, although it had originally been constructed to the highest standard. It consisted of a curiously shaped bench of mahogany, well padded with a cushion of stained and faded black leather, and fitted with straps on each of four legs and in the middle. Each strap ended in a heavy buckle of somewhat tarnished brass. Not only did this allow its user to be immobilised, but the shaped padding and central strap clearly acted to keep the back down and the bottom high, and also vulnerable. The configuration suggested an instrument more of erotic torture than simple hygiene.

A victim, he could see, would be forced to flaunt her bottom, while the wedge-shaped end would keep her thighs well apart and her quim and anus available. The other end was flat and angled somewhat downwards, to support the unfortunate girl's stomach. A narrow section was clearly designed to leave her breasts dangling free and pushed out to either side, and also left no doubt that the thing was designed with a female body in mind.

The bench stood on a broad, heavy stand, evidently designed to prevent it from overturning however vigorously the victim might struggle. At one side this stand extended someway beyond the feet of the bench, and in the corner that would be beside a victim's head stood a peculiar tower. This was in the same dark mahogany as the bench and stand, and consisted of an open framework within which was enclosed a large vessel of thick glass. The top of this bore a wide lid and a valve, while the side was calibrated to indicate the volume of whatever liquid it might hold. At the bottom a tap led to a thick rubber tube, suspiciously new, and then a complicated device with a handle and various taps. The function of this was not immediately apparent, save that it obviously controlled the flow of the fluid in the reservoir. From its end another tube led out, thinner, longer and terminating in another tap, several leather thongs and a round brass nozzle, evidently designed for insertion into the victim's vagina or anus. This was hung on a hook, around which several loops of the tube were twisted. Further hooks supported a variety of instruments, most of which seemed to be designed for poking into bodily cavities.

'Weird indeed,' he remarked. 'Have you put Cora on it yet?'

'Well, no. I, er ... I couldn't really think of an excuse.'

'Who needs an excuse? She may be in the Air Force now, but she's still a whore at heart. Always will be. Now little Molly, on the other hand, is not a natural whore ...'

'But you said all women are whores at heart, I remember, the first time we managed to squeeze a bit of fun out of ... what's-her-name, the cook's daughter ... Sarah, and she wanted a shilling.'

'Did I? Yes, I did, but that was at school. I have developed my philosophy since then. You see, a girl like Molly will whore if she has to, but it is not her instinct.'

'Her upbringing, I suppose?'

'It has nothing to do with upbringing, nor background. In fact, rich women generally are natural whores, having married for money, and thus used sex as currency. Molly, on the other hand, fucks for pleasure. Her true place in life is as a wife.'

'You intend to marry her?'

'Good heavens, no! Me, married to some Irish guttersnipe? Don't be absurd!'

'Oh. Are you going to make her go on the clysopomp, then? Can I watch?'

'Dirty bugger, aren't you, Puffer? Yes, of course, to both.'

'Now?'

'No, not now! For goodness' sake, man, we do have some responsibilities, you know. I mean, damn it, we're a meteorological station, not a whorehouse! We have to get all the gear up and running, make a wireless report, check the strip, all sorts of things. How's Cora on the radio, by the way?'

'Fine. She's a clever girl, got the hang of it a sight faster than I did, that's for sure. I say, shall we do both at the same time, perhaps make one watch while the other gets it?'

'For goodness' sake, Puffer, don't you think of anything but sex? Duty first, remember, otherwise the brass will cotton on and we'll lose our cushy billet.'

'Right. Yes, of course. There's not much that Cora and I haven't done, though. I mean, we've managed to get the balloon thingamajig working, and we got a farmer over to mow the strip, and we've put that orange thing like a cake-icer up . . .'

'Balloon thingamajig? Cake-icer? Good God, man, at least learn to act the part! And if you think I'm bringing a plane down on a strip prepared by yourself, some Yankee tart and a West Country farmer without checking it myself, you've another thought coming.'

'We've got the plane?'

'Yes. A Gloster Gladiator, an adapted one. It's all right, but I'm damn glad we're out of range of Jerry's fighters, that's all. I have to collect it from Exeter aerodrome tomorrow.'

He stepped back from the bathroom at the sound of a dull thump. Molly was on the landing, her pale face a touch red, resting with one of his cases to either side of her. Alexander gave Herbert a meaningful look.

'In here,' Herbert said, reluctantly pushing open the door to the master bedroom. 'I'll have Cora move my things in a while.'

'Where will I be, sir?' Molly asked.

'In with me, naturally,' Alexander answered, 'but you'd better have a room of your own for form's sake. What have you done with Cora, Puffer ... or Flying Officer Puffer or whatever it is?'

'I've turned the Long Room into a dormitory,' Herbert answered, as Molly strained to lift the two huge cases once more. 'I thought –'

'Very little, evidently,' Alexander cut in. 'How is she supposed to come to you when we're allocated more staff, you great ass?'

'I just thought a dormitory ...' Herbert went on sulkily.

'Oh it's not a bad idea, just not for Cora. These things have to be handled carefully, you know. We mustn't let the little dears think they're being put upon, must we?'

'No. Look, Alexander, I'm not really sure ...'

'Just leave it to me, Puffer. Everything is in order. Have you heard from the Ministry yet?'

'Well, yes. I was meaning to talk to you about that. You see ... er ...'

'Spit it out, man!'

'Well the thing is, apparently, Sappho Yates didn't do exactly what she was expected to. She's joining the WAAF, but she's applied to be trained as an officer.'

'Hell. I told uncle Reggie he was laying the class stuff on a bit thick.'

'There's more. A couple of friends of hers have also joined, or servants maybe. Sisters or cousins, I think, from the papers.'

'They're coming here?'

'Yes, I thought . . .'

'For goodness' sake, man! Why couldn't you wait until I . . .? Oh, never mind, we'll just have to make the best of it. Now, Molly, when you've finished with the luggage, tidy the room a little, sort out your own, try to find some flowers, yes, definitely flowers. Nip down to the radio shed, which is outside somewhere, I believe. You'll find Aircraftwoman Jackson in there. The two of you are to report to, er . . .'

'The library?' Herbert suggested.

'Library!' Alexander snorted. 'The AOC's office, which is what the library is now, or will be. Eighteen hundred hours sharp, that's six o'clock.'

Molly was visible in the master bedroom, a fine oak-panelled room looking out over the carriage sweep. She was bending over a case, the blue cloth of her uniform skirt taut across her neatly rounded bottom. As she answered, Alexander stepped forwards to give the target a firm swat. Molly squeaked.

'That's "yes, sir", Leading Aircraftwoman MacCallion, and how many times do I have to tell you to salute when I address you, and preferably with your face rather than your backside towards me, delectable though it is?'

He had put his hand on her bottom, to feel the softness of her flesh beneath the thick blue serge. Molly giggled. Alexander spent a moment more fondling, and took his hand away with an effort.

39

'Yes, sir,' she answered him, but stayed bent, quite clearly making her bottom available.

Alexander gave her another, lighter smack and turned from the room. Together they walked down the stairs to the hall. Herbert spoke as soon as they were out of earshot.

'Did you spank her then? Properly, you know, bare botty?'

'No, not yet. She hates it. I'll do it, naturally, but I want to make it something special, really let her get her confidence up before she gets it.'

'Splendid. I can watch, yes?'

'Naturally. I want to use an excuse too, so she thinks it's for real. Otherwise she won't get half so upset.'

'I'd have thought she'd be jolly ashamed anyway, more so if it's done for a wheeze.'

'Not really, no. She's odd that way. In some ways she's remarkably rude, in others utterly naïve. Three months she spent whoring for Tweedie, and she didn't know that self-abuse means masturbation. Her parents seem to have worked on the principle that if she knew absolutely nothing about sex she wouldn't get into any mischief.'

Herbert laughed as they passed out into the weak autumn sunlight. Rounding the building, they came out to where the full sweep of Dartmoor was visible, a great spread of brown and green and grey rising to a ridge, which in turn rose to a granite-topped peak. Higher hills stood beyond, most capped with their mounds of crumbling rock, some, more distant, curves of dull lavender against the blue of the sky.

'That's Mill Tor,' Herbert said, pointing to the nearby peak. 'Climb that and keep going and it's ten miles before you even get to a road, more or less.'

'Wonderful!' Alexander remarked, drawing in a deep breath of air. 'This is the real England. It makes you realise what we're fighting for.'

'Or not,' Herbert remarked.

'We're doing our bit,' Alexander answered. 'Very important work, meteorology. Ah, drink in that air!'

'It smells of sheep shit.'

'You have no romance in your soul, Puffer, that's your trouble. Now, where's the strip?'

'In the home field,' Herbert answered, 'over that wall.'

They walked forwards to a gate in a wall of granite blocks. Beyond was a field, more or less flat, with a central swathe of paler grass where it had been cut.

'It's a bit short,' Alexander remarked. 'We'll have to knock the end wall down.'

'The sheep will get in from the moor,' Herbert pointed out.

Alexander answered with a snort.

'It'll do, I suppose. We'll need a chance light. Are either of these girlies we're getting engineers? We'll need a couple, but I want to avoid other men if we possibly can.'

'Both. Newly trained, of course . . .'

They continued talking as they walked out to the strip and around it, then back to the outhouses, one crowded with equipment but otherwise empty, the other with Cora sitting in front of the radio. Her uniform jacket was open, also the top two buttons of her blouse, revealing a deep slice of rich brown cleavage above the third button, which seemed on the point of giving in under the strain. As the two men entered she just smiled, making no effort whatever to adjust her uniform. Nor did she salute.

'I don't think much of discipline around here,' Alexander remarked. 'Look lively, girl. Do your buttons up, and salute when an officer enters the room.'

'I can't,' Cora answered.

'That's "I can't, sir",' Alexander snapped. 'For heaven's sake, girl. You did basic training, didn't you?'

'Yes . . . yes, sir, but . . .'

'But what?'

'But this is . . . this is us . . .'

'Yes, it is, but one day I'll walk in here and there'll be some brass hat behind me. For now, we're alone and, as you so rightly say, this is us. On your feet.'

'What are you going to do?' Herbert asked nervously as Cora stood.

'Whack her arse for her.'

'Oh . . .'

'Don't tell me you haven't?'

'Well, no . . .'

'You do bed her, don't you?'

'Yes, of course . . .'

'But you haven't spanked her?'

'Well, no . . . but you haven't done Molly, you said . . .'

'That is different. There always was a wet streak in you, Herbert. Come on then, Aircraftwoman Jackson, the party's over. Up with your skirt and touch your toes.'

Cora didn't answer, and threw Herbert a pleading look even as she began to inch up her skirt. Herbert had gone pink, and looked away. Alexander didn't, but kept his attention on Cora as she pulled up the woollen skirt, revealing well-turned calves, plump lower thighs, the tops of her stockings with the bands cutting into her soft brown flesh to make her still plumper upper thighs bulge. She hesitated, her look of appeal changed to resignation and the skirt was rising again, exposing her big, round bottom as she wiggled to get the hem over it, the meaty cheeks quivering within her huge white knickers. The skirt was turned up and tucked into the top of the knickers. Reluctantly, she bent down, to reach back and flip her tails up, then take hold of her legs.

'Well, she knows how to pose for it,' Alexander remarked, 'but if she thinks she's keeping her drawers up she's very much mistaken.'

As he spoke he had reached out to take hold of the waistband of Cora's knickers. They came down with a single, hard jerk, stripped away to leave the fleshy brown bottom quivering and bare. She gasped, but made no effort to get up, despite the sudden exposure of her bottom and the fleshy rear purse of her quim. She was wet, white juice showing between the plump, silky lips. Alexander chuckled and pushed the handle of his swagger stick at her hole. It slid in easily, and came out sticky with thick, white juice.

'By God, she juices easy, unless she'd been playing with herself. Well, Aircraftwoman Jackson?'

Cora shook her head, dislodging her cap. Alexander gave a deep sigh.

'Hopeless. That's "No, sir, I have not been playing with myself".'

He chuckled and held the swagger stick out. Cora took it in her mouth without hesitation, to suck up her own juices. Alexander could feel his cock starting to stiffen, in response not just to her nudity and the strongly feminine smell of her sex, but also his power over her.

Pulling the swagger stick from her mouth, he reversed it and tapped the end to the ample black bottom before him. Herbert took a step back, his face red, his eyes fixed to Cora's rear view.

'Twelve, I think,' Alexander announced as he brought the stick down across Cora's shivering bottom. 'You should have done this weeks ago, Puffer, and regularly since. Not that it'll do much good, I don't suppose. My stick's too short by half, when you consider how well padded she is.'

He had continued to apply the stick as he spoke, and the black girl's reaction suggested that it was far from ineffective. She had taken the beating in a series of gasps and high-pitched squeals, all the while hopping from one foot to the other and clenching her bottom cheeks.

Rather enjoying the show, especially the way it made her flash the jet-black knot of her anus with each movement, Alexander made no effort to stop her.

The stick was leaving marks, purple on brown, and by the end her skin was prickly with sweat and juice that had begun to splash from her sex at each blow. Alexander gave the last three hardest of all, and on the twelfth Cora jumped up, to clutch at her now well-marked bottom. She went into a little dance, bouncing up and down on her toes with her face screwed up in pain and her big breasts bouncing wildly in her blouse. Alexander waited until she had calmed down before speaking.

'There we are, Aircraftwoman Jackson, all done, but remember, there's more where that came from.'

'Yes, sir,' she managed, snivelling a bit as she began to adjust her clothing.

'Did I say you could cover up?' he demanded. 'No, I didn't. Bend over again, I'm going to fuck you.'

'But Alexa–' Herbert began, only to be cut off.

'Shut up, Puffer, and get your cock in her mouth.'

He had been pulling at his buttons as he spoke, and his cock came free, hard and ready. Cora had bent again, her face set in a resentful scowl, only to change abruptly as his cock slid up into her well-lubricated quim. He began to fuck her, watching in delight as the meaty, well-smacked bottom bounced and quivered to his thrusts. Soon she had begun to moan, and when Herbert at last managed to present his cock to her mouth she took it in, to suck noisily.

'Fore and aft, eh, like we used to ride Sarah, only without having to worry about having her damn father come in.'

Herbert said nothing. His eyes were shut in bliss, his mouth slightly open. Cora was sucking hard, spittle already running down her chin where it had escaped from her mouth. She was clinging on to Herbert too, and using the thrusts into her rear to make her mouth work on the cock inside it, a practised trick Alexander had seen before. He was feeling thoroughly pleased with himself, grinning as he fucked her, until at last the effect of what he'd done to her and now being in her body became too much. Pulling his cock free, he pressed it down between the silky black buttocks to rut in her crease, fast, and faster still, jamming it hard in as his orgasm hit him. Suddenly her cleft was slimy with sperm, but he kept rubbing, emptying himself between her buttocks until there was no more to come.

Satisfied, he sank down into her radio operator's chair to watch Herbert finish off. If Cora had been reluctant to take her beating, she was now all eagerness, mouthing on the thick, stubby erection in her mouth and tickling the fat white balls that protruded from Herbert's fly with her long red fingernails. He had begun to masturbate in her mouth, and seemed in no hurry to fill the hole Alexander had so recently vacated.

Cora made the decision, pulling Herbert down. He went, the black girl climbing on immediately, to lower her body on to his erection. Alexander shook his head in amused contempt as Herbert was mounted. Cora was in charge, plainly, with no sign of embarrassment or reluctance whatever. Her fingers went to her blouse, popping open the buttons as she wiggled and bounced on the cock inside her. Two quick movements and her huge breasts were free from her bra, fat and round in her hands, the jet-black nipples sticking out firmly to attention between her fingers.

Alexander said nothing, watching as his friend was used by the black girl, not commenting even when she came suddenly forwards to straddle Herbert's face. Only her bottom showed, two big black cheeks peeping out from beneath the hem of her jacket, but he could hear the wet noises of her quim being licked, and see the ecstasy on her face. Herbert was wanking, pulling on his cock with desperate urgency as his face was smothered in her flesh.

Herbert came first, the spunk bubbling out from his cock and over his hand. He kept licking, even when he had begun to go limp, and by the time Cora gave a squeal of delighted ecstasy, his cock was already deflated. She climbed off, grinning, and turned to Alexander.

'I've learned my lesson, sir, thank you, sir,' she said, smiling sweetly as Herbert pulled himself up from the floor.

'Impudence, eh?' he answered. 'Well, I may just have the remedy for that. Has Leading Aircraftwoman Mac-Callion been to see you?'

'Molly's here? Neat . . .'

'For goodness' sake, Aircraftwoman Jackson. Do you want another dozen across that fat backside?'

'No, sir,' she said hastily.

'Good,' he answered. 'Now tidy yourself up and report to my office at eighteen hundred hours.'

'Sir. Sir, where is your office?'

'The library.'

He shook his head. She began to dress, both men watching as she returned her breasts to the ample bra she had been told to wear, pulled up the big white knickers and wriggled the blue skirt down over her hips. As they left she was still doing her buttons. Alexander spoke as the door closed behind them.

'You mustn't let them take control like that,' he stated. 'Remember, you're the man, and an officer to boot.'

'I er . . . ah . . . I rather like it that way,' Herbert answered him.

'You like it that way? For God's sake, man, get a grip on yourself. No wonder she's so damn slack if you let her ride you like that all the time. Never mind, I'll keep her in order, and I haven't made Molly up to Leading Aircraftwoman for nothing, you know.'

'No?'

'No. She may be a little thing, but she's the eldest of seven. She'll soon have Cora in order, and we can just pray that these two you and uncle Reggie have landed us with are either innocent, tarts, or both. So, where's the shed with the other devices in it, then?'

'The dairy shed, across the yard.'

Herbert led him between two buildings, to a yard entirely concealed from outside view by a wall and the sides of the house and various buildings. Against the back wall of the house a large old-fashioned black-iron pump stood at the centre of a stone trough. The place had an air of desertion, and so did the long building into which he followed Herbert.

It looked as it might once have been used for milking cows, or some such agricultural drudgery. Where the milking machines might normally have stood were six devices of dark wood, black leather, glassware and brass, not unlike the clysopomp. Unlike the clysopomp, they had clearly not been used for years, but were filthy with dust and cobwebs, the leather cracked, the brass black with inattention. The rubber fittings were also gone, cracked and discoloured, some fallen away.

Their poor condition was not the only difference. Like the clysopomp, the bench was designed for a girl, with space for her breasts. The bench was higher though, so that even with a girl as busty as Cora there would be plenty of room beneath her. It was also flat, marginally reducing the degree to which the victim's bottom would be flaunted. There were straps too, and more tubes, and while it was hard to tell with the rubber in such poor condition, there had evidently been cups and some sort of valve system. Further tubes, badly perished, connected all six machines together and to what was evidently some kind of hand pump at the far end.

'These will need some work,' he remarked, ducking down to investigate one of the cups.

'I was hoping the girls' engineering skills might come in handy there,' Herbert answered him.

'No doubt. How about power?'

'It's all hydraulics, or rather, it was. I was thinking we could use the generator?'

'Yes, why not. It's beyond me, though, I confess. Leave it to the erks, I suppose. In fact, there's rather a fine irony in that, don't you think? We have them repair the things, and it's only afterwards they find out what they're for!'

Herbert's fat, boyish face split into a wide grin.

'Splendid,' Alexander went on. 'In fact, I take back what I said. You're not completely mad. It's a lark.'

'I just hope we can make it work.'

'Of course we can. Old Jervis did it, didn't he, and look at him?'

'I think it was uncle Archibald originally.'

'Well, he was as mad as a hatter by all accounts, and Francis St John was pretty eccentric.'

'I was never sure if the story was true about Francis.'

'Must be. You wouldn't make that sort of thing up, would you?'

'Well, no . . .'

'There you are then, and if a couple of bright lads like us . . . well, me, can't manage it, I shall eat my cap, badge and all. We've got the erks too.'

'I still don't know, Alexander. I mean, what if . . .'

'Oh, do dry up. We can keep a tight lid on it, and if any of them do object they'll be too damn embarrassed to say anything. It's just a shame we won't be getting Sappho Yates, that's all.'

'I understand she's rather slim, as it happens.'

'So I hear. Not such a loss after all, then. What's the time?'

'Ten to six.'

'Splendid. Time Molly was introduced to Madame la Clysopomp!'

Herbert's face went abruptly pink. Alexander rose to walk briskly from the shed. There was a back door, leading from the yard into the house, which proved unlocked, and to lead into a scullery and the kitchen. He pushed through, quickly orientating himself to find the hall, then the library. Neither of the girls had arrived, and he paused to look around, immediately impressed by the air of old-fashioned refinement. The room had a high ceiling, like all the lower story, and was almost square, with high, arched windows on two sides and rank upon rank of books on the others. Various display cabinets stood about, showing collections of stuffed birds, eggs, china, silverware and more. A large rug of dark, rich colours occupied the centre of the room, surrounded by four well-stuffed armchairs.

There was no desk as such, only a writing table between two of the windows. As sitting at it would leave his back to the room he opted for an armchair instead, settling himself into it just as the girls' voices became audible. Both were chattering happily and instantly recognisable, Molly's strongly accented Irish and Cora's southern United States. He folded his hands in his lap, wondering whether to concoct an excuse or simply to demand obedience. The answer came immediately. As with the spanking, Molly's reactions were sure to be stronger if he didn't admit his reasons were purely sexual. A speech delivered by the fitness-obsessed headmaster of his school came to mind as the girls trooped into the room, still chattering.

'Attention!' he barked.

Molly reacted promptly, coming smartly into position at the centre of the carpet and saluting. Cora followed suit, more slowly, and the corner of her mouth was still twitching as she settled.

'Aircraftwoman Jackson,' he stated. 'Are you acquainted with the name Jervis Maray?'

'Yes, sir,' she answered, struggling to suppress a titter. 'Flying Officer Maray's cousin, sir. Used to own this house.'

49

'Yes, he did,' Alexander went on, 'and, what is more, he had rather a nasty reputation. Now, I'm sure he left one or two implements around that would prove considerably more effective than my swagger stick when it comes to disciplining insolent girls. Do I make myself clear?'

'Yes, sir. Absolutely, sir, but, er . . . sir, I don't really think you're supposed to spank us and things, sir.'

She burst into a fit of giggles. Alexander drew in his breath. Clearly the idea of tricking her into accepting discipline wasn't going to work. Yet she had made very little fuss earlier, at least about accepting his right to punish her. From the expressions she'd been making and the way she'd jumped around, there was no question in his mind that she'd found the punishment both painful and humiliating. For one moment he caught the uneasy feeling that she was a great deal more intelligent than he was, and more knowing, only to push it down as absurd. Falling back on another favourite phrase of his ex-headmaster, he spoke again.

'I think we understand each other, Aircraftwoman Jackson.'

'Yes, sir. You just go ahead and warm my buns any time you feel the need.'

There was more than a touch of mockery in her voice but he ignored it, telling himself that she would be more valuable as an ally than an antagonist if he was unable to subdue her personality. He went on.

'I shall, Aircraftwoman Jackson, rest assured of that. Now, from tomorrow we become an operational station. I know you're both barely out of training, and Flying Officer Maray likewise, but I intend to run a tight, efficient operation in any case. If we don't, none of us is likely to stay here very long. Understood?'

Both responded, this time seriously. He nodded, relieved.

'You know your duties?'

Again their response was prompt and confident.

'And that what goes on here is strictly secret. There is to be no gossiping in the village. There are to be no leaks.'

This time there was a touch of mirth in Cora's response and something different in Molly's. He paused, once more deciding between truth and deceit. Once more deceit won, despite the suspicion that at least Cora and perhaps both would know exactly what was going on.

'Good,' he continued, warming up to his headmaster's set-piece. 'Now, as I say I want this station to be efficient. There will be no room for slack behaviour, laziness, any of that sort of thing. I want you in peak condition. *Mens sana in corpore sano*, a healthy body in a healthy mind, that's my motto. We've plenty of opportunity for clean, outdoor living up here, plenty of fresh air and space. I intend to implement a regime of callisthenics and other exercises, for all non-commissioned personnel.'

He looked at Molly, who seemed slightly surprised but nothing more.

'As part of this programme,' he went on, 'I intend to implement a system that both improves personal health and makes one more alert. This is known as Internal Hygiene, a system of proven benefit to the health, as used by many of our most prominent citizens. Any questions?'

Prominent citizens that included Genevieve Maray, he reflected, a woman capable of the most extreme sadomasochistic excesses and now in a lunatic asylum.

'What actually happens?' Molly queried.

It took Alexander a moment to recover, wondering if she could have walked into his trap quite so blindly.

'I'm glad you asked that question, Leading Aircraftwoman MacCallion,' he said, recovering. 'Clearly a demonstration is in order, for which I am sure you will volunteer?'

'Yes, sir.'

If she had any suspicions, they were not betrayed in her face. Cora looked composed, perhaps too composed, but she said nothing. He went on.

'At present, we have only one working model of the device designed by Mrs Maray for this purpose, which is installed in the bathroom.'

He stood. Neither girl moved.

'Come, come, Leading Aircraftwoman MacCallion. To the bathroom, on the double.'

Molly immediately gave a string of orders, doing her best to sound commanding. Cora responded, the two of them marching from the room. Alexander followed, his pulse picking up at the prospect of what he was about to do. He and Herbert shared a nervous grin as they reached the door with the girls' shoes already clattering on the stairs.

By the time they reached the bathroom, both girls were there, waiting at attention in the passage. Alexander pushed in, wedging the door behind him to make as much space as possible.

'At ease,' he stated, indicating the clysopomp.

Molly came in, her face registering first curiosity, then concern.

'No time like the present, eh?' Alexander said cheerfully. 'If you would be good enough to disrobe, we may have a demonstration.'

'Disrobe?' Molly asked.

'Naturally, after all, we wouldn't want to spoil your uniform, would we?'

'In front of everyone?'

'Yes, of course,' Alexander answered, genuinely surprised by her sudden coyness. 'It's not as if we haven't seen it all before, after all.'

Molly shrugged, and her face coloured slightly, but she began to disrobe. Alexander sat down on the edge of the bath to watch, delighted by her slight uncertainty and occasional hesitation as she removed first her belt, then her shoes, as if trying to decide which article of clothing would reveal least. Her necktie followed, then her jacket, both passed to him. Her uneasiness grew markedly as she began to unbutton her blouse. From the way she was glancing at Herbert, it was obvious that his presence was making her uneasy. It seemed astonishing that she could have recovered so much modesty in the short space of time since he had arranged the cover for her entry into the WAAF, yet she was clearly embarrassed.

Her display of emotion was making his cock grow, despite his recent orgasm. With him, she was uninhibited, and it was delightful to discover that exposure in front of others made her blush, yet that she was still obedient. It was perfect, and considerably more appealing than Cora's attitude, for all the black girl's lush curves and willingness.

With her blouse half open Molly stopped to sit down on the bench of the clysopomp and work on her stockings instead. To do it she was forced to tug up her uniform skirt, exposing most of her neatly formed legs and a little slice of creamy thigh. One stocking came off, then the other, unclipped and rolled down, to leave her bare legged. Her skirt followed, pushed down with a somewhat peevish motion and an irritable glance at the leering Herbert Maray. He appeared not to notice.

Alexander took her skirt and she went back to her blouse, popping each button open with trembling fingers and shrugging it off as the last one came loose. Underneath she had a girdle to support her stockings, big white knickers with a half-inch of lace trim and a bra designed to raise and part her little round breasts. Her fingers were shaking hard as she unfastened her girdle, and harder still as it dropped away to expose her tummy and the lower slope of her back. Alexander gathered the fallen garment up and bundled it with the others.

She sat down again, awkwardly, her knees together but her feet kicked apart. Her hands went behind her back, to her bra strap, but she was shaking so hard she couldn't manage the catch. She turned to him, her face now bright pink and her eyes full of mute entreaty. He leaned forwards to help, pinching the catch between forefinger and thumb, to open it and let her breasts loll forwards. She took hold of a shoulder strap, her gaze directed to the floor as she pulled it free. The other followed. Her bra hung for a moment on her breasts, supported only by their shape and weight, one nipple half showing. Then she had pulled it clear, baring two breasts the size of big fists, each topped with a soft, rose-pink nipple.

Alexander adjusted his cock, which had grown uncomfortably hard. He'd seen her breasts before, many times, but there was something in her attitude that made her slow, reluctant strip immensely appealing. Even as she lifted her bottom and stuck her thumbs firmly into the waistband of her big knickers, he resolved to make the best of her attitude, making her exposure in front of others a rare treat, something to be indulged only occasionally, and then savoured.

She had paused, hesitant, looking at Herbert in a mute appeal to his decency, expecting him perhaps to at least turn his back for her final exposure. He just stared, apparently oblivious to her embarrassment, which now had her cheeks and neck flaring scarlet. Seeing that she was not to be spared, she shrugged, made a face and pushed down her knickers, providing Alexander with a brief glimpse of the pouted rear of her sex as she bent to pull them off. He took the discarded knickers from her as he stood up.

'Thank you, Molly, my dear. I think we may dispense with ranks, as you're out of uniform, ha, ha. Now, I'm as new to this as you are . . .'

Molly shook her head.

'You're not new to it?'

'Not like this, but .... but, I'm to have an enema, aren't I?'

'Er ... yes.'

'And the straps are in case I struggle, aren't they? I just used to have my hands and ankles tied up.'

Herbert made a gurgling noise in his throat. Alexander turned him a disapproving look. Molly took no notice, but went down, draping herself carefully over the bench to leave her breasts hanging down and her bottom high. She was also open, with the lips of her quim showing in detail and her anus a tiny knot of palest pink flesh between her well-spread cheeks. She was shaking hard, and had closed her eyes, but gave no resistance as Alexander began to strap her in place.

He did the belly strap first, then those that held her thighs, and lastly her arms. It left her utterly helpless, and him with a cock so hard it ached. She was perfectly placed, and not just for enemas. All he need to do was pull out his erection and kneel behind her and he would be able to plunge his cock into her unguarded and very wet quim, or even up her bottom. She would have no choice.

Restraining himself with difficulty, he began to examine the workings of the machine. The water went into the glass reservoir, that much was obvious, and it was equally obvious that the nozzle went up the girl's bottom. What happened in between was not so clear. There was a system of valves, one or more of which appeared to control the rate of flow. Others seemed to be designed to bleed air out of the system, or possibly for evacuation of the girl's enema. More than one looked as if it was intended to allow other substances to be introduced to the flow.

Molly waited patiently as he studied the system, shivering slightly in her nudity, with goose-pimples roughening the pale skin of her flaunted bottom. At last he decided he knew how it operated and twisted all the valves to off. He turned to Cora.

'Aircraftwoman Jackson, fill the reservoir.'

'OK . . . yes, sir,' Cora answered. 'I'll fetch a jug, sir.'

'I think soapy water is the right thing,' Herbert suggested.

Cora disappeared, leaving Alexander and Herbert to contemplate Molly's naked body. Again he bit down the temptation just to mount her, contenting himself instead with an exploration of her bottom, stroking the skin. Briefly, he allowed his finger to linger in her cleft, and tickled her anus with a nail, to make the little hole twitch and draw a sob from Molly. Only when the clatter of shoes on the stairs signalled Cora's return did he step back. Only then did he notice that Molly's quim had opened a little more at his touch, the centre now wet and puffy, inviting entry.

'Here we are, sir,' Cora stated, holding up a large ewer before dropping the soap from the bath into it and putting it beneath the tap.

Water gushed out, Molly turning her head to look in horrified fascination as it filled, and as Cora filled the reservoir in turn. Two ewers left the reservoir full of milky water, to a volume of one gallon.

'She'll never take that,' Herbert remarked, 'not a little thing like her.'

'Well, no,' Alexander conceded. 'Anybody any idea how much we're supposed to use?'

'One quart, sir,' Molly said miserably.

'One quart? Thank you, my dear,' Alexander answered. 'Now, the nozzle. Evidently we tie it into place, but it is quite large, and I imagine it would be kind to provide some sort of lubricant. Is there anything in the way of grease in that cupboard, Cora . . . er . . . Aircraftwoman Jackson or whatever.'

The urgency of his cock was breaking down his reserve as well as his attempts at formality. The smell of

Molly's sex was strong in the air, and her pale, helpless body was growing ever more tempting. Cora seemed to take forever rummaging through the cupboard, which was filled with vials, bottles and tubes of every description. All the while Molly's shivering grew worse, and her anus had started to tighten and relax to a slow, lewd rhythm. At last Cora produced a large tube.

'This looks possible, "Tremaine's Applicant Unction, The Indispensable Aid to Husbandry, as recommended by the Veterinary Profession for horses, cattle, pigs, sheep and all kinds of livestock".'

'That doesn't sound right,' Herbert responded. 'Even if it is a lubricant, it's hardly the sort of thing a lady of Genevieve's status would have used.'

'What's it doing in the bathroom cupboard, then?' Cora pointed out as she twisted the lid from the tube. 'Ugh, it stinks!'

Alexander's nostrils twitched as a thick, oily smell reached him.

'Put a dab on her fanny,' he suggested. 'See if it stings.'

'Sir!' Molly protested, but Cora had already ducked down, her full lips curled up into a wicked smile as she smeared one greasy finger to her friend's quim.

Molly's buttocks tightened immediately, but relaxed again.

'Well?' Alexander demanded.

'It doesn't hurt, sir,' Molly answered, her voice sulky and resentful.

'Splendid!' Alexander stated. 'Here we go, then.'

He took the nozzle and the tube, smiling as he squeezed out a thick worm of the lubricant on to the rounded brass head. The smell grew stronger than ever, but he ignored it as he smeared the grease evenly over the nozzle and squeezed out a second worm, directly on to Molly's anus. The tiny ring twitched as the cold unction touched it, then again as Alexander applied the nozzle.

Gently, he smeared Molly's bottom hole with grease, watching in ever-growing delight as the muscle spread like a fleshy pink flower. Soon she was clearly loose enough to take the nozzle without pain, and he pushed gently, imagining his cock-head doing the same as Molly's anal ring gaped wide to take the insertion. She moaned as her hole stretched, and gave a low sigh as it closed again on the neck of the nozzle, but said nothing.

Alexander leaned back a little, grinning. The way the thick hose stuck out from the girl's anus was deliciously obscene. It was undeniable, thoroughly rude evidence of what he had done, and of what he was about to do. Breaches of propriety had always delighted him, and it was hard to imagine a more flagrant breach than a man inserting an enema tube up a young girl's bottom. The presence of an audience made it all the better, while the use of an unction apparently designed to allow vets to examine pigs and horses as an anal lubricant added an exquisite detail. His mother, his nanny, his teachers, all those who had attempted to invest him with a sense of morality, he knew would have been utterly outraged.

He began to fasten the thongs which would hold the nozzle in place up Molly's bottom. She was shivering harder than ever, her buttocks twitching, and the glistening ring of her anus pulsing and squirming on the brass shaft inside it. With all four thongs done up tightly enough to make her soft white flesh bulge around them, he stood. Ignoring the subtleties of the valves, he simply twisted the one designed to let the water run to full. A huge bubble rose up in the water reservoir, to burst from the surface even as Molly gasped, then went into babbling speech.

'No . . . too fast . . . please, no . . . ow! Ow!'

She had begun to writhe in her straps, making her bottom wiggle and her hair shake in the most appealing way. Alexander twisted the valve off with a twinge of regret. Her struggles subsided, her body growing slowly limp as she let out a long, low moan, which broke to a sob as he once more turned the valve, adjusting it to about a quarter of the maximum. Her breathing grew abruptly ragged, but otherwise she stayed still.

'Is that better?' he asked.

'Cold,' Molly managed in between gasps. 'It stings.'

Alexander decided to take her remark as assent and turned his eye to the reservoir. Less than a half-pint had gone up her bottom, but already there was a swollen look to the flesh around her anus, and he began to wonder just how much pressure there would be inside her. The angle at which the bench forced her to hold her bottom suggested that the consequences would be both spectacular and filthy.

'It's quite a high angle,' he stated. 'Isn't she going to spray rather?'

'I think that's the idea,' Herbert answered him.

'Damn messy!'

'I think you're meant to use this double one if you want it to be clean,' Cora suggested, reaching up to the rack for a larger nozzle with two holes and two tubes. The shaft was easily as thick as his penis, the bulb half as much again.

'A bit big,' he said doubtfully. 'Molly, would you rather take that, or just spray and clean up afterwards?'

She gave an anguished sob but said nothing.

'Perhaps if we held a bucket under her behind?' Herbert suggested.

'Well it wouldn't really be under her, would it?' Alexander pointed out. 'More behind. I suspect you'd have to be pretty quick off the mark to catch it all.'

'We could unstrap her and let her go on the loo,' Cora pointed out.

'I doubt there'd be time,' Alexander commented, tugging at his chin reflectively.

'I really think she's supposed to spray,' Herbert insisted, 'and probably clean up after herself. After all, if she just needed an enema —'

'Nonsense!' Alexander cut in. 'She said herself that she used to need her wrists and ankles tied.'

'I don't think she needed to, exactly . . .'

'Don't be obtuse, Puffer.'

'No, Alexander. Sorry.'

Molly had begun to whimper softly as they talked, and her whole body had begun to tremble again, hard, with her buttocks clenching and unclenching to a slow rhythm. Suddenly she started to sob, then to gasp and shake her head. Alexander glanced to the reservoir, to note that there was now over a pint up her bottom. Her whole anal area was now pouted out, and there was a swollen look to her sex and what was visible of her belly, as if she had suddenly grown fat, or pregnant.

Her sobs grew louder, then turned to little, pained grunts. She began to wriggle her bottom again, also her toes. Thoroughly excited by her condition, Alexander gave the valve another twist, increasing the flow. Molly cried out and once more began to writhe, and to clench her buttocks in a desperate effort to keep her anus tight. Suppressing a chuckle, he twisted the valve to full. Molly screamed, and once more began to babble.

'No . . . I can't . . . sir . . . please! Please! No! It's going to happen!'

She broke off into a scream. Alexander stood back hastily as her bottom hole started to expand, the nozzle emerging, her ring pulsing as she struggled to keep it in.

'I think she's going to blow, chaps . . .'

Even as he spoke Molly gave in, surrendering to the pressure in her bowels with a cry of utter despair. The nozzle burst from her anus. Water exploded from the gaping hole, only to hit the nozzle where the straps held it to her flesh and burst out in every direction, over Molly's bottom and legs, the clysopomp, and the floor.

Herbert had retreated into the passage. Alexander and Cora were pressed into one corner. All three watched as Molly expelled her enema, the full contents of her rectum spurting out, against the nozzle, then in a high arc over her sodden and filthy buttocks as the nozzle was pushed fully away. She had gone quiet, but she was still shaking, her whole body quivering to great racking sobs and gulps as she fought for air. Her anus began to pulse, cutting the stream off, only to erupt fresh fluid a moment later. She cried out again, then went abruptly limp. Alexander stepped closer, both fascinated and repelled, to watch her finish.

Fluid was still bubbling from her anus, to trickle down her thighs and quim, where it dripped from her sex-lips and the rich ginger tangle of her pubic hair. She lay still, making no effort whatever to restrain herself, but allowing it all to come out, liquid and solid. Tears of humiliation were running down her face, and as the trickle died to a series of weak farts, she began to snivel, and to urinate, her pee running out to form a broad yellow puddle on the floor. When at last she was done, Cora bent to work on the straps. Alexander steepled his fingers thoughtfully.

'Clearly we still have something to learn,' he remarked.

'Yes,' Herbert agreed, with a doubtful glance at the mess on the floor.

'Still, not a bad effort, first go, and really quite stimulating, although rather too messy at the end, perhaps. Right ho. Clean up your mess then, my dear, take a bath and present yourself to me spick and span in, shall we say, half an hour?'

Molly responded with a miserable nod, not even raising her eyes.

'Good. Dinner at eight then, Cora . . . that is, twenty hundred hours. Dress uniform, I think, Puffer – we mustn't be sloppy, must we?'

'Absolutely,' Herbert agreed.

'I shall see you downstairs then.'

Alexander pushed in at the door of the master bedroom as they reached it. His cock was painfully stiff, his head full of images, of Molly's reluctant strip, of her bottom spread and vulnerable, of her helpless writhing as the enema was put up her, of her agonised distress as her anus had erupted and she had defecated on the floor. It faintly occurred to him that he might have pushed her too far, have broken her down so absolutely that either she would rebel and refuse to do as she was told sexually, or become so crushed it was no longer enjoyable. Not that it mattered. For the moment the needs of his cock were paramount.

He went to the bed and lay down. Trying to seem nonchalant, he lit a cigarette, propping himself up on the pillows to smoke it. Time passed, ten minutes, twenty, twenty-five, as he nursed his erection and waited. A minute before the hands of the clock registered a half-hour a timid knock sounded at the door. He called out. Molly came in, still naked, downcast, her hands folded in front of her, her head hung so that her wet red fringe covered her eyes. Alexander patted the bed beside him.

She came, shuffling slowly on her feet, to climb on the bed. In no mood for discussion or a scene, he swiftly undid his buttons. Molly watched, wide-eyed, and the moment his erection sprang free of his fly she took hold, to tug on his shaft with earnest determination. Alexander relaxed, fully aware that she was in an extremely emotional state, but happy so long as she was attending to his cock. She was keen too, quickly moving round to lie her head on his lap and take him in her mouth. He began to stroke her hair and back as she sucked, enjoying the feel of the wet strands and the smooth, cool skin. She seemed tiny, fragile, clinging to him with all the desperate urgency of a drowning animal, and yet she was sucking his cock with real passion. He let his fingers wander lower, to the softness of her bottom, opening the little bare cheeks to show off the tiny hole between. Her anal flesh was puffy, the central hole a little open, inviting buggery.

With her mouth working so hard on his cock and his balls cupped in her hand, he knew he would come in her mouth if he didn't act quickly. Taking her firmly by the hair, he pulled her up. She came, still gaping, with spittle running down her chin as he pulled her to him. He kissed her as she came into his arms, her body trembling, full of life yet unresisting as he took her by her bottom to push her up on to her knees. She went, allowing herself to be positioned with a doll-like passivity even as her huge green eyes stayed fixed to his erection.

He got behind her, took hold of her bottom and spread her cheeks, stretching out her anus. She'd been washed, thoroughly, yet her quim was already sticky with juice again. Briefly, Alexander plunged his cock up, working it in her body to the sound of her gasps and moans. As he fucked her the urge to come rose up again. He pulled back, knowing that in two or three more pumps it would become irresistible.

Again he spread her buttocks, this time pressing the head of his cock to her stretched anus. She gave a loud sob as she realised she was to be buggered, but gave no resistance, instead letting her ring go loose as he smeared the come cream from her quim on to it. Her anal flesh felt rubbery, and oddly cool, tight too, drawing a grunt from him as he tried to force the head in. Molly gasped and reached back, pushing his cock aside to apply a spit-wet finger to her hole.

Alexander watched as she prepared her anus. Her finger delved deep, to come out wet and sticky, her hole opening, closing again as she once more pushed the finger up. He waited, nursing his cock and watching her ring move in and out. At last she pulled her finger free, to leave her bottom hole ready, moist and red, the centre showing a black hole into the cavity of her body. He pushed his cock in again.

This time it went in, the head squashing in past the sloppy ring, and deeper as he pushed. She cried out as

63

he tried to force it deeper still, and began to clutch at the bed clothes. He pulled back a little, pushed again, pulled back and pushed again, lubricating his cock shaft with her natural fluids as he buggered her, thrusting deeper and deeper into her bowels. She was tight, and hot, the flesh of her rectum forming a sheath around his cock, an ecstatic sensation that grew with each push, bringing him closer and closer to orgasm.

He was determined to make a thorough job of buggering her, but his head was swimming with dirty images of her strip and her enema. Suddenly it was all too much, and he was jerking frantically at the shaft of his erection where it emerged from her bottom hole, his knuckles smacking on her flesh, his cock head working in the warm, slimy interior of her rectum . . .

She cried out as he came, somewhere between despair and ecstasy as her gut filled with spunk, and then she was masturbating, rubbing her quim with desperate urgency and calling him 'sir' over and over again. Alexander barely noticed, too busy milking out the last of his sperm up her bottom to worry about her reaction, until her anus abruptly began to pulse on his cock, sucking out the last of what he'd been pumping up her.

Molly screamed and went into a frantic, ecstatic dance, clutching and biting at the bed covers, kicking her feet on the bed, writhing her bottom on his cock. He let it happen, her orgasm peaking as his faded, but kept his cock in, even when he had completely finished. At last she subsided and he pulled out, to leave her bottom hole a gaping red cavity into her body, with sperm dribbling from the lip and down over her quim.

Both collapsed on to the bed, Molly crawling up to lay her head on Alexander's chest. He put his arm around her shoulders and gave her a squeeze, feeling thoroughly content and well pleased with himself as his mouth twitched up into a happy grin. She cuddled close, showing no inclination to move, or speak. Alexander relaxed, letting his mind play over the events of the afternoon with ever increasing satisfaction. Only one detail jarred, arousing yet not perfect, her reaction to being made to take her enema in front of an audience. He considered, then spoke.

'You didn't want Herbert Maray watching, did you, earlier?'

She shook her head, a tiny, timid gesture, and snuggled closer to him.

'But you let him, without complaining.'

For a long moment she was silent, and when her voice did come, it was barely more than a whisper.

'I want what you want for me, sir.'

Alexander allowed his grin to spread across the full width of his face. Downstairs the gong sounded to announce dinner.

5

Kerslake Manor, Devon – November 1939

As Holly came slowly awake, the day before seemed like a bad dream, the crowded trains, the weight of her kit bags across her shoulders, the long walk from Okehampton Station to Kerslake Manor. The months before were little different, her training, the unfamiliar discipline and routine of military life, the whole concept of ranks and orders and responsibilities, the details of a trade she had never expected to learn. She had succeeded, though, Hazel with her, each relying on the other for support until they gradually became adjusted to their new life.

By the time they had reached the Manor it had been dark, and cold, with a sharp wind blowing down from the heights of Dartmoor to the south and west. They had been exhausted. Both had collapsed into bed after making a brief meal of bread and soup and stowing their kit. A black girl of their own rank had helped, and shown them their room, a fine bedroom converted to a three-bed dormitory.

Outside it was just beginning to get light, soft greyness stealing in beneath the heavy curtains that blocked off the window. It was cold, the air chill on her face where it rose above the bedclothes. Hazel was still asleep.

For a while she lay still, feeling slightly homesick, yet also relieved. Most of those she had trained with at Innsworth had gone to the aerodromes of south-east England, which seemed more likely to bear the brunt of any attack that came than north-west Devon. She had been surprised when both she and Hazel had been ordered to report to Kerslake, and while she had felt an odd sense of having cheated in some way, there was no denying the relief.

At length she got out of bed, pulling her thick flannel nightie around her as she rose. Even for early morning everything seemed strangely silent, muffled almost, while there was an odd quality to the light. Peering through the curtains, her suspicions were immediately confirmed. It had snowed during the night. The window looked out on to Dartmoor, which was a sheet of white, broken only where rocks and the larger gorse bushes thrust black through the crust.

It was a beautiful scene, serene and lonely, making the crowds and bustle of the camp and her journey seem more distant than ever. Her immediate thought was to go outdoors and make a snowman, for which she immediately felt silly, then homesick, more sharply then before, at the memory of how she and Hazel and Sapphie had done exactly that the winter before. It had ended in a playful fight, and the others holding her as they stuffed her knickers with snow . . .

The boom of a gong broke her daydream. Pushing back through the curtain she found Hazel stirring, looking out bleary-eyed through a curtain of brown curls. A moment later footsteps sounded outside, the door was thrown back and the black girl appeared.

'Rise and shine, you two. Exercises, ten minutes, in the yard. Knickers and tops.'

The door shut, leaving Holly standing with her mouth open, framed around the first syllable of the question she had been going to ask.

'You're catching flies, Holly,' Hazel remarked. 'Come on, show willing or they'll make our lives a misery.'

'Yes, but . . .'

'Don't get precious, Holly. You know what they're like about keeping us in our place from the camp.'

'Yes, but, what did she mean by knickers and tops?'

'It means the corporal's a bully. That or she's ragging us, and if she is, she'll be the one who lands in it. Come on, just pretend it's Sapphie making us do it.'

'But there's thick snow outside!'

'Like I say . . .'

Holly made a face but began to scramble among her things immediately. She had barely started to unpack the night before, and nobody had made her, so she had left it. Now she regretted the choice as she scrabbled among her clothes for her largest pair of knickers. Another thought occurred to her.

'Do you think it's blouses, or bras?'

'Bras, count on it,' Hazel answered.

'Oh dear . . . and what about the bathroom?'

'Ten minutes.'

'Yes, but I need my . . . oh!'

Hazel was already in a pair of white knickers, large, but too thin to conceal the generous contours of her bottom and hips, nor the shallow crease of her sex. She was holding up a bra too, and was scowling as she began to pull it on.

'I hate these things! They're never big enough!'

She gave a grunt of effort as she pulled the catch to, fastening the bra to leave two plump bulges of breast flesh pushed up over the top of the cups.

'I tell you, those ones are meant to go with evening gowns,' Holly insisted, pulling on her own knickers beneath her nightie.

'They're the only ones that fit!' Hazel answered. 'Now come on!'

Holly whisked off her nightie as Hazel went to the door. The cold air immediately set her skin tingling and made her nipples pop out, adding to her embarrassment. She rummaged for a bra, grateful when she immediately found a full-cupped one, but less so as she started to pull it on to find that it was one of her older ones and too tight. Again she began to rummage.

'Holly!' Hazel snapped. 'Do come on!'

'I . . .' Holly began and gave up, pulling the bra on and going abruptly pink as she looked down to see just how much flesh was spilling from the sides.

She followed Holly through the door, consoling herself that however much boob she was showing, her knickers concealed her bottom a great deal more effectively than her friend's. Both were thigh length, and came well up, but while Holly had slimmed a little during training, Hazel had filled out, and the seat was distinctly taut across her buttocks.

They found the bathroom, each hurriedly splashing water on her face, brushing her teeth with frantic haste and pushing her hair back into some semblance of order. The strange machine against one wall caught Holly's attention for a moment only, before Hazel had pulled her back through the door. They ran for the stairs, only to stop short at the sight of a man coming up, in full, immaculate uniform, complete with Squadron Leader's insignia. Both came to attention, Holly's face flushing crimson with embarrassment as she saluted.

'Hurry along, girls,' the officer answered, returning the salute in an offhand manner.

He gave a low chuckle as they passed, and his swagger stick flicked out to tap Hazel's bottom.

'Pervert!' she hissed as they reached the bottom of the stairs. 'Men! Come on, the yard must be out the back.'

They found the right door at the second attempt, rushing into a kitchen and through a scullery before tumbling into the back yard. The black girl and a tiny woman with striking red hair and a single chevron sewn on to her chemise top were already waiting. The wind hit Holly immediately, and she hugged herself tightly as she staggered out through the six inches or so of snow that carpeted the yard.

'We'll soon have you warm, sprogs!' the tiny woman called. 'In line! Arms extended, feet apart! Jumping on the spot, begin!'

Holly began to jump, too shocked by the cold and the suddenness of it all to do anything but obey, yet instantly grateful she had chosen a sensible bra when Hazel's breasts fell out at the first bounce.

In the window above the yard, Alexander lit a cigarette.

'Oops!' he remarked as Hazel's breasts bounced free.

Herbert laughed.

'I think that's ten shillings you owe me,' Alexander remarked, holding out his hand.

'Well, I'm still amazed,' Herbert answered. 'I really didn't think they'd fall for it, especially with the snow.'

'How could it be otherwise?' Alexander queried. 'They're only country girls, after all. They don't know any better. And they've spent the last few months being told to obey orders without question and all that rot. I reckon they'd have done it in the nude. Not that it makes much difference, not for the curly one anyway.'

He laughed and drew deeply on his cigarette, blowing a smoke ring before turning his attention back to the girls.

'You don't see a trio of top hampers like that everyday,' Herbert remarked wistfully. 'We were lucky there.'

'Absolutely. Now, let's see if there's anything we need to know. Pass their papers, would you?'

Alexander took the sheath of orders passed to him, keeping half an eye on the exercising girls as he leafed through. Molly had changed the exercise, making the girls bend to touch their toes, a position that strained all three well-fleshed bottoms against the thin seats of their knickers.

'Shame they're not facing the other way,' Herbert remarked. 'Still, look at the way their tits hang!'

'You'll get your chance, Puffer, you'll get your chance,' Alexander assured him. 'Now, that's odd.'

'What?'

'I thought they were sisters, and the original papers had them both down as Mullins, only she's put herself down as Bomefield-Mullins instead, Holly Bomefield-Mullins. She'd be the one with the straight hair, I think. Yes.'

'What's so odd about that? A half-sister probably, after all, look here, they're the same age, so if they're sisters, they'd have to be twins. They look fairly alike, after all.'

'Not that alike. You know who the Bomefields are, don't you, or rather, who they were?'

'No.'

'They owned Ashwood House, in Somerset.'

'Cissy Yates's place?'

'No, it's not her place. She just lives there. It belongs to Lord and Lady Cary. Lady Cary was a Bomefield.'

'So?'

'Well it's damn peculiar, don't you think? Here's this girl, calling herself Bomefield-Mullins, and she's from Lady Cary's estate, and knows Sappho Yates?'

'I don't get it.'

'No, you wouldn't, would you. Have you ever met Lottie Cary?'

'No.'

'Well, take twenty years odd off her and she'd be the spit of that girl.'

'What, you think she's some sort of by-blow or something? Surely not!'

'No? From what Uncle Reggie says, she very well might be. By all accounts Victor Cushat saw Lottie heavily pregnant, before she was married. So where's the child?'

'Farmed out somewhere, I'd suppose, but then . . .'

'I'd risk ten pounds she wasn't, or at any rate, not very far, a hundred pounds as it goes, and the same that she's down there praying the seam of her knickers doesn't split.'

'So you really think that's her?'

'Has to be. Why else should she called herself Bomefield-Mullins, save in an effort to salvage some pride from being illegitimate?'

'Well, yes.'

'I'll soon make sure of it, and by God but that'll bring Uncle Reggie out of the sulks if it's true, won't it just!'

6

Whitehall, London – January 1940

'It's Lottie Cary's brat, no question,' Alexander stated confidently, blowing a smoke ring as he settled back into a chair in Reginald Thann's office. 'The dates match, she's got the same looks, and the woman who's supposed to be her mother is the maid at Ashwood.'

'So who's the father?' Reginald Thann demanded.

'Goodness knows. Can't be Toby Cary, or they'd have married when she got preggers. Some hayseed, I suspect.'

'The little bitch!' Reginald Thann spat as the Air Ministry pencil he had toying with snapped between his fingers.

'Steady on.'

'You have no idea, Alexander, you have no idea. I offered the woman marriage, Alexander, marriage! By God, you should have seen her when she was young, so damn airy, as if butter wouldn't melt in her mouth. And all the time she's whoring around with half the farm boys in Somerset, and Cicely bloody St John into the bargain if half the rumours are true. That's Cicely Yates to you, Sappho's mother.'

'Really, Lottie Cary and Sissy Yates together?'

'Yes. Cicely was a notorious invert, yet she managed to get pregnant by Yates, who must be the biggest quean since Oscar Wilde. Utter debauchery, absolute pollution . . .'

'And you didn't get a look in, eh? Tough luck.'

Reginald Thann's face, already red, abruptly took on the colour of a beetroot. Alexander hastily changed the subject.

'So you're happy to forget Sappho if you can have Holly Bomefield-Mullins instead?'

'Yes, absolutely, far more satisfying, far more direct. Both would be good, in an ideal world, but I think I've lost Sappho. The wretched girl's already a Section Officer, in the Air Transport Auxiliary if you please. But yes, the daughter will suffice. I want her devoted to me, utterly.'

'That should be possible, I would imagine, although it would be a sight easier if you were actually there. It's in women's nature to subordinate to one man, I think, most women's anyway. My little Molly's like that, a perfect firebrand to the girls, but she'll do anything I want, and I mean anything, even –'

'I do not wish to know about your sordid conquests, Alexander.'

'No?'

'No.'

'Suit yourself. So how am I suppose to get her fixed on you when you're not around?'

'I've been considering that. There are certain techniques which can be used to make a person suggestible – sleep deprivation, starvation, fear, pain, anything to break the spirit. According to what I've read, rather than hating their persecutors, people who've been treated that way eventually become completely dependent. That's how I want her, Alexander, broken down completely, grovelling to me, crawling to beg at my feet . . .'

'Well, yes, so you say. We're doing our best. We have her out at six every morning to do exercises in her undies, and we've instituted a hygiene programme she absolutely loathes. It's superb, the girls have to take turns to give each other enemas on this bizarre machine the Maray's had installed, and believe me, you have never seen a girl blush so red as when she's got a quart of water up her back passage and she realises she can't hold it any more. It's hilarious, and –'

'Yes, yes, that's all very well. What about beatings? What about her diet? Have you made food a privilege? And sleep, no more than four hours, remember.'

'That's all a bit strong, isn't it? I do have a Wing Co, you know. I have to keep the place in shape, and I can't have Holly wandering around looking half-dead. I mean to say, it's bad enough with Puffer around, who's a complete penguin . . .'

'A penguin?'

'Has wings, can't fly.'

'Oh. Well, maybe I can bump you up a rank, but I don't suppose inspections are exactly common, not at Kerslake?'

'We've had a couple. There hasn't really been all that much for the brass to do, you know.'

'There will be. This is the calm before the storm, believe me. You want to see some of the intelligence reports. The Luftwaffe has three times as many planes as we do, over a thousand fighters . . . no, forget I said that. So, a few exercises and this hygiene regime, that's all you're doing?'

'Well, yes, and that's about all I can do, realistically. It's pretty humiliating for them, you know. I need my engineers, Uncle Reggie, and she's good. Besides, you want her to keep her looks, don't you? Otherwise, what's the point?'

'It's not enough, Alexander, not nearly enough. I have gone to a great deal of effort for you, Alexander, and I wish to be repaid. Do you think it was easy to get a fit young pilot posted to a meteorological station in the middle of nowhere?'

'Well, no, not for a minute . . .'

'Then keep your end of the bargain. Yes, physically, she has to be in prime form, and of course she must remain a virgin . . . She is a virgin, I take it?'

'Oh, yes, no question there. There's not a lot a girl can hide when she's on a clysopomp . . . that's the machine, and the design is wonderful. It leaves the girl with her arse in the air and her cunt stretched open . . .'

'Good, good. Yes, I need her in prime physical condition when she comes to me, but I need her broken mentally. Considerable physical suffering will be necessary for that, from which she can recover. In fact that's the way to get around the problem of my absence. You are to channel her dependence past yourself as it grows. You must make it clear that her torment, and more so her recovery, lies in the hands of somebody above you, a controller. Yes, that's it, refer to me as the Controller.'

'Do you really think that will work?'

'Yes. I have studied the theory in detail. It is mainly Russian work, but I see no reason why the system shouldn't apply to all peoples equally. But you must do as you are told. I need you to work on her constantly, on three main angles, sleep, food, pain.'

'Well, I suppose I could probably get away with spanking her . . .'

'Not enough, I say. She must be treated like an animal, like . . .'

'An animal? Now there I can probably help you. I have a little surprise in store.'

7

Kerslake Manor, Devon – January 1940

'Do you really think they'll buy it?' Herbert asked excitedly as he surveyed the line of six machines in the dairy.

All had been repaired, the wood polished until it shone, the brass gleaming, the glassware rubbed free of every stain and smudge. Even the rubber hoses and cups had been renewed, which had taken some creative entries in the stores book. Hazel and Holly had also harnessed the entire apparatus to the generator, so that individual machines or the entire system could run under power at the flick of a switch. The dairy had also been refitted, repainted and was scrubbed clean every morning, despite not yet being in use.

'They'll buy it,' Alexander responded confidently. 'Molly and Cora will see to that. It would be nice to have a clearer excuse, yes, but I'll put my mind to that. One thing at a time, that's the secret. After all, they're only just getting used to having their bums flushed.'

They turned from the machines to walk out into the yard. The girls were just finishing their morning exercises, their faces flushed, their skin shiny with sweat, despite the cold of the early morning. Alexander paused to watch for a while, admiring the way the sweat-soaked cotton of their underclothes clung to the flesh beneath.

Cora in particular looked appealing, her dark skin in strong contrast to the white cloth, her buttocks showing as quivering globes as they moved in her ample knickers, her huge breasts straining against the fabric, both nipples stiff and prominent. The white girls were not far behind. Both were showing an abundance of flesh, with their wet knickers clinging to the dark of their pubic hair at the front and the contours of their bottom to the rear. Both their bras were inadequate to hold in their breasts.

He paused to admire them for a second, trying to decide who was the more appealing. Both were tall, both well built and unequivocally feminine. Holly was a little more elegant, her proportions classic, her face delicate, Hazel more fleshy, fuller, more rustic in her beauty. Holly projected innocence, shyness with a wilful edge that made the prospect of taming her appealing. Hazel was more earthy, less reserved, yet with a tendency to pout very prettily indeed when challenged.

It was true that they might have been sisters, especially when their more intimate detail were considered. Hazel was more busty, and her nipples were larger, but once their legs were spread there was very little difference. When Molly put them on the clysopomp nothing was hidden, and both he and Herbert had frequently stolen the chance to watch. Both girls had big, opulent bottoms, the cheeks firm and fleshy, and clefts deep. Both had plump, fleshy cunts of pale flesh, the outer lips swelling and full around the soft pink folds of the inner. Both were equally hairy. Both were also virgin, their hymens closing off each vagina to a tiny, ragged hole. Even their bottom holes were similar, brown, well puckered and fleshy.

Reginald Thann, he reflected, was an idiot. To want a fine girl like Holly Bomefield-Mullins as a sexual slave was only common sense, but to attempt to reduce her by starvation was a fool's game. Her body was glorious, magnificently feminine, her bottom and breasts most of all. She was beautiful too, her face delicate, fragile, her hair thick and a rich, healthy brown, her complexion like thick cream. Only a madman would want to reduce her to the sort of grovelling wretch his uncle seemed to expect, especially when it seemed highly unlikely that she would fully recover. While there was no question that it would be an effective revenge on Charlotte Cary, spoiling Holly's beauty seemed to be rather missing the point.

In fact it seemed a shame to surrender Holly at all. Molly's devotion was a delight but, having grown used to it, he wanted more. He also knew that she would accept whatever he did, or so she had frequently assured him, apparently not just willing, but keen that he should take on other girls. Of the three, Holly appealed the most. Cora was willing, perhaps too willing, but with her it was impossible not to feel that she was somehow laughing at him. However degrading the orders she was prepared to obey, it was always ultimately by her own choice, a game.

Hazel appealed. She was fuller, more abundant, her figure more exaggerated in every way than Holly, and also pretty, with her bold eyes and her luxuriant brown curls. Yet there was something slightly bovine about her, a passivity, a placid acceptance of events that was less than entirely satisfying to him. Even when he had come in to watch her take an enema she had betrayed no emotion beyond a faint resentment when she started to pout. Holly had been crimson with blushes.

Molly snapped out an order. The three girls turned as one to run from the gate and out across the frost-laden turf, Molly following. Alexander smiled to himself, impressed by their ready obedience. He watched them as they went, admiring the four jiggling bottoms. Holly, if anything, had put on a little weight, certainly muscle.

So had he, and Herbert had lost none despite Alexander's demands that he diet. Food was good, and plentiful. With all but a small proportion of the Manor's land allotted to local farmers at peppercorn rents, a regular supply of lamb and pork was assured. The same sources provided eggs and vegetables, while there was no shortage of bread or potatoes, and combining his own cellar with those of Herbert and his cousins had ensured a good five years' supply of wine and spirits. Cora, who had originally come over with a wealthy New Orleans family as an assistant cook, was also a great asset, with a particular flair for pastries.

'Quite a view,' he remarked, turning at last from his contemplation of the girls. 'Come along, Puffer.'

Herbert turned reluctantly away and followed Alexander into the house. In the hall a large brown envelope lay on the mat. Alexander collected it and brought it into the study. He had had a table brought in to use as a desk, and he took a seat behind it as Herbert settled himself into one of the armchairs.

'What do we have here, then? Ministry of Food. The rationing bumph, I expect . . . Yes, it is. Now let me see.'

For a moment he studied the thick sheaf of information in silence while Herbert looked on with the expression on his podgy face growing increasingly concerned. Finally he spoke.

'Does that affect us?'

'Yes, directly as we don't have our own canteen, in theory at least.'

'Are we going to have to cut down at all?'

'Yes,' Alexander answered. 'They're not doing things by halves. Good grief, meat is to be rationed by price, at one shilling's worth per week. What are you supposed to buy with that?'

Herbert had gone pale.

'Not that it should affect us too badly, although beef may prove a bit of a problem, and pork if things get really bad. We should do well enough for lamb though, and you're the squire, so there'll be no difficulties with game. Fish may be a problem, but we should manage locally for trout. No, not everything affects us, by any means. Hmm, they're introducing some sort of coupon system, very complicated. That's for clothing and such like, apparently you have to hand over the coupons when you pay. That won't affect uniforms, naturally, but it would be a shame to see the girls go bare legged.'

'If it comes to that. What about chocolate?'

'Let me see . . . three ounces a week.'

'Three ounces a week?'

'Afraid so.'

'Sugar, marmalade?'

'Eight ounces of sugar a week, not good. Cora will have to cut down on the cake making, I'm afraid. We're allowed a pound of jam or marmalade every two months, but we've plenty in stock, and we get an extra pound of sugar if we make our own jam, so that's good. Hmm . . . there are some truly revolting suggestions here, you know. They recommend dried egg, powdered milk and margarine. Damned if I will!'

'What's margarine?'

'Margarine? Don't you know the line from Belloc? "And I with these mine eyes have seen, A dreadful stuff called margarine, Consumed by folk in Bethnal Green." I don't remember the rest, but it more or less sums it up. Not that I've ever tried it, of course, but it looks vile and it smells like that stuff we use to grease the girls' arses. In fact it's probably similar. I believe they make it by some sort of chemical process anyway.'

'How revolting!'

'My thoughts exactly. Now that's not good. Only two ounces of tea per week. Not good at all. You can make a woman strip, you can spank her bottom, you can make her take enemas in front of an audience, and she'll curl up at your feet like a kitten. But take away her afternoon cup of tea and she'll turn into a monster. We'll have to do without to make sure they get enough.

What else ... One egg per week! Oh, well, I don't suppose that will affect us much, not here, but still.'

'Terrible!'

'Yes, shame the girls can't lay them, really, but we know what they can do, and by God they're going to need to! Two pints of milk, per week! They have to be joking! And butter, two ounces, good God! Cheese, two ounces! Two ounces! By God I'd want more than that with my after dinner glass of port! Not only that, but it's all subject to availability, which undoubtedly means that half the time we won't get any at all.'

'Oh, dear,' Herbert whined. 'Those beastly Germans, why do they always have to go and spoil everything! And our lot! I mean, I knew we'd have to tighten our belts a little, but this is awful.'

'No it's not, Puffer, my boy. It's a heaven-sent opportunity, that's what it is. Get Cora in here.'

Holly made a final adjustment to her tie. It still felt strange to be wearing what she had always considered masculine clothing, but considerably less strange than it had done at first. The same was true of the uniform as a whole, which was a great deal tighter and more restrictive than the dresses she had been used to.

It was still an enormous relief to put it on, after nearly an hour exercising in nothing but her knickers and bra, and with both the male officers watching at one point. Just the thought sent the blood to her face. Squadron Leader Gorringe was bad enough, but he was handsome, and there was no denying that it made being near naked in front of him easier. Having Flying Officer Maray watch was worse, far worse. There was a leering, prying intensity about the way he stared. Gorringe made her blush. Maray made her blush and shudder, invariably bringing her an uncomfortably intense awareness of her sex.

Content with her appearance, she made her way quickly downstairs to help with breakfast, only to draw up short at finding Leading Aircraftwoman MacCallion in the hall.

'Briefing in the AOC's office,' MacCallion said bluntly, nodding towards what Holly found herself thinking of as the library regardless of its current use. She changed course. Both Hazel and Cora where already there, also the two officers. MacCallion entered behind her and shut the door as Holly got into line.

'At ease,' Squadron Leader Gorringe ordered. 'Right, I know you all want to get your breakfast down you, and so do I, so I'll keep this brief. We had a letter from the Ministry of Food this morning, laying out the details of the rationing policy that has been introduced. Leading Aircraftwoman MacCallion has posted the relevant documents on the board. I will distribute individual items at the end of this briefing. I fear that this will mean considerable restrictions, if not actual hardship. Now, while we don't do badly for ourselves up here, and we're certainly not in any danger of starvation, I would nevertheless appreciate any little wrinkles you might have. Anyone?'

Nobody answered. He looked from one face to another.

'No? Well, perhaps something will come to you later. For now . . .'

'Excuse me, sir,' Hazel said suddenly.

'Yes, Aircraftwoman Mullins?'

'There might be whortleberries on the moors, sir . . . in season.'

'Yes, Aircraftwoman Mullins, in season. Thank you in any case. Now . . .'

'Seagulls' eggs are edible, sir,' Molly put in.

'Yes, yes, another good idea, if we can spare the time to search for them on some suitable cliffs. Now . . .'

'There are some jolly big snails around, I've noticed,' Flying Officer Maray stated. '*Escargots*, the French call them. They're good.'

'Perhaps, yes. Anybody else?'

The was silence.

'Right then. There is something else, something I had been hoping to avoid, but now becomes too important to overlook. Mullins, Bomefield-Mullins, it may have occurred to you to wonder about the nature of the machines in the dairy you have been working on over the past few weeks?'

'Yes, sir,' Hazel answered him. 'We thought they were milking machines, patent milking machines, for goats we thought.'

'Close, Mullins, very close. They are in fact milking machines, but not for goats. I won't beat about the bush. They are for women.'

'I beg your pardon, sir?' Holly asked before she could stop herself.

'For women,' Gorringe replied. 'They are for extracting breast milk.'

'Whose?' Holly asked, forgetting to address him properly in her shock.

'Originally?' he responded. 'I have no idea. Now, any woman who sees fit to volunteer. Naturally I wouldn't attempt to order any of you, but when you see the restrictions on dairy products the Ministry will be imposing, you will appreciate that you might be of very considerable service. Nor do I wish to rush you into a decision. Consider the matter, and let me know by lunchtime. Any questions?'

Holly hesitated, struggling to take in what was being suggested, glad to have been given the opportunity to decline such an outrageous request, but too embarrassed to ask the question she wanted to. Hazel did instead.

'Yes, sir. Wouldn't we need to be having babies to make milk?'

'Good question,' Gorringe answered. 'Apparently not.'

'Isn't . . . isn't it all rather indecent?' Holly blurted out, her outrage finally getting the better of her shyness.'

'Indecent?' Gorringe answered immediately, raising his eyebrows in surprise. 'There's nothing indecent about it. *Mens sana in corpore sano*, my dear girl, health and exercise. The human body is not indecent, and for the female of the species to produce milk is a natural function. It might be considered a little indelicate perhaps, but never indecent. As I understand it, it's not even all that unusual in this part of the country. Flying Officer Maray?'

'Yes, thank you, sir,' Maray answered, rising to his feet. 'It seems, although there are no actual records of this fact, that the practice was carried out during the last war, both here, and at least one of the local farms. Hence the milking machines. The locals are perhaps rather, er . . . secretive about it, and I would advise against bringing the topic up in village, any more than one might a delicate matter such as . . . ah . . . um . . . illegitimacy. That's er . . . it, I think, sir.'

'So there we have it,' Gorringe went on. 'And besides, I like to think we have come beyond the narrow values of our grandparents' generation. As I have explained before, health and exercise, *mens sana in corpore sano*. The human body is God's gift, and nothing to be ashamed of. We should make the best of it, should we not?'

Holly didn't answer. What he was saying seemed to make sense, as it had when he announced the hygiene programme, yet the implications of it still seemed hideously embarrassing and deeply improper.

'No?' he went on, his voice as bland as if he had just announced some minor variation in the day's routine. 'Well then, to breakfast. Pick up your bumph on the way out.'

MacCallion gave a brief order and the girls stepped forwards one by one to take an envelope from Flying

Officer Maray. They then trooped from the room, pausing only briefly at the notice board in the hall to take in the details of rationing. In the kitchen, they hastily began to prepare breakfast. Holly said nothing, wanting Hazel to speak first before she voiced her opinion. Cora got in first.

'Well, I'm going to volunteer.'

'Really?' Holly demanded, more shocked by the casual tone of the black girl's voice than anything else.

'Yes,' Cora went on. 'Why not? We drink human milk as babies, don't we? Why not as adults?'

'Yes, but . . . ,' Holly stammered. 'I don't know . . . it's just not normal!'

'It seems to be normal enough around here,' Hazel put in.

'I don't think so,' Holly answered her. 'I just think the AOC's a pervert, and Flying Officer Maray too.'

'There are six machines, Holly. That means six girls at a time. It's got to be normal, hasn't it, if so many of them were doing it?'

'They could have made the machines specially.'

'Those machines were old, and they'd been used a lot. Come on, Holly, you repaired them, you saw.'

'OK, so his cousin Jervis and his wife were perverts too. That's no surprise if they were anything like him.'

'So they'll get a thrill out of it. That's just men for you. I don't want to have to put up with two pints of milk a week, not to mention the miserable amount of butter and cheese. We'll be able to have cream too, and –'

'You're not going to volunteer, are you?'

'Yes, I thought I would, and so should you. The more of us do it, the more there'll be to go around.'

'Hazel!'

'Makes sense to me,' Cora said.

Holly went silent. Her cheeks were flushed with blood and her nipples were inexplicably and embarrassingly hard. Her breasts seemed bigger too, enormous balloons of flesh hanging from her chest, each one like a cow's udder. She gave a shiver at the thought and tried to stop herself imagining how it would feel to be on one of the machines, the big rubber sheathes on her breasts, sucking out the milk into a pail. Flying Officer Maray would be stood to one side, leering at her in her nudity, his cock in his hand, ready for her mouth, for her quim . . .

She shook herself to rid her mind of the disturbing thought. As had happened so many times before, the most disgusting, perverted thoughts always seemed to push themselves uppermost in her mind. It was like the time Sapphie had made Hazel masturbate the notorious Peeping Tom they called Mr Peeper. Hazel had actually done it, and even taken him in her mouth, yet it hadn't seemed to trouble her too much. Holly had thought about it for months, pictures of Mr Peeper's grotesque penis constantly forcing themselves into her mind. It had happened even when she was playing with Sapphie and Hazel, even when she was actually coming, with one or other of her friend's faces buried between her thighs.

'Do you think it really happens a lot down here?' she asked timidly after a while. 'I mean, I've never heard of it before.'

'I have,' Cora asserted. 'It happens back in the States, in the corn belt mainly, where there aren't many dairy cattle. OK, so women aren't actually brought into milk, but mums keep it up once they've started.'

'Oh.'

'It's just one of those taboo things,' Hazel added. 'I mean, it's not something that's going to be talked about much, is it? But that doesn't mean it doesn't happen. Like playing together, or the curse.'

Holly nodded, remembering the shocked reaction of some of the other girls at Innsworth Camp to her casual intimacy with Hazel. She hadn't really understood at first, assuming everybody did it, and had been amazed to discover just how strongly sexual play between girls was disapproved off, especially when the same girls seemed to take sexual activity with men for granted. Many had not even been virgins. She had known that her own upbringing had been unorthodox, and had still been astonished by just how different other women's attitudes were. The same seemed to be true of the idea of being milked.

Molly MacCallion bustled in, breaking Holly's train of thought. She threw a quick glance around the kitchen before addressing Cora.

'Isn't that porridge ready yet, Jackson? Look sharp.'

'Nearly done,' Cora answered.

'I take it you all know your duty?' MacCallion went on, glancing around once more. 'I realise that the AOC has only asked for volunteers for milking, but if any of you should back out, believe me, I'll make your lives hell. That's all.'

She turned abruptly on her heel and left the kitchen. Holly heaved a deep sigh.

Squadron Leader Gorringe pulled off his gloves, then his goggles and flying helmet, handing each to Molly as she hastened to keep pace beside him. The morning flight had passed without complication. As usual, he had taken the Gloster Gladiator up to the regulation sixteen thousand feet in a broad spiral, paying more attention to the magnificence of the Devon countryside beneath him than to his implements. It was a part of the day he enjoyed, bringing a sense of freedom and also superiority. Better still, it was the best time to think.

With both Molly and Cora playing their parts, it was proving easy to manipulate the other two girls. Hazel simply seemed to take cruelties and humiliations as they came, as if they were an expected part of life. She never showed more than her resentful pout, even with the contents of her bottom dribbling down over her sex, or afterwards, when scrubbing the mess up, naked and on her knees. Holly pouted more and blushed a lot, but she did it, and that was what mattered.

Herbert's scheme, to bring girls into milk as his cousin and uncle had done, no longer seemed a far-fetched fantasy, but a simple matter of time and patience. They had the girls, they had the machines, and if Herbert was right, the girls would in due course start producing milk. Herbert would then be able to indulge his obsession to the full, while he himself would have an extra dimension added to his enjoyment of the power he held over the girls.

The situation with Reginald Thann was less satisfying. The original idea had been simply to corrupt Sappho Yates, preferably making her a whore, perhaps leaving her pregnant. Since then, Thann's demands had grown increasingly severe, and increasingly difficulty to fulfil. His hold over Holly relied on his own authority, and it was simply not practical to introduce some mysterious 'Controller' from whom all orders flowed. Nor was it practical, or sensible, to degrade her to the extent Thann was demanding. She might rebel, which would be potentially disastrous. Even if she didn't, Hazel might, even Cora and Herbert. Molly he felt he could rely on.

Despite that, he clearly had to make some effort to keep Thann happy. Providing false reports was the obvious answer, and yet it was entirely possible that Thann might choose to make an inspection, especially if he thought Holly would be waiting for him as a broken and cringing slave. It was therefore better to claim that he was making every effort, but that progress was slow. He could then put forward the argument that she should not be turned over to him until she was ready. As Thann wanted her absolute surrender, it seemed likely to be an argument he would accept.

How long he could string it out he was uncertain, and there was also the problem that while Thann wanted Holly starved, it would clearly benefit her milk production if she was well fed, even fattened up a little. Her breasts were a good size, but smaller than Hazel's, and smaller still than Cora's. Two or maybe three stone of extra flesh seemed to be about right, filling her out without making her inefficient.

By the time he had landed, the full plan was clear in his mind. He would keep Holly in good physical health and work on her subservience. He would make sure she stayed a virgin, but make no effort to groom her for Thann. His reports to Thann would show slow yet definite progress, never too little, never too much.

'So, what's for lunch, darling?' he asked as they reached the yard.

'A pheasant,' she answered, 'a fine cock bird, served on a bed of watercress, with roast parsnips and croquette potatoes.'

'Splendid.'

'I've a little surprise for you too, sir.'

'Oh yes?'

She had opened the door for him and he had marched through and into the hall before she spoke again.

'Our volunteers, sir.'

He stopped, to return the salute of the three girls lined up in the hall. All were stood smartly to attention, and if Holly's face betrayed a touch of the sulks, the others were expressionless.

'Excellent! Excellent!' he declared happily. 'All four of you! That's the spirit! With girls like you in England, we'll have this war over in a trice!'

Holly drew her breath in. She was doing her best to ignore Flying Officer Maray's stare as she undid the buttons of her blouse. Suggesting he leave, or turn his back even, was obviously pointless. He was quite capable of standing in the bathroom door while she was taking an enema without the slightest suggestion that he felt he was being intrusive. At least now it would only be her breasts on display, and not every rude detail between her legs, or so she told herself. It seemed to make little difference. Her face was still hot with blushes, her chest pink, her nipples and quim uncomfortable. He had a stiff cock too, just as he did when watching her take her enemas, a short yet wide bar in his trousers that suggested an alarming width.

When she was on the clysopomp she always half expected him to pull it out and simply stuff it into her body. She was sure the straps were only there to allow the operator to persecute the girl, and that several of the implements had no hygienic function whatsoever. The straps also gave her a strange sense of irresponsibility, while she knew her quim was always ready, and that he could see. It was as if being in restraint made it reasonable for her to have her virginity taken, as if she had no reason to feel bad about it because she was not obliged to make a conscious act of surrender.

He hadn't done it, but she was very sure he had wanted to. Now she was going to be in a position only marginally less vulnerable, and if he wanted to have her, it would be a simple matter of tugging up her skirt and pulling down her knickers. It didn't bear thinking about, but at the same time it was impossible not to think about it. He would pull her uniform skirt up, jerking it up over her thighs, her bottom, her hips, to leave her showing behind, protected only by the flimsy cotton of her knickers. Not that they'd last long. He'd do it slowly too, drawing them down to prolong the agonising humiliation of her exposure, his breath hot on her bottom as her cheeks came on view, her crease, her bottom hole, her quim . . .

She shook her head, hard, trying desperately to rid herself of the awful images flooding her mind. Her blouse was open, her jacket off. She shrugged the blouse away, drawing out the moment before she had to expose herself by hanging it neatly with her jacket and tie. Her fingers went behind her back. Her bra came open. The weight of her breasts lolled forwards. She shut her eyes, took the cups, lifted, and she was bare, her chest on show, pink and fat and wobbly, the exposure made so much worse by the fact that her nipples were hard. She hung the bra up and went to stand in front of the machine.

The thick belly strap that would hold her body in place hung down to either side of the bench. It wasn't necessary, she would stay put, but she knew it would be used, and that deep down, she wanted it to be used. That way she could give in. When the time came for the thick, ugly cock to be inserted into her virgin quim there would be no guilt, no remorse, only the knowledge that the fat pervert Maray had tricked her into surrender . . .

The dairy door slammed. Holly turned her head, to where the other three girls stood beside her, each topless but otherwise immaculate, creating a strange contrast between naked chests and neat WAAF skirts. Squadron Leader Gorringe had come in. He was fingering his moustache was he walked towards them, his swagger stick in hand, the stick he so often used to flick their bottoms. He stopped beside Molly MacCallion, the first in line. She was stiff to attention, her back ramrod straight, her little breasts straining upwards, the nipples perky and taut. Holly quickly turned her face to the front.

'Splendid,' Gorringe remarked, 'that's what I like to see, proper military style, no slacking. Now, as you know, this is nothing more than a trial run, and I don't expect for a moment that we'll get any milk today. Still, twenty minutes a day after lunch, and we'll soon have you in, I would imagine. A little massage in your spare time wouldn't go amiss either, I don't suppose. In fact, to provide a little encouragement, here's five pounds for the first girl to provide a taster.'

He had drawn a large white note from his pocket and was holding it up. Holly immediately found herself trying to calculate how long it would take for her to earn five pounds on her wages of fourteen shillings a week. The simple answer was that it would be over seven weeks, giving her a sudden greed followed by immediate guilt. Squadron Leader Gorringe was still talking as he walked behind the line of topless girls.

'Very fetching you look too, if I may so, ladies. Once you're actually in milk, I think we'd better say knickers only, for the sake of hygiene and practicality, you understand. After all, I would not wish to place any unnecessary strain on your modesty.'

Holly had to stifle a gasp at the outrageous lie, but succeeded in holding herself in. Gorringe had reached the end of the line and was standing beside her, just inches away.

'Yes,' he continued, 'fine, healthy girls, all four of you, for which, to an extent at least, I believe I may thank my regime of exercise and hygiene. I don't think it will be long at all before we have all four of you in milk, no, not long at all.'

As he spoke he had reached out, to take hold of her right breast. She struggled to keep still, the muscles of her chest and shoulder jumping as his thumb brushed over her nipple, to make it harder still. He lifted, as if weighing her breast, and his face set into a thoughtful frown. Finally he released her.

'Yes,' he remarked as he started back down the line, 'very fine. Now, this is something I intend to do scientifically, and I do feel that the weight of your breasts may provide us with valuable data, both on your progress and your capacity. It will also answer some interesting questions. For instance, do girls with larger breasts produce more milk? If so, how does that extra production relate to size, or weight? Yes, we will take measurements. Aircraftwoman Jackson, how accurate are the kitchen scales?'

'To one-sixteenth of an ounce, sir,' Cora answered immediately.

'Excellent. Very well, by the left! One step forwards! Mount your machines!'

Holly obeyed, her now ingrained urge to follow an order making it a great deal easier for her as she climbed on to the bench. Only as the weight of her breasts shifted downwards did she realise that with all four of them on the milking frames it was going to mean that the men had to attend to any adjustments they could not make themselves.

Sure enough, the two officers did not even wait to see if the girls could manage, but stepped forwards immediately. Gorringe took hold of Molly's strap, binding it tight around her tiny waist as Maray went to Cora. Holly waited, wishing the machine didn't make her bottom stick out quite so blatantly, and praying that it would be the Squadron Leader and not the Flying Officer who attended to her.

Her prayers went unanswered. By the time Maray had fixed Cora's belly strap in place, Gorringe was already working on Hazel. Maray came to her, and she was already fighting down the disturbing images of having the big cock hidden in his long-johns pushed up into her defenceless body as he took hold of the strap. A moment later the buckle had been pulled tight and she was helpless. It got worse. Rather than going back to Cora, Maray stayed with her, fixing her arms into place first, then going to her legs. As he began to ruck her skirt up to allow the strap to be fixed around her lower thigh, the images in her mind grew stronger than ever. Her skirt was up, and it didn't need to be up much further before her stocking tops would be showing, the legs of her knickers too. Then it would be the seat of her knickers, which could be pulled down so easily, and up would go his cock, as simple as that, plunging deep into her body, bursting her hymen on the way . . .

Her legs had been secured. She was now completely trapped, able to move only her head, forearms and lower legs. Her skirt was tight across her bottom, making it feel more prominent, and more vulnerable than ever. In ways it was worse than being on the clysopomp. She was covered, it was true, but it wasn't going to take much to expose her. Not just that, but on the clysopomp she had the hose up her bottom to make entry awkward. She couldn't imagine even Maray being perverted enough to mount her while she had a quart of soapy water in her gut ready to squirt out.

She shut her eyes in shock as he moved forwards to take one of her breasts in his hand, his fat, damp fingers squeezing her flesh, fondling her for a moment before he picked up the cup. The rubber touched her breast, Maray fumbling with the unfamiliar device, so that his fingers seemed to be loitering on her flesh for a long, long time before he finally managed to get it done. He managed, though, introducing her breast to the suction cup. Her nipple protruded downwards, pointing into the pail placed below just in case.

Maray went to her other breast, taking just as long to fix the cup into place, and again making sure he had a good grope. Holly took it with her eyes closed, her face dark with blushes and the same awful fantasy running over and over in her mind, her bottom stripped and her quim penetrated as she lay bound and helpless.

As Maray finally stood up she cursed herself and wondered why it was always the most unappealing of men who forced themselves into her fantasies. It had been the same with the ghastly Mr Peeper, and others, even the fat old butler at Babcary where her mother lived. It was different now, though. It could become real, all too easily.

She waited as the others were strapped up, acutely aware of the feel of the suction cups on her breasts and the bonds on her limbs. Her breathing had picked up, her need for air rising until she wondered if she was going to panic. She fought the feeling down, determined not to seem weak in front of the others, particularly Hazel. So many times it had been the same, when Sapphie whipped them, or other things, Hazel always coping so much more easily.

'All done, sir,' Maray announced, rising from where he had been feeding Cora's fat black breasts into the suction cups.'

'Splendid,' Gorringe answered. 'Molly ... Leading Aircraftwoman MacCallion is a bit loose in her cups. I've had to use a couple of bits of string to make sure they stay in. Otherwise, ready for take-off, I think?'

'Right we are, sir,' Maray answered and casually reached up to flick the switch.

Holly gasped as both her breasts were suddenly squeezed, so hard that for one awful moment she was sure they would burst. They didn't. The pressure went, only to come back a second later, and again. She found herself gasping for air, barely under control, dizzy, her vision hazy. She started to struggle, barely conscious that she was doing it, yet with a tiny, mocking voice in the back of her head telling her that now she knew what the straps were for. Soon she was writhing in her bonds, and calling out over and over for it to stop. It made no difference. The sucking went on, relentless, hard, her breasts alternately squashed and pulled, squashed and pulled, until she was sure she would faint. Her bladder went, completely unexpectedly, pee squirting backwards from her quim, into her big drawers and down her legs. She cried out in shame and misery as the hot fluid began to patter on the floor behind her, but still it went on. She started to kick, her feet drumming on the floor behind her, to shake her head, her hair flying in every direction, to hammer her fists on the hard wood of the stand. Spittle was running from her mouth, piddle still gushing from her quim, in little spurts and jets, to the same rhythm as the pump.

It stopped, suddenly, leaving her gasping on the bench, her vision red. Her whole body was prickling with sweat. Her breasts were in agony. Her stomach was fluttering. She felt sick, dizzy and completely out of control. She was too far gone to even think of holding back the last of what had been in her bladder as it ran down the inside of her thighs to join the puddle on the floor. When Gorringe spoke his voice seemed to come from a great distance.

'Hmm, yes, I think you two riggers have fed rather too much power into the system. Is she all right, Puffer?'

The answer was a splash of water. Holly managed to turn her head, to see Maray standing with a bucket upended over Molly MacCallion's head, as if through a heat haze. She realised the little Irish woman had passed out, and wondered how close she had come to doing the same. Nearer to her, Hazel was wide-eyed and wide-mouthed, but managed a weak smile as their eyes met. Holly slumped down, exhausted.

Molly was released first, and stood up, swaying slightly in Gorringe's arms, her eyes unfocused. Maray set to work on Cora's straps, then Hazel's, and finally Holly's. Released, she struggled to stand, finding her legs weak and her head still swimming. The suction cups came off and she cried out in fresh pain, then gritted her teeth as her circulation came slowly back to normal. At last she looked down.

Her breasts had swollen to two huge, bloated, angry pink balloons of flesh, each with the agonisingly swollen nipple protruding a good inch from the tip. Her skin felt impossibly sensitive, too tender to touch, yet at the same time itching so badly that the urge to scratch and to pull at her nipples was close to irresistible. She forced herself to stand to attention instead, as the Squadron Leader approached.

'Ah, Bomefield-Mullins,' he said, prodding the very tip of his shoe into the pool of urine in which she was standing. 'I see you've had a little accident.'

'Yes, sir,' she managed weakly, the blood rising to her face despite the state she was in.

'Never mind,' he went on. 'These things happen. Mop it up in a minute.'

He patted her bottom and turned to face the line of girls, three standing, Molly seated on her milking frame.

'Well,' he began, 'an interesting trial, and I think we have learned something. Yes, we have definitely learned something. So, less power, the straps are a clear necessity, we need a supply of water on hand, and it ought to be done nude in case of unfortunate accidents. So, Mullins and Bomefield-Mullins, if you could spare a moment this afternoon to make the necessary adjustments?'

'Yes, sir,' Holly managed.

'Splendid,' he went on. 'Then I think we'll call it a day, even though that was only about eight minutes. Until tomorrow then.'

He made for the door, leaving Holly amazed that what had seemed like one minute had in fact been eight, and with a vague sense of disappointment.

8

Kerslake Manor, Devon – March 1940

Holly placed her left breast gently on the scale. The two-pound weight on the other plate immediately lifted. Molly MacCallion removed the weight to replace it with a four-pounder, the largest of the set. Slowly, Holly's boob rose up. Molly switched the weights once more, peering close as the scale shifted once more. Holly held perfectly still as a one-pound weight was added, then an eight-ounce one. Still the weights remained up. Molly frowned and added the four-ounce weight, then the two. Slowly, Holly's breast rose up.

'We'll call that three pounds, fourteen ounces,' Molly stated.

Cora made a mark on the clipboard she was holding. She too was topless, her huge black breasts thrusting out, as round and firm as melons, and as big. Hazel was also bare from the waist up, and her naked breasts nearly as impressive in bulk as Cora's. Molly alone was covered, and that only by a thin chemise that did little to hide her plump breasts, now small only by comparison with the others.

'That's an increase all round, Corporal MacCallion,' Cora announced.

'Good,' Molly answered. 'Maybe it will be today.'

Holly nodded. Her breasts felt swollen and tender, as they always did now, while her skin had changed in texture, growing tauter and more rubbery. She was having to treat her nipples with fat as well, using the margarine to which their ration entitled them, but which everyone but Molly and Cora refused to eat.

If her breasts were bigger, that wasn't all. She had put on nearly two stone, despite rationing, both officers doing their best to keep the food rich and plentiful, and never stinting on the supply of wine, port in particular. Her bottom was both bigger and more muscular, the cheeks high, round and firm, so that she'd had to let out the seams on her knickers.

The knickers did at least fit, just. She had had to abandon a bra altogether, partly because none of hers fitted any more, and partly because it was more comfortable without one. Her blouses and jackets were hard to do up, and she was more than a little grateful for the officers' now casual attitude to undone buttons. The display of her cleavage to Herbert Maray's prying gaze was a small price to pay when she spent so much of her time with not just her breasts but her whole body naked.

She fell into line behind Hazel, waiting as Cora and Molly MacCallion completed the report and put away the weighing scales. The time set aside for breast weighing and milking practice, Squadron Leader Gorringe's 'Hampers' Half-hour', was now directly before lunch, following digestive problems brought on by the machines. The suction cups had also been adjusted to provide a less violent motion, so that the girls' breasts were now squeezed to a slow, even rhythm. It still left Holly pink and tender after every session, but none of them had passed out or wet themselves since the adjustments had been made.

Molly MacCallion, now a Corporal, snapped out an order. The three girls set off, marching in a neat line to the dairy, each to take her place at a machine. Molly selected the last in line, and all four came to attention as the two officers entered the shed, the cotton of their blouses creaking faintly as it took the strain of their breasts.

'Well, girls,' Gorringe stated. 'How about some milk today, eh? You certainly look ready. In your own time, Corporal MacCallion.'

'Sir,' Molly snapped back. 'On command, squad disrobe . . . Disrobe!'

Holly began to strip, as always finding it a lot easier when there was no choice in the matter. Stripping had become a familiar and precise routine, and deviations were likely to lead to the application of the Squadron Leader's swagger stick to her bottom. First went her cap, jacket and skirt, in that order, each to be hung on the double peg installed on the wall behind her. Her shoes followed, placed under a chair also provided and on which she had to sit to remove her stockings. Standing again, she unbuttoned her blouse, took it off and folded it on the chair. Her bra or chemise would have followed if she'd had one. Last came her knickers, leaving her to return to attention, stark naked.

'Now that's what I call a parade,' Maray remarked as the four girls formed their line in perfect timing.

He was walking behind them, setting Holly's stomach fluttering as he came near. The images of being fucked by him as she lay helpless on the milking machine had never gone away, despite the increasing familiarity of the embarrassing routine. He had not done it, though, restricting his attentions to fondling her breasts, on the pretext of checking their development, and familiar pats on her bottom. Sometimes he made Cora wait behind, and Holly suspected that the black girl was made to go down on his cock, but that was all.

She got her pat, his hand lingering briefly on her bottom to feel the shape of her cheek. Then he had moved on, beyond the end of the line.

'Squad, ready!' Molly snapped. 'Mount your machines on my command . . . Mount!'

Holly went forwards, mounting the machine in the now familiar but still hideously embarrassing posture, breasts hanging down, bottom thrust out, quim well spread behind. Her muscles twitched as Maray began to strap her in place, and the fantasy started to rise up again, too strong for her to fight, of being mounted and casually, contemptuously, fucked. As her belly strap tightened her bottom lifted and spread, adding the exposure of her anus to her woes. She was sure that no man's cock could possibly fit into the tiny hole between her cheeks, but she did know men liked to do it. Cora, who seemed to know everything about male behaviour, had told her. She was sure Maray was no exception. Tied and helpless, she could be buggered, whether his cock fitted properly or not.

She could feel his breath on her skin as her legs straps were fastened, then his red, sweating face appeared beside her as he came to strap up her arms and put her breasts in the suction cups. He was better at it than he had been, but he invariably treated himself to a quick feel, and for Holly, every single touch of his fingers seemed magnified a thousand times. It also left her nipples erect, even before her breasts had been squeezed into the cups.

Soon she was ready, all five straps tight to hold her in position, both breasts encapsulated in thick, pliant rubber, her nipples jutting out over the milk pail. Squadron Leader Gorringe had gone to the machine. She winced as his hand went to the switch, and it had started, the shock of the first, sudden squeeze making her gasp for all that it was perhaps the fiftieth time she had been on the machine.

She closed her eyes as the pumping began, her breathing growing deep and changing to the rhythm of the machine. Each squeeze sent a little shock through her, painful at first, but changing to pleasure as it went on. Her flesh began to ripple gently in time, each pulse focussing on her quim, so that she had quickly begun to juice so liberally that it was trickling down into her pubic hair. The men could see, she knew, and it seemed astonishing to her that either could hold back from plunging a stiff cock into her all too obviously ready hole.

A clock had been installed, ostensibly for efficiency's sake. When both men had watches this was clearly a lie. It was loud, the ticking drawing out the twenty minutes she spent on the machine to what seemed an endless agony of embarrassment. Her ears were constantly straining for the half-hour chime that would signal an end to the ordeal, bringing relief but also disappointment: that it was over, that she hadn't been fucked.

The chime came, at the very point Holly was beginning to wonder if she wouldn't come to orgasm simply through the endless stimulation of her breasts. She was close, she knew, and she was terrified that if it did happen she would cry out, begging to be mounted as she came, and that one of the men might very well oblige.

As the squeezing stopped, she let out her breath in a long, exhausted sigh. She had been closer to orgasm than ever, so close she knew no more than a light touch would have been needed to get her there. She also knew that if her hands had been free she would have been masturbating, and realised that there might be another reason for the strap, to spare her modesty.

Her breasts were pink, swollen and felt agonisingly tender, as always. They were also wet with sweat, but that was all. She still inspected each as soon as she had been released, thinking of the crisp white five pound note Gorringe had pinned to the notice board and hoping for milk. There was none, but as she gently lowered her breasts Hazel gave a squeak of excitement.

'Sir! Holly, look!'

Holly turned, to find Hazel holding up both her breasts, now so big that the flesh bulged from around her spread fingers. Like Holly's, Hazel's breasts were flushed pink, with the nipples straining to erection, also like Holly's, they were slick with sweat. Unlike Holly's, each big nipple was covered with spots of a thick, yellow-white fluid, milk.

'By God, she's done it!' Gorringe exclaimed as he stepped close. 'Puffer, look here, Hazel has done it. She's in milk! Look, girls, I said you could do it!'

They gathered round, protocol forgotten, Hazel proudly holding up her boobs to show off the milk-wet nipples. Cora reached out to touch, stroking a finger on one of Hazel's teats to gather up a drop of milk, which she put to her mouth. Molly immediately pushed forwards to do the same.

Hazel was smiling, clearly proud of herself as she soaked up the attention of the others. Even when Squadron Leader Gorringe ducked down to take one stiff teat in his mouth and suck she simply giggled, complaining only that his moustache tickled. He paid no attention, but drew deep, sucking in his cheeks. When he did come away, there was a trace of white on his lips. Immediately the spots of fluid on Hazel's teat reappeared. They were larger now, fat beads of milk, growing as she gave her breasts a gentle squeeze.

'Splendid!' Gorringe crowed, 'and jolly nice too, hmm, sharp, yet rich . . . very fine! Five pounds to you then, my dear, and we'd better celebrate. Cora . . . that is Aircraft . . . oh, the hell with it . . . Cora, my sweet, rustle up something special for dinner. Herbert, fetch up some of the twenty-one. I think this calls for a celebration!'

'Port,' Alexander declared happily, placing the basketful of black and cobwebbed bottles down on the sideboard. 'The twenty-one Croft, among the finest we have in stock. Don't stint yourselves, and no titles either, or ranks. Tonight we are equal, and the hell with convention too. Molly, my love, how about wrapping that pretty face around old John Thomas while Puffer sees to the decanting?'

He caught the look of shock and surprise in Holly's eyes as he made the suggestion, and suppressed a chuckle. Molly also looked doubtful, but only for a moment. Then she had come to him, her eyes full of mischief as she got down on her knees in front of an armchair.

Alexander sat down. Herbert had gone to the sideboard. Cora and Hazel were talking and did not seem to have noticed what was going on. Holly was trying not to stare. As casually as he could, he reached down to unbutton his fly. His cock was already stiffening, the prospect of making Molly suck him in front of the other girls highly arousing. He pulled it free; the head was poking out through the mouth of his foreskin, red and shiny with fluid. Holly's mouth came a little open.

Molly took his cock in hand and he relaxed back. His favourite brand of cigar was running low, but he had brought a box up for the occasion, and reached for one as Molly began to roll his foreskin back and forth in her hand. Holly was now staring openly, and the other two girls had noticed, Cora giggling behind her hand, Hazel's face unreadable.

Determined to make the best possible show of casual superiority, he kept his attention on the cigar, removing the band, clipping each end, lighting and drawing it while Molly worked on his penis. By the time he had the tip glowing bright orange and the rich, hot smoke had begun to flow, he was erect in her hand. She took him in, between pretty, painted lips, to suck on his helmet as she masturbated him into her mouth. He took a mouthful of smoke and blew a large ring into the air, watching it rise as her dainty hand scooped his balls out of his long-johns.

He felt content, absolutely at ease with the world, replete after an exceptional dinner, with a good cigar, good port to come, and a pretty girl sucking his cock. Cora had prepared a true feast, using all her skill. Snails had been washed down with a rare old Mosel, its German origin conveniently ignored. Tiny trout had been served grilled with a hazelnut butter and accompanied by a white Graves from his own collection. Hare from the moor had followed, stewed, as the guns of the Gladiator had negated any possibility of it being served whole. He had managed to find a Hermitage from before the Great War for the hare, and finally there had been a steamed treacle pudding with an Yquem of even more venerable vintage. The only thing missing had been cheese, and it was an omission he intended to put right as soon as possible.

Hazel's milk had come in fully. She was even having to wear two pieces of flannel over her breasts to soak up the excess, which still came, just minutes after she had been relieved. They had put her on the milking frame in the afternoon, and while she had only been able to produce a couple of fluid ounces, it had been enough for everyone to have a taste. There had even been a little over for tea. It now seemed realistic to expect to be getting worthwhile volumes within weeks if not days.

Molly was doing extraordinary things to his cock, using lips, tongue, the tube of her throat and both hands to excite him. He decided to come, but also to ensure that his orgasm did not mark the end of the entertainment. He reached out to pat her head.

'Come along, bubbies out, my darling, and your behind too, make a show of yourself!'

Molly kept sucking, but her hands went back immediately, to ease up her skirt over the seat of her knickers. She wiggled, took hold of the waistband, tugged it out from beneath the girdle she was wearing, and pulled them down. Alexander could see that she had pushed the rear pouch down just far enough to make a bold display of bare bottom framed in raised skirt, lowered knickers and taut suspender straps. It was a sight he was sorry to miss, but the soft, wet feel of her mouth was just too good to allow him to break away. He was going to come at any moment.

With her bottom bare, her hands went straight to her top, to open her uniform jacket, then her blouse, all the while sucking and licking at his aching cock. He felt as if he was about to burst by the time she had rolled her chemise up over her breasts to leave them sticking out, plump and bare, the rosy nipples erect and quivering slightly to her sucking motions.

The sight was too much. He came, full in her face even as she opened her mouth to take his cock back in. A thick streamer caught her in the eye and she gasped in shock, pulling back, only to catch the second spurt in her open mouth. He took her head, pulling her down to make her suck and drain what remained of his sperm deep into her throat with his cock pushed deep to make her gag on the helmet. She took it, unresisting after her first instinctive withdrawal, even though she had one eye closed with a thick blob of sperm, and more squeezing slowly out from beneath the lid. One cheek and the side of her nose were also streaked with it.

When he finally let her go she swayed back on to her heels. She was gasping for air, with bubbles of sperm escaping from around her lips and from her nose, while the mess on her face was running slowly down, in streaks discoloured by her make-up. Alexander chuckled and reached out to pat her head. Molly responded with a weak smile and began to do her blouse up again.

'Not yet, my girl,' Alexander ordered. 'I'm not wasting having you like that. How about a floor show, the sort you used to give for us when you worked for that cretin Tweedie?'

Cora's response was an immediate giggle. Molly looked doubtful for one instant, threw a shy glance towards Holly where she sat on the sofa, then nodded meekly.

'That's my girl!' Alexander called. 'Oh, and keep your uniforms on, that should add a certain something. Nothing like a pretty girl with her clothing disarranged, eh, Puffer? And haven't you got the port ready yet, man?'

Herbert had stopped to watch Molly expose herself, but immediately went back to the bottles. Working with practised efficiency, he assembled a corkscrew, decanters, coasters, a candlestick, glasses and other necessities. Cora stepped into the middle of the room, her face set in a bright, slightly vindictive smile. She beckoned to Molly, who hesitated, then began to crawl across the carpet.

'No, no, no,' Alexander interrupted. 'We'll have none of your tricks, young lady. She's the Corporal, show some respect.'

'I thought you said no ranks, sir?' Cora asked.

'Maybe, but you look a damn sight too smug. So you can start by kissing Molly's arse.'

Cora's expression changed abruptly, to consternation, but she went down to her knees even as Molly stood. Molly struck a pose, hands on hips, chin raised a trifle, to look down on Cora as the black girl came crawling to her feet. Alexander settled back, reflecting that Molly's bare boobs, bum and quim hardly seemed to detract from the authority of her pose, yet the sperm still running down her face definitely did.

'A moment,' he stated, rising to his feet. 'Stay still, my dear.'

Molly obeyed, standing motionless as he put a finger to her face and scraped up the sperm. Her mouth came open in expectation as soon as the come had become thick enough to force him to roll it on his finger. He shook his head.

'It's not for you, my dear. Would I be so cruel? Turn around and stick out your bottom.'

Molly obeyed immediately, swivelling to push her neat, pale bottom out, directly at Cora's face. Alexander leaned down, taking hold on one cheek to pull it wide, stretching out the pink dimple of Molly's anus. Placing his finger in her crease, he wiped off the sperm, using the lip of her anus to catch it, until the hole was clogged with a thick blob of dirty come. He let go and Molly's cheeks closed with a faint squashy sound.

'That's better,' he said happily. 'Now, Cora, you may lick.'

Cora made a face. Molly giggled and pushed her bottom out further. Her cheeks peeled apart, so that the half-open crease was just inches from the black girl's mouth, the sperm-soiled anus on show. Alexander settled back, accepting the glass of port Herbert was holding out to him. He sniffed and sipped, savouring the rich scent and abundant flavours of the magnificent vintage, then chuckling to himself as he wondered how it compared to a taste compounded of spunk, make-up and Molly's anus.

It was obviously something Cora was reluctant to try, because while she had puckered up and given Molly a full, wet kiss on each bum cheek, she was still holding back from her dirtier task. Molly looked back, fighting to hold a look of lofty disdain on her face, and snapped out an order,

'Aircraftwoman Jackson! On my command, lick . . . Lick!'

Cora seemed to break. With a final grimace she went forwards. Her tongue came out and she was licking, lapping up the coating of dirty sperm from Molly's bottom hole, first slowly, with her face screwed up in disgust. Then it was in mute resignation, lapping and swallowing her load as if performing a disagreeable yet necessary task. Finally her reserve broke.

Holly could only stare in amazement as Cora buried her face between Molly's pert buttocks, licking with an enthusiasm that could not possibly be faked. She took the glass of port offered her by Flying Officer Maray without a word and swallowed half its contents at a gulp.

Her sex was tingling, her head spinning with drink and dirty thoughts. Taking a kiss on the anus had been a favourite trick of Sapphie's to make both Hazel and herself say thank you for punishments. Sometimes it had gone further, Sapphie perching, bare bottom, on one or other of their faces to have her bumhole and quim licked until she came. Once, when the two of them were alone at Ashwood, she had even been made to kneel by the toilet door and use her tongue to do the job normally reserved for a couple of sheets of paper. To watch Molly and Cora was compelling, and hugely arousing.

Hazel was also watching, no less fascinated. Molly had gone down to the floor, slowly, Cora never once taking her face away from between the Irish girl's buttocks, until both were on their knees. Once down, she licked more firmly than ever, lost in the delight of Molly's bottom, her eyes closed in bliss.

Alexander Gorringe still had his cock out, and was stroking it lazily in between sips of port and puffs of his cigar. Herbert Maray was equally excited, squeezing a thick erection through the material of his trousers and staring fixedly at the girls on the floor. Holly's heart gave a jump at the sight, a picture of him entering her from the rear as she licked at Hazel's bottom coming unbidden into her mind. Alexander spoke.

'Come on, girls, make a show of it. Pay attention now!'

Molly reached back to pull her bottom cheeks open, and allow a full, unimpeded view of Cora's tongue-tip working in her little pink bumhole. Holly swallowed hard, wondering if she dared squeeze her quim, which desperately needed touching. She could feel her control going, lust and drink threatening to push aside everything else, yet still frightened of what she might do, and have done to her.

Cora moved, poking the broad tip of her nose into the open bumhole she'd been licking as she began to lick at Molly's quim. Molly sighed. Herbert gave a low moan and began struggling with the buttons of his fly. His cock sprang out, erect, every bit as fat and fleshy and ugly as Holly had imagined it, and her throat went dry at the sight.

Molly was going to come. Her eyes were shut, her mouth open, and coming wider as the muscles of her legs and bottom began to twitch in climax. Herbert moved quickly, laughing as he filled her gaping mouth with cock just at the point of no return. Molly's eyes sprang open as her mouth was invaded, but then she was sucking, hard, and making lewd gobbling motions on the thick erection as she came under Cora's tongue. Herbert lasted seconds, sperm bursting from around Molly's lips even before she had come down from orgasm, to splash on the floor beneath her as both Herbert and Cora pulled back.

Holly took another drink. She knew that if Herbert had come to her and demanded his erection be tossed or even sucked, she would have done it. She also knew that if she and Hazel had been ordered to provide the same sort of lewd display Molly and Cora had given she would have done it. Something would happen anyway, she was sure. Her inhibitions were fading, her need strong, all that remained of her reserve a desire to have it done to her rather than have to take the lead.

The others had settled. Molly was curled at Alexander's feet, her breasts still out, her knickers off. Hazel had made herself comfortable on the sofa beside Holly, close enough to touch hands. Herbert was bringing round port, placing decanters on various tables, including the one by Holly. Cora had gone to another sofa, and Herbert joined her, to whisper into her ear as he sat down.

Cora giggled and immediately began to fiddle with the buttons of her jacket. They came undone, her tie was tugged off, her straining blouse buttons tweaked open, and her boobs were out, two huge, dark balls of flesh, the jet-black nipples tight in erection. Herbert licked his lips and leaned forwards. Cora was smiling as she held one huge breast up for his attention. His mouth came open. He took the nipple in, an expression of almost divine contentment spreading across his face as he settled down to suckle on her. Cora was smiling too, her eyes closed, her mouth just a little open, an expression as much of contented relief as of pleasure.

Holly suppressed a giggle and shared a glance with Hazel. Hazel's hand tightened in hers, and without really thinking she shifted her position, to lay her head against her friend's abundant chest. Sipping at her port, she watched Cora suckled, the sight of the girl's face, slack with pleasure, and the two huge breasts pushing out from the open WAAF uniform both shockingly improper and arousing in the extreme. Again she wondered if she dared play with herself as she watched, or maybe with Hazel.

Nobody was watching, or if they were, nobody cared. She let her hand sneak to the front of her skirt, to press the bulge of her pubic mound. It felt glorious, but only made her want to touch again, while the blood had gone to her face. She cuddled more tightly to Hazel, rubbing her face into the plump pillows of boob flesh as she wished her friend would make her suckle, just as Herbert was suckling Cora.

Only he wasn't. He had pulled back, grinning, and as he turned Holly saw that a trickle of white was running from one corner of his mouth. Molly burst out clapping. Alexander gave a drunken cheer, echoed by Hazel. Holly began to clap too, despite a sudden burst of jealousy. Cora stood, taking a boob in each hand, to make a proud display of her wet nipples with the milk beading on the teat.

'Splendid!' Alexander called out. 'That's my girl! Right, time a for toast, in girls' milk, no, rum punch. Herbert, fetch a bottle. Empty your glasses, everyone!'

Holly obeyed, downing her port in one.

'Up to the sideboard, you two milkers,' Alexander ordered. 'Boobies out, Hazel, my girl, and see if you can't do better than this afternoon. There are pint glasses somewhere, I'm sure.'

He ducked down, to rummage in the sideboard, coming up with the glasses. Hazel had stood, and already had her top open, her face showing a blissful relief as her breasts came bare into her hands. Both girls went forwards to take a glass, giggling as they squeezed their fat breasts. Spurts of milk erupted from Hazel's teat immediately, and a little puddle of yellow-white fluid had already begun to form in the bottom of her glass before Cora's milk started to come. When it did, it was sudden, milk spraying out to wet both the sides and base of the glass.

Holly watched with growing jealousy as the two girls milked themselves. Hazel always seemed to be the one who got the attention. Sapphie had always seemed to prefer Hazel, which hurt, even when it was for some painful or degrading punishment. Now Hazel was in milk first, and the centre of attention, while Cora's success just made it worse.

Before she really knew what she was doing she was pulling at her jacket, determined to get her boobs out and at very least have a share of the attention. Alexander saw what she was doing, and gave her a friendly leer, which sent the blood to her face but put a smile on it too. Encouraged, she quickly opened her blouse, just as Hazel and Cora had done, with her jacket wide and the open blouse supporting her bare breasts. She began to play with herself, squeezing her breasts and pulling her nipples out between forefingers and thumbs, wondering if she could get her own milk started.

113

Herbert came back, holding a bottle of rum. He gave one pleased glance at Holly, then turned his attention to Hazel and Cora, peering low to see how much milk each had produced. There was plenty, as Holly could see. Alexander stepped close, and planted a firm smack on the seat of Cora's skirt as Herbert twisted the closure from the rum bottle.

'Rum punch all round,' Alexander declared, 'and a smacked backside for the last tart to down hers!'

Nobody objected and Holly found herself with a new concern. Hazel stood back, her teats wet with milk. Her glass was half full, almost exactly. Cora gave her boob a last firm squeeze and stood back too, leaving the milk level in her own glass a fraction below that of Hazel's. Alexander poured the rum in, a liberal shot to each glass, leaving the bottle well down.

'Glasses in one then!' he called. 'Remember what I said.'

Holly suddenly realised that he was going to cheat, and that it was almost certain to be her who had to suffer the indignity and pain of a spanking. Always when there was a particularly dirty or unpleasant task he made sure she got it, and she had no doubt he enjoyed seeing her suffer. Snatching her glass, she jumped up, to take hold of a pint mug and pour the contents out. The others had had to fetch their glasses, and she had swallowed her punch before Molly had even tasted hers. Alexander laughed.

'Scared of a smacked bottom, are we, Holly, my girl? Well, we shall have to see what can be done about that but, for now, you're safe. Another glass?'

She accepted, feeling rather pleased with herself as the other girls struggled to down their glasses. Cora took hers in one, Molly finishing a fraction of a second later on her second gulp. Hazel failed, catching the punch in her throat and going into a coughing fit that left her with the milky liquid running out of her nose and mouth to splash on to her breasts. Alexander laughed.

He was rubbing his hands as he went to sit on one of the sofas. Hazel was left coughing and wiping the mess from her front and face, but she came to him as soon as she could, as always, accepting her fate with no more than a touch of resentment. Alexander patted his lap.

'By God, I've wanted to do this for a while. Come on, my girl, over you go.'

Hazel went, down across his lap, to leave her boobs dangling down at one end and her bottom lifted at the other, her hips a little way off his lap, obligingly, so that her skirt could be pulled up.

'You know the form, don't you?' Alexander chortled, taking hold of the hem of her uniform skirt. 'Been spanked plenty of times before, eh? Your mama a bit of a Tartar, is she? Used to spank you plenty, I'll be bound, eh?'

Holly giggled, thinking of all the times she'd seen Hazel spanked, almost without exception by Sapphie. The skirt was coming up, and Holly moved to where she would be able to see Hazel's bottom properly, a position she always felt gave the best view of a girl's spanking. She had refilled her glass, and sipped at the punch as Hazel was exposed. It tasted good, the rich, spicy rum blending well with the smooth, slightly sharp taste of the girls' milk, and she smacked her lips in appreciation even as Hazel's uniform skirt reached the small of her back. The blouse tails were lifted, and Hazel's knickers were on show, the thin cotton seat absolutely straining with plump, womanly bottom, undoubtedly muscular, yet more than a little overweight. Alexander gave the quivering globe of girl-flesh an experimental pat and tugged Hazel's waistband out from under her belt.

Every eye in the room was fixed on the scene as Hazel's knickers came down, exposing her big pink bottom, with the puffy, moist tart of her sex on clear show between her thighs. She was plainly ready, and plainly virgin, with the taut red crescent of her hymen

115

showing in her glistening hole. Alexander took hold of one already straining suspender strap and let it smack back against the plump flesh of Hazel's thigh. She squeaked in pain, then gasped as he kicked up his knee and her buttocks came wide to reveal the rude brown star of her anus.

She tried to close her thighs, but the next instant the spanking had started and she had forgotten all about the humiliation of her exposure. Instead she was kicking wildly, her lower legs flying up and down, her thighs opening and closing like scissors. It was hard, Holly could see plainly, but then Hazel had always been a baby about spankings, big girl though she was.

Alexander was laughing in drunken merriment as he spanked, his hand rising and falling across Hazel's bottom, to wring pig-like squeals from her lips as her big cheeks bounced and quivered. In no time her flesh had begun to redden, an all-over flush marked here and there by the imprints of his fingers. Still she kicked and writhed, with Alexander holding on to her waist with all his force. One shoe flew off, then the other, but still he spanked, laughing all the more and spanking all the harder as her struggles became increasingly frantic.

Even when her knickers tore wide he carried on, ignoring her wail of distress. By then her whole bottom was a rich crimson, bumpy with goose-pimples and slick with sweat. Her bumhole was pulsing and her quim sodden with juice, but if she realised how rude she looked from behind, she no longer cared. Only when she let out a loud fart did he stop, and then only because he was laughing too hard to continue.

He let go. Hazel jumped up immediately, to snatch at her bottom, rubbing and squeezing the fat cheeks with desperate energy as she jumped up and down on her toes to make her flesh quiver and jump, buttocks and boobs as well. Alexander shook his head, grinning as he reached for his glass.

'Ow! That was hard, sir!' Hazel protested. 'I thought it was just going to be for fun . . . a friendly one!'

'It was for fun,' he answered. 'I enjoyed it anyway. Besides, you've plenty of padding, and well, I had to do justice to the target, didn't I?'

Her answer was a reproachful look. He went on.

'If you're sore, get Holly to kiss it better for you. Yes, that's the ticket. Come along, Holly, we've had too little from you this evening.'

Holly could only stare, unable to respond. Hazel had no such doubts, but threw Holly a demanding look and stuck out her bottom. Holly found herself going to her knees. She shuffled forwards, her face crimson, a huge lump in her throat. It didn't stop her. She reached Hazel, took her friend by the hips, pushed her face close, scenting hot, ripe quim, fresh sweat and a new, milky tang. For one last moment she hesitated, and then she was kissing the hot, roughened cheeks, her desire rising up, stronger and stronger still until she finally felt able to abandon herself completely. It was what they wanted to see, she knew it, and it was what she wanted to do . . .

She was doing it, her face burrowed between Hazel's hot smacked bottom cheeks, her tongue in the juice-filled quim hole, her nose wriggling on the soft, wrinkly anus. Hazel cried out in pleasure and began to wiggle her bottom in Holly's face, drawing claps and calls of encouragement from the audience, male and female alike. At their response, Holly gave up the last shred of her reserve and put her tongue to Hazel's anus, burrowing deep into the soft, fleshy ring just as Cora had done to Molly's.

Hazel sighed, pushing back to smother Holly in hot bottom flesh. A hand caught in Holly's hair and she was being forced deeper between the fat cheeks, until she could barely breathe. Still she licked, revelling in the feel and taste of Hazel's bottom hole, with all the memories of the glorious pleasure it had brought when she had been made to clean Sapphie flooding back.

The audience no longer mattered. She was going to come, come with her tongue up Hazel's bottom, and they could think what they liked of her. Her hands went down and she was wrenching and jerking at her uniform skirt, determined to get at herself. She heard Cora's delighted giggle, as if from far away, then a wet, sucking sound as one or other of the girls went down on a cock.

Her skirt was up, her hand pushing impatiently past the tangle of cloth and down her knickers, to her quim. She began to rub at the little bump down between her lips, then touching the hole to feel the tight ring of flesh that sealed her. She was creamy, more so than she had ever been before she had begun to try to bring herself into milk, her quim awash with thick, slimy juice.

Hazel's grip tightened in Holly's hair, pulling her face in. Holly, unable to breath, smothered in hot, wet bottom flesh, could only lick at Hazel's now open bumhole, probing as deep as her tongue would go. She was coming, and even as strong male hands took hold of her knickers she made no effort to pull away. They were whipped down, something fat and firm pressed to the wet mouth of her quim. It was going to happen, and there was nothing she could do. She was helpless, Hazel's grip and her drunkenness taking the place of her bonds, her arousal too, her orgasm still rising up even as the fat cock-head pressed in against her straining flesh.

Her hymen burst at the very peak of her orgasm. She cried out as a sudden, sharp pain tore through her quim. The cock was in her, right in, deep up her hole, pushing deeper still as a warm trickle of blood ran down between the lips of her sex. The man pulled back, slowly, his cock grating against the newly split skin, to make her gasp and grunt, still riding her orgasm as she was given her first ever fucking. The cock went in again, hard.

Fresh blood ran out around the mouth of her sex, over his balls, to wring a new cry from her throat as he began to fuck her in earnest.

A cheer broke out from among the others, then clapping, from all of them at once. It was Gorringe who had cheered. Holly realised that it was Maray whose cock was inside her. Her orgasm lifted one last time to the humiliating knowledge, and it had begun to die. Herbert Maray went on fucking. Gorringe began to sing a perverted version of a Christmas carol, and to beat out the time on Molly's bottom. Maray responded with a laugh, and adjusted his thrusts to the same time. The girls joined in as Gorringe hit the chorus. Hazel dropped Holly's head. Her mouth came away from her friend's bottom hole, sticky and warm. The song rose to a wild, obscene crescendo. The pumping got faster. Maray's fat belly began to slap on Holly's bottom, stopped, and suddenly the fluid trickling down over her quim felt different, thicker and stickier. Vaguely, through the haze of sex and alcohol clouding her brain, she realised that he had come up her cunt.

Alexander moaned. His head hurt, his eyes were glued shut, the inside of his mouth had the texture of granite and a flavour unpleasantly reminiscent of how sheep dung smelt. Only slowly did he become aware that he was not in bed, and that his body was certainly not in any position he'd have chosen voluntarily.

He tried to open his eyes, unsuccessfully until he had managed to wipe them. Vision came slowly, and he realised that he was slumped against the sofa, where he had passed out, and his half-full port glass was still clutched in one hand, unspilt. Molly's head was in his lap, her mouth slack, with a runnel of drool coming from one corner to wet his balls. She was nude save for her stockings and her chemise, which was rucked up around her neck. He swallowed the port, grateful for

119

anything to take the revolting taste out of his mouth, and looked around for more.

The rum bottle was where they had left it, empty, with the tot glasses still lined up, also empty. Of the six bottles of port he had brought up from the cellar, all were now finished save for dregs, while no more than a couple of inches remained in the decanters. He groaned again, and forced himself to move, sitting up so that Molly's head fell to the floor with a bump. She gave a low moan but her eyes stayed shut.

Slowly, he forced himself to his feet. His body ached, his back especially. Staggering to the sideboard, he downed what remained in one decanter, then another before turning to survey the room. It was a shambles. Cora lay spreadeagled on the floor, stark naked. Of Hazel and Holly there was no sign, save their uniforms and underwear, strewn across the floor along with everyone else's. Herbert was there, asleep in an armchair, dressed, but with his clothes open to leave bare the pasty white bulk of his stomach and also his genitals. His penis was curiously dirty, streaked with the red-black of dried blood.

'Hell!' Alexander swore as he remembered the sight of his friend's huge cock-head pushing in at Holly's virgin quim. 'Damn and hell!'

He tried to remember if he had fucked her himself. The answer was yes, at the very climax of the orgy, making a spit roast of her with his cock in her quim from behind while she sucked on Herbert's. If he remembered rightly, Cora had been sucking on his balls at the time, or possibly Molly. He had come inside Holly as well, he was sure, too drunk to remember to pull out at the last moment and make an iced bun of her bottom.

Again he cursed, the full implications of what they'd done sinking in. Herbert had come up her too, and from what he could remember of the state of her quim, she'd been in prime form for a fucking. If she'd been bleeding, it had not been as a result of her monthly cycle.

He made for the window, in desperate need of fresh air. The lights were still on, the shutters and heavy curtains obscuring the window completely. He wrenched them open, to find brilliant sunlight outside, already burning the night's frost from the stones of the carriage sweep.

'What the hell is the time?' he demanded of nobody.

He turned, one hand on a chair to support himself and struggled to focus on the glass-domed clock that stood on the sideboard. It showed twenty minutes to ten, and he realised that he should already have made his early morning report. Cursing freely, he forced himself to stand upright.

As he stumbled from the room he tried to yell an order, but only a feeble squeaking issued from his throat. He staggered to the kitchen, wondering where Holly and Hazel were, and if he should rouse them or try to get airborne without help. A glass of water went some way to clearing his head, the cold morning air outside further. The upper works of the Gladiator were visible on the airstrip, white with frost and sparkling in the weak sunlight.

He cursed and pushed back inside. Reasoning that Holly and Hazel might have found the strength to go to bed, he pulled himself up the stairs. Sure enough, they were there, fast asleep, in the same bed, cuddled into each other's arms. He pulled the covers off and planted a heavy slap on the nearest bottom, Holly's, an effort that caused a fresh twinge of pain in his head.

Twenty minutes later he was airborne, with the others hurrying about their morning duties. Only when he was high in the air did he at last manage to force himself to focus on his problems. The situation was now worse. Not only was Holly in rude good health, but she was no longer a virgin.

For a moment he considered trying to sew up her hymen again, only to abandon the idea as impractical. Pretending that Hazel was Holly was more useless still. Hazel was still virgin, but the two of them did not look all that alike, and Hazel's body was even fleshier than Holly's. Thann was thorough, and would notice the substitution, just as he was sure to notice a ruptured hymen. If lying to Thann had seemed a good idea before, now there was no choice.

When he finally returned to earth, landing so badly he nearly upended the aircraft, he found the station in some sort of order. Everybody was dressed and the drawing room had been tidied up. There was also post, including a letter for himself in a plain envelope. He tugged it open irritably, expecting some new directive or minor alteration to his orders. To his surprise there was no heading, just a single passage of typed text. Puzzled, he began to read ...

I have given some thought to our difficulty and have found a solution. Presently a Ministry circular will arrive stressing the need for rigorous discipline. When it does, you are to construct a box to the specifications shown overleaf – the Hotbox. This is to be used for disciplinary confinement, and it should not be beyond your imagination to ensure that our subject transgresses, and that the box is employed to make an example of her. Proceed urgently, have it made elsewhere and delivered as if from the Ministry. As matters stand, I hope to be able to pay you a visit in the near future.

There was no signature, but it was all too obviously from Reginald Thann. Alexander turned the sheet over, to find a rough but highly detailed diagram of a device apparently compounded of a barrel, a medieval iron maiden and stocks. For a while he just stared at it, then threw the letter down on the table with a curse.

9

Ermecombe Village, Devon –
April 1940

Eliza Grant sat darning in front of the fireplace. A
big-boned, handsome woman of sixty-five, her expression was one of placid determination as her big fingers
worked the needles in long practised motions. Opposite
her, her husband Nat sat at his ease, a mug of cider in
one hand. Both looked up at the sound of an engine
outside the cottage, and they shared a glance of surprise
as it stopped directly outside their front door. Nat
leaned back to twitch the lace curtain aside. There was
an army-green Austin 10 parked in the road. One man,
an officer, was getting out. A woman sat at the wheel.

'It's them from Kerslake Manor,' Nat remarked. 'The
officer fellow and that red-haired Irish baggage.'

Eliza put her work down, immediately curious. There
was a sharp rap at the door.

'Come in,' Nat called, the door immediately swinging
open to reveal the officer.

'Mr Nathaniel Grant?' he enquired, after nodding to
each of them.

'That's me, sir,' Nat answered. 'Nat Grant.'

'Pleased to meet you, Mr Grant. I'm Squadron
Leader Gorringe. I command at Kerslake Meteorological Station.'

'The Manor. I know.'

'Yes, exactly. Now, the thing is, Mr Grant, I understand that you are a carpenter of some skill.'

'You'll be wanting my son, young Nat.'

'Ah . . . I see. My mistake. He's . . .'

'In France.'

'Ah . . . that's a nuisance . . .'

'What is it you're wanting? A job of work? I can turn my hand to most things.'

'Yes, to rather exact specifications. It will pay, naturally . . .'

Gorringe leaned forwards, to pass across a piece of paper. Eliza caught a glimpse of a complicated diagram. Nat frowned.

'Whatever is it? Some machine?'

'Something of the sort,' Gorringe answered. 'Ministry business. Can't say. Careless talk costs lives, you know.'

Nat nodded and reached for a pair of spectacles, to peer closely at the diagram.

'Could you do it?' Gorringe asked.

'Dare say,' he answered. 'I've the tools, and the time.'

'Splendid. May I offer you ten shillings then, to cover your initial costs?'

'Ten shillings? Thank you kindly. When would you be wanting it?'

'As soon as possible, if you would, and do let me know if there are any materials you have trouble getting hold of. Discretion, you will appreciate, is essential.'

'I'll tell nobody, be sure.'

'Splendid, I have every confidence in you, Mr Grant. Perhaps you would allow me to offer you a little tobacco in appreciation of your hard work?'

He had reached into his pocket and was holding out a good-sized packet of tobacco, which disappeared into Nat's pocket as quickly as it had left the Squadron Leader's.

'Splendid,' Gorringe went on. 'I'll call in a week or so to see how you are doing. Meanwhile, I don't suppose you could advise me on something? I'm trying to locate somebody who knows all about cheese-making.'

'Cheese?' Nat answered. 'You'd be wanting Jan Linnel.'

'Jan Linnel,' Eliza agreed. 'Lucy Linnel, if you want any work done.'

'Splendid, and where does Mr Linnel live?'

'To Kerslake dairy, back the way you came. Only he's in France.'

'Lucy's the one you want, as I said,' Eliza answered. 'Lucy Endicott as was.'

'At the dairy?'

'Yes.'

'Thank you both then, much obliged.'

Gorringe turned for the door, retreating with a polite and slightly embarrassed nod to each of them. Nat raised his hand, then went back to studying the diagram.

'What is it, do you suppose?' Eliza demanded, leaning close.

'I wouldn't like to say,' Nat answered. 'Looks like you have some fellow sitting in a barrel.'

'In a barrel? Don't be foolish, whatever would a body want to sit in a barrel for?'

'He wouldn't want to, I reckon. Seems sure it's for German prisoners, to make sure they tells what they know. They used to have something similar Lydford way, in the castle dungeon, so I've been told.'

'That'll be it then. I'll be off to Judy's then, for a half-hour, no more, so don't fret for your lunch.'

'I shan't, but no gossiping, mind. You heard what the man said.'

'I'll pass no idle gossip. It's another matter I'm thinking of.'

Nat's reply was a thoughtful nod. As Eliza rose to collect her coat and hat, he was reaching up to the mantelpiece for a large and blackened pipe.

Outside the air was flecked with mist and a heavy overcast hung so low that the tree-tops were obscured. Eliza drew her coat close, hurrying towards the village, where her sister Judy lived, one of four, all still within a few miles radius of Ermecombe. Judy, a few years younger than Eliza but similar in looks, was at the back of her house, throwing grain to a group of chickens and ducks. Eliza pushed in at the back gate, to open the conversation without bothering with greetings.

'That fellow Gorringe, to Kerslake Manor, he's after somebody who has a hand with cheese.'

'He is?' Judy demanded.

'He is,' Eliza confirmed. 'And what with this new Squire being a Maray . . .'

'And the way those girls of theirs have been growing. I was taking the eggs over yesterday, for the rent on our venville, and I'll swear that big up-country girl was wet where she shouldn't be. Even that little Irish baggage as drives the car has plenty enough, and her no higher than my chin . . .'

'No question then. I'd best have a word with Lucy, and May'll want to know, and Becky, to Kerslake.'

'Alice too. I wonder if this Herbert's as generous as old Jervis?'

'My concern's more whether he's as wicked.'

10

Kerslake Manor, Devon – April 1940

Holly stretched as she came awake, then shook herself to fight down the slight sense of sickness she felt. One arm was beneath Hazel's neck, and she pulled it free gently. Hazel stirred.

'Come on, lazy bones,' Holly yawned, and reached down to pinch Hazel's bottom.

Since the drunken orgy to celebrate Hazel coming into milk they had slept together. Nobody objected. A good deal of the station's formality had been abandoned, at least outside of their daily duties. Molly and Cora now slept with the two officers openly, while it was not uncommon for one or both of the men to demand their cocks sucked as they relaxed in the drawing room after dinner. Spankings had also become a regular occurrence, with the three girls' infringements noted on the public boards and dealt with each evening as circumstances required. It was treated as entertainment as much as punishment, at least for the men and Molly MacCallion, who was exempt. Holly, Hazel and even Cora took it with a blend of resentment and acceptance, but none could have honestly denied their own pleasure at seeing the others dealt with.

To Holly it had become routine, shameful, painful, but still routine. Five times since the orgy she had ended up across Alexander Gorringe's lap, bare bottomed and squealing as she was spanked to a rosy glow. She was sure she was being picked on too, but in a way she didn't mind. If she was singled out for punishment and humiliation, at least it showed that the men found her as attractive as Hazel and Cora, if not more so. So she put up with it, even accepting such perverse additions as having to remove her knickers under her skirt before punishment. She knew the cruel detail was designed to make sure that everyone got an unobstructed view of the rudest parts of her body when she began to kick, but made no complaint.

Of more concern was her failure to come into milk. Hazel's production was approaching a pint a day, and even then Holly often had to relieve her at night. Cora was doing better still, exceeding the pint mark on most days, despite Herbert's devotion to suckling her. Holly felt left out, and with Molly's breasts now two hard, fat little balls of pink flesh, she was concerned that she would be last, or worse, that it might never happen.

Morning exercise had also become an efficient routine. They had a jug of cold water and a chamberpot in the room, and both splashed their faces and peed before pulling on knickers and chemise tops. It saved time, the bathroom often being occupied, and lateness adding a black point towards their punishment tally. Five black points meant a spanking.

They arrived in the yard before Molly MacCallion, and the exercises were completed without fault. The morning went on smoothly, Holly avoiding criticism, while both Cora and Hazel were given points. By lunchtime she was feeling thoroughly pleased with herself, and not just for her good behaviour. Her breasts felt different, as heavy and sensitive as ever, but also somehow loose, uncontrolled, rather as her quim had felt when she'd wet herself. It was disconcerting, but filled her with hope that she might finally be ready.

Sure enough, ten minutes into the milking session she felt a curious, damp sensation on her teats that was not sweat. She called out, an inspection was made, and Alexander Gorringe confirmed that she was in milk. Both men immediately began to clap, and even the trussed and gasping girls managed to congratulate her. By the time milking was over, a small puddle had collected in the pail beneath her breasts, enough to be worth pouring into the collecting jug.

She went about her afternoon duties in a happy daze. The feeling of being left out was gone. Cora's attitude to her had changed, even Hazel's, bringing her a feeling of womanly significance she hadn't felt since starting her periods.

Alexander Gorringe put the sheaf of Air Ministry instructions to one side as Herbert Maray's head appeared around the study door. His friend's round, red face showed a self-satisfied smile.

'Something up, Puffer?' Alexander asked.

'Yes,' Herbert answered. 'There's something I'd like you to see. This list, something old Jervis wrote.'

'Oh yes?'

'Yes, look here, there's a column of names, and at the top it says – Cream, Butter, Erme Head, Dartmoor Blue. I think it's a list of his customers, the ones he used to sell girls' milk to. There are ticks, and figures too. Look, Charlie Truscott's down for butter and Dartmoor Blue. Dartmoor Blue must be cheese.'

'Hmm, so it would seem. Blue, eh?'

'Yes, do you think this Linnel girl will be up to it?'

'I don't see why not. She runs a dairy, doesn't she?'

'I think it's rather specialist, a blue. Something to do with putting the veins in.'

'Well, if Jervis could do it. Anyway, she's coming up this afternoon, so we can discuss it then. Hmm . . . let me see that list.'

He took the sheet of paper, scanning down the list of names with ever increasing interest. Finally he spoke.

'Good God, but Jervis had a select clientele, didn't he just? Look here, Bertie Soames, he's Lord something-or-other now, and Larksmead, and George Templeton, and Jennings, and Napier-Sale ... this isn't a list of customers, Puffer, it's a ruddy gold mine!'

'I say, you're not thinking of blackmailing them, are you? I mean, it's not really ...'

'Don't be an ass! We'd get blackballed from every club in the country. No, Puffer, look at the prices, and this was in the twenties. Think what we could charge now, in the middle of a ruddy war!'

'Well, yes, but we don't have enough, really, do we? I mean, even with Holly up and running, and Molly too, at full strength, that'd be no more than four pints a day ...'

'Don't be such a damn pessimist. Cora and Hazel are both still on the up, and with the others I reckon we'll be getting a full gallon a day at maximum production. There's another thing too. There are six machines, remember, and to judge by this list Jervis had a pretty impressive supply. Where do you suppose he was getting his milk?'

'I don't know.'

'I'll tell you. Local girls, most of who will now be the village matrons at Kerslake and Ermecombe, the farms too. Oh, you may be sure they kept it to themselves, but they did it, rest assured.'

'Erme Head's a farm, south across the moor, below Hangingstone Hill. That's what the other cheese was called.'

'I'll bet one of the girls came from there then. Know anything about it?'

'Not a great deal. A Colonel Penrose and his wife run it as a tea shop. I know who Jervis's maid was too, a Rebecca Apcott. She would know, surely.'

'Find out about the farm, and this maid. If these little tarts were prepared to do it for Jervis, they'll be prepared to do it for us.'

'Very well, Alexander, but um . . . I mean to say, the girls, they won't be, er . . . little tarts any more, will they? I mean, this is from twenty-two, so even if the youngest girls were maybe sixteen, they'd be . . .'

'Thirty-four, prime producing age.'

'The youngest, yes, but it started much earlier, right back to the turn of the century, I think. They'll all be in their fifties and sixties now . . .'

'With daughters in prime fettle. One thing's for sure, this Linnel girl knows something. She could barely keep the smile from her face when I saw her. She'd be game too, I'm certain, and for more than milking. I mean, look at it from her point of view. Her husband's away, she's struggling to make ends meet, and we come along with an offer of easy money and perhaps a portion of best sausage into the bargain. Mark you, she's more your type than mine, fifteen stone if she's an ounce.'

'I'm sure she wouldn't wish to be unfaithful, not with her husband fighting in France!'

Alexander responded with a snort, then went on.

'No, Puffer. It'll be easy. We pay, naturally, but these country trollops think a few shillings are riches. Then we have to sound out our market, maybe visit the old customers, discreetly, of course, see if we can't find a few new ones . . .'

'What about Reginald Thann?'

'I wouldn't have thought so, joyless old bastard . . .'

'No, not as a customer. I mean, what's he going to say?'

'He won't know, not if I get any say in the matter! I see what you mean though, hmm . . . tricky one, that . . . D'you think we could take young Holly into our confidence, get her to play along?'

'No, not really.'

'Hmm . . . I dare say you're right. We'll have to stick her in this barrel contraption then, when he comes down, or he's sure to kick at how plump she's grown. He doesn't want her to know he's the mysterious "Controller" until she's ready, so that's to our advantage. He's becoming a damn nuisance. Now, we need this Linnel woman on our side, so nip down to the cellar and fetch a bottle of brandy, nothing fancy.'

'Right away.'

Herbert Maray left and Alexander once more picked up the list, scanning down the names again and again with ever increasing satisfaction. Jervis Maray had supplied an impressive selection of twenties socialites, mainly known debauchers, although there were a few names, the inclusion of which was astonishing. Most were now respectable and wealthy members of society. A knock sounded at the door. He called out, looking up to see Molly's head appear around.

'Mrs Linnel, sir,' Molly announced.

'Show her in,' Alexander responded, hastily composing himself.

As Lucy Linnel stepped into the room, Alexander immediately found himself assessing her potential for milk production. It had to be good. She was tall, well made, and extraordinarily buxom. He guessed her age at thirty, while her breasts were simply enormous, two huge balls of flesh straining out her dress, with both nipples showing as substantial lumps in the fabric. They had to be larger even than Cora's, and he found himself wondering if she would not merely be aware of Jervis Maray's habits, but have been involved. She was smiling.

'Do sit down,' he offered, indicating a chair. 'My number two has . . . ah, here he is.'

Herbert came in, his face growing abruptly redder as he focussed on Lucy Linnel's chest. In one hand he held a bottle of brandy.

'Do have a drink,' Alexander offered as Herbert poured.

'I don't mind if I do,' she answered, reaching out to accept the glass and wrinkling her nose as she sniffed it.

'Brandy, French,' Alexander explained.

She sipped and swallowed. Her smile grew broader than before.

'Now,' Alexander began, 'as I mentioned when we met at the dairy, we are interested in contracting you to produce certain dairy products – cream, butter, cheese . . .'

'Blue-veined,' Herbert cut in.

'Yes, ideally a blue-veined, but also a straightforward cheese after the style of Cheddar or Wensleydale. You seemed to indicate that there would be no difficulty?'

'None whatever, sir.'

'Splendid, and you understand that we will be supplying the milk, and that you are on no account to mix it with any other milk?'

'Certain sure, sir.'

She now looked as if she was about to burst out laughing.

'Good, good. Hmm . . . tell me, Mrs Linnel, do you . . . do you, um, know Erme Head Farm at all?'

'I was born there, sir.'

'You were born there?'

'Yes, sir. Polly Haldon, Polly Endicott as was, used to keep house there. She's my mother.'

'Ah, I see. Splendid, splendid. And er . . . does the name Dartmoor Blue mean anything to you?'

'Yes, sir, that's the cheese we used to make for Mr Jervis, sir, just as we'd be doing for you.'

'Good, and this cheese, it's not a cows' milk cheese, is it?'

'No, sir.'

'Goat, sheep?'

'No, sir.'

'You were perhaps closely ... er ... intimately involved with the production?'

'Yes, sir.'

'Good. I think we understand each other, Mrs Linnel ... Lucy, may I call you Lucy?'

'Certain you may, and certain I do. If you're needing my help, sir, I can be back in within the month, and I can manage a quart a day.'

'A quart a day!' Herbert exclaimed, losing the face of calm superiority he had been wearing as they spoke.

'A little over, at my best,' Lucy said proudly. 'Time was when I was the best in either village.'

'The best between how many?' Alexander asked.

'Twelve at most, before Mr Jervis died,' she answered.

'Twelve, eh? And these twelve women, might they also be interested?'

'Could well be, sir, if you can match what Mr Jervis used to pay.'

'Oh I'm sure we can manage that. Let me see, with ordinary milk at threepence a pint, I think we could be generous and say sixpence.'

'Ten shillings the quart, Mr Jervis used to pay, sir.'

'Ten shillings a quart? Great Heavens, woman ... I mean to say, Lucy my dear, you must realise that we can't match that nowadays. After all, there's a war on, and ...'

'Oh, there's no real difficulty there, sir. Mr Jervis, he used to sell our butter and cream and cheese to wealthy gentlemen all over the country, for a fine profit. The blue-veined was especially popular, sir.'

11

Ermecombe Village, Devon –
May 1940

Eliza Grant peered from the side of the thick curtain
which shut off the window. The street was empty save
for a large black and white cat. She gave a nod of
satisfaction and turned back to the interior of the
church hall, shutting the curtain carefully behind her.
Fourteen young women occupied the centre of the hall,
sitting or standing, most visibly nervous or excited. A
few were calm, around whom little groups had gathered.
There were also older women, Eliza's sisters, Becky,
Judy and May. Most, young and old, bore a family
resemblance, tending to dark curls, large dark eyes and
pretty, full features. Even the youngest had womanly
figures, big breasts, round, heavy bottoms, soft, plump
curves at belly and hip.

Eliza looked over them with mixed emotions, pride
and a great deal of motherly affection, but also concern
and not a little embarrassment for her own time spent
on the milking machines at Kerslake Manor. Both Lucy
Linnel and Alice Barracombe were among the girls, and
both were the illegitimate daughters of Jervis Maray.
She was not even certain if her two eldest were Nat's, or
Jervis's, or from one of the many men she had been with
at his wild orgies. At the time she had been accepting,
even eager. Looking back, she felt she had been taken

advantage of, and was determined that it should not happen to the younger girls, every one of whom was either a daughter, a niece or the child of a close friend.

She could see her own emotions of so long ago reflected in them, the giggles, the sidelong glances, the blushes, the feigned indifference, all reactions she had shown. Irritation rose up at the thought that, left to their own devices, every one of them would make the same mistakes as she had, her sisters too. May was stood by the doors. Eliza nodded to her and she promptly slid the heavy bolt across the doors.

'That'll keep them as aren't wanted out,' Eliza remarked. 'We've a full house, I reckon, Judy.'

'We have that,' Judy answered. 'I hadn't hoped for better than eight or ten.'

'We wouldn't have above five, but for the war,' Eliza answered, stepping up to the platform.

The girls settled with a murmur as she went to the single chair set in the middle of the platform, all but a group of three which included a particularly tall girl with striking blonde hair. Eliza waited a moment, but the three continued to chat.

'Alice Barracombe!' Eliza snapped. 'You may be one of the bettermost folk hereabouts nowadays, but you're not too high nor too old to feel the palm of my hand.'

Alice went abruptly quite and sat down, blushing fiercely. Absolute silence had fallen over the audience, every girl sitting primly to attention with her hands folded in her lap.

'That's better,' Eliza stated. 'We'll have none of your crams today, any of you. First off, you all understand why you're here?'

The girls nodded, many blushing, some giggling behind their hands. Eliza gave them a stern look and went on.

'I'll be speaking plain, otherwise you won't get the sense of what I say. You've all of you heard what used

136

to go on over to Kerslake Manor. Some of you were there, as I was myself in my time, so there's no call to blush so, Mary Athwell, you're no better than the rest of us.'

One of the youngest of the girls immediately mumbled an apology, but the pink flush suffusing her face only grew darker.

'Last time, as it goes,' Eliza continued, 'matters were a sight too much the men's way, and this time I intend it to be different. If this new Squire's anything like Mr Jervis, he'll be wanting all sorts of extras, and cabaret and what have you. Before you know it, half of you'll be in trouble.'

There was a chorus of titters, quickly quelled as Eliza glared about the room.

'It would take a bit of explaining, that,' she said, 'what with your menfolk away. So listen. You stay together, three or four at a time, with one of us four, and one of the more sensible ones, and you don't allow no liberties. Any as strays, they'll get their backsides walloped, for all the others to see, and I don't mean by hand. I mean with a good thick stick, or mayhap a razor strop.'

Absolute silence had fallen again. Several of the girls exchanged nervous glances. Eliza smiled to herself as she went on.

'We're doing this proper, as I say, all organised. First off, we'll have a call of names, same as the men do in the army, and I'll tell who's to be with who. Just say yes when I call out your name . . . Anna Wescott?'

'Here, mother,' a particularly voluptuous woman in the front row answered. 'You know I'm here, mother, and you know every other body in the hall . . .'

'Are you in mind for a walloping?' Eliza demanded. 'This is to be done proper, and that . . .'

She stopped. One girl, a touch less buxom than the others and with straight, dark hair, had raised her hand.

'What is it, Hannah?'

'I was thinking,' Hannah answered, 'if we're to make an organisation, and we're to make them at the Manor sit up and take notice, shouldn't we give ourselves titles, same as in the orphan's home to Exeter, where I was? Matron, and Sister, and the like.'

Eliza paused, then nodded.

'That's what I was just coming to, Hannah Smith, if you'd bide your yap. I'll take on as Matron, and that means you've to do as I tells you or there'll be trouble. Same goes for Becky, and Judy and May. You four, Alice, Lucy, Roberta Slater and my Anna, you'll make the Nurses, with three to four girls apiece.'

There was an immediate buzz of conversation, and some moving between seats.

'Quiet, the lot of you!' Eliza roared. 'Elseways there will be a walloping, here and now, and I won't be too choosy as to who gets it. I'll say who's with who, as a matter of common sense, not who fancies yapping to who while you're on the machines.'

Once more there was quiet. Eliza sighed and cast a glance over the assembled girls. Some were sensible, some less so, some far from it. Some lived in Kerslake, others in Ermecombe, some on farms, a few on the moor. Hannah Smith's suggestion came back to her, and when she spoke it was with confidence.

'Write all this down, Alice, if you would be so kind. You four who've been before, you're to take charge of the little ones, so four groups there'll be. First, Ermecombe Group, led by my Anna ... Nurse Anna Wescott, with three girls, Sophie Athwell, Mary Athwell and Sally Grant. Next off, Farm and Moor Group, led by Alice Barracombe, with two girls besides, Jenny Penrose and Nellie Causey. Then there'll be the Dairy Group: Nurse Lucy Linnel, along with your two as works there, Anne Linnel and Mary Draycott. Last off, Kerslake Group, Roberta Slater as Nurse, seeing as she's done it before, even if . . . never mind, she's Nurse, and with Hannah Smith, Anne Apcott and Emily Arrish. There, see how it goes smooth when there's somebody with a bit of sense in charge.'

One or two of the girls had opened their mouths to speak, but changed their minds as Eliza's glance swept over them. A few exchanged smiles or threw worried glances to those chosen as nurses; most stayed attentive as Eliza continued.

'It'll be down to the Nurses to keep order, and the Matrons to make sure it's kept. Mr Gorringe, who's the fancy officer fellow to the Manor, he'll be asking for girls to help out on his land. Some Government scheme behind it, seems, so there'll be no trouble there. That's once you're in milk, and that's where the trouble comes in. Some of you are giving natural, I know, and you'll have to judge what you can spare. For the others, it'll take a bit of time, and there's a knack, which I'll show, with my Sally, so there's no question of it not being proper. Sally.'

Her youngest daughter stood, pink faced. A giggle ran through the room. Some girls were smiling behind their hands, others looking worried or shocked.

'Come along,' Eliza urged. 'There's no cause to be over modest.'

Sally stepped forwards, the colour of her face rising from fresh pink to scarlet. Slowly, she made her way to the platform, looking back again and again, as if seeking some way out.

'Do get on with you!' Eliza snapped. 'You'll be bare enough when you're on the machines, my girl, and a penny to a shilling the men'll try and sneak a look, and more.'

'But, Mother . . .' Sally protested with yet another glance to the other girls, most of who were now giggling behind their hands.

'Do as you're told, Sally Grant,' Eliza ordered.

139

Sally made a face, but her hands had already gone to the buttons of her dress as she mounted the platform. She turned her back to the audience, many of who were now showing open amusement at her discomfort.

'Quiet, the lot of you!' Eliza demanded. 'There's no cause for that. We're all as God made us and, if you're to do this, there's not a deal of room for modesty, believe me. Now do come on, Sally!'

Sally half turned. She had undone the top buttons of her dress, just enough to allow her to show her bra. Her face was scarlet and her fingers were shaking as she scooped out first one plump boob, then the other. A fresh ripple of amusement ran through the onlookers. Sally bit her lip and turned fully, showing her chest, the two plump globes of flesh supported by her disarranged bra, flushed pink in her embarrassment, the nipples erect. Eliza shook her head.

'That's no way to do it. You need plenty of space, for comfort's sake, and to make a proper job of it. These foolish new brassières are no help, neither. Open your dress properly, girl, and off with your brassière.'

Blushing hotter than ever, Sally complied. Her dress came open, and was pushed down to her waist. The bra came off, her boobs spilling free. Topless, she stood trembling. Eliza stood.

'Now, lean on the back of the chair. That's right.'

Sally had gone forwards, letting her breasts swing beneath her. She jumped as her mother took hold of one.

'Whatever's the matter with you?' Eliza demanded. 'Why, it doesn't seem yesterday I was changing your towels . . .'

'I'm nearly thirty, Mother!' Sally said miserably.

'Then it's time you got some sense in your head,' Eliza answered. 'Remember you've nothing I haven't seen before, and you'll be doing nothing I haven't done myself.'

'Not in front of everybody!' Sally wailed.

'Don't go giving yourself airs,' Eliza answered and turned to face the audience. 'There's a way to this, done by yourself, or with help. You must imagine you're milking a cow, which you are, after a fashion. Firm and soft, and regular too, that does the trick.'

She had taken her daughter's breast in both hands and was massaging the fat, dangling globe. Sally's nipple had grown stiffer still, and her eyes were closed in an agony of embarrassment. The crowd had gone quite, some hiding amused smiles, some embarrassed themselves, one or two touching their own breasts through their clothes, every single one in rapt attention. Eliza went on massaging, her big hands working on her daughter's boob in a slow, regular rhythm.

'Firm and regular, that's the trick,' she stated. 'See the way of it, and how the teat goes stiff? Twice a day, evening and morning, that's the best way, for maybe an hour. It won't come at once, but it will come, perhaps in three weeks or a month. So be patient. And see how Sally's standing, so as her chest hangs down, that way the milk wants to come out. Now you try, Sally.'

Eliza let go of her daughter's breast. Sally took hold, cupping the fat globe, her face a rich crimson as she began to massage herself, her flesh rippling gently to the motions, her nipple growing longer and tighter. Eliza watched in approval for a while.

'That's the way of it,' she stated. 'Do them turn and turn about. It works best with a friend to help, in truth, and bent down, that's the way Polly Endicott showed me.'

Sally continued to massage, now holding her other breast. Her eyes were tight shut, her mouth slightly open, both nipples fully engorged. Eliza spoke suddenly.

'Come on, girl, you can put those away now, whatever are you thinking?'

Sally seemed to come awake, dropped her breast and hastily scrambled for her bra, still blushing as she covered herself with frantic haste. Eliza paused, wondering how best to express what she knew she had to say and thinking back to her times at Kerslake Manor. Sally was fully covered by the time she spoke.

'As I mentioned before, if the new Squire's at all like the old, he'll expect all sorts, and give you a fine parcel of old crams to get it. Then there's this Gorringe fellow, who I reckon's not the sort of gentleman as is a gentleman, if you follow my meaning. They may ask for all sorts, and the way of it is, that after a time on the machine, you'll more likely than not be of a mind to give it. That's when trouble starts, and I'll not have it. It's nature, certain sure, but any who gives way to temptation will feel a stick across their behinds, and you needn't doubt that. Should you ... if it's all too much ... well, there's ... there's always one another ...'

Eliza stopped. Most of the girls were giggling. Lucy Linnel winked. Suddenly she was filled with burning embarrassment, all the emotion she had been struggling to keep inside welling up to burst out into the open. Two brisk steps took her to the platform steps, another three to Lucy's side.

Lucy started back, her face working with alarm, then pain as Eliza's thumb and forefinger closed on her ear in a tight pinch. She squealed, and a gust of laughter swept through the room as the other girls realised what was going to happen. So did Lucy, pleading and squealing and batting at Eliza's body as she was dragged to her feet and pulled across the room.

It made no difference. Eliza sat down on the bench by the wall. Lucy came down across Eliza's lap with a wail of raw frustration. One swift movement and Lucy's skirts were up, another and her fat pink bottom was bare. Eliza laid in, spanking the big, wobbly bottom with all the force of her brawny arm. Lucy's screams of protest turned to screams of pain, and she began to kick at once, her legs pumping and parting, her knickers flying free, the fat, hairy split of her sex coming on show. Still Eliza spanked, her face set in grim determination, puffing and blowing as she belaboured Lucy's bottom, smack after smack, until the big cheeks had turned from pink to an angry red.

Every woman in the room was watching, some giggling or laughing out loud, many with their hands over open mouths in shock or delight, or both, Eliza's sisters in smug satisfaction. Finally, with Lucy blubbering and contrite across her lap, Eliza lost her breath. She stopped, but kept her grip, with her spanking hand lying on her victim's hot red bottom. Lucy stayed down, snivelling faintly.

The other girls had gone silent. All were watching, bright eyed in trepidation, each face flushed and full of emotion, each one quite clearly pleased with what had happened, scared that she would be next, and fully aware of the consequences. Lucy's legs were open. Her quim showed, swollen and moist.

Eliza shook her head in despair.

12

Kerslake Manor, Devon – May 1940

Holly watched as the Gladiator rose into the air. Squadron Leader Gorringe had been in a foul temper all morning, and for no obvious reason. Two days before, Molly MacCallion had finally come into milk. Their total production was now two quarts a day, and no less than fourteen girls in the local villages were doing their best to add their own milk to the yield. Carefully worded enquiries to those on Jervis Maray's list of customers had also borne fruit. Many had declined politely, a few with gruff refusals. None had threatened recriminations, and just over half had expressed an interest. Gorringe had been expecting a third at most.

There was some bigwig from the Ministry coming at lunchtime, but it wasn't the first inspection and, other than the bulk of the girls' chests, there was nothing to excite suspicion. The dairy could be disguised as a store room within minutes, and had been that morning. The clysopomp had been moved to an outside shed and was now used only for the amusement of the officers, the girls occasionally being given a choice between an enema or a spanking.

Everything seemed to be going smoothly, and yet Gorringe had been snapping at the girls all morning, and singling her out for especially rough treatment. He had come out to watch their exercises and shouted at her for not keeping up, although she had been. He had chided her for taking her time over breakfast, although she was encouraged to eat as much as she could to keep her milk production up. He had even shouted at her for being slow to bring the accumulator out on to the strip, despite having put the other girls on different duties so that she had to cope alone.

She was feeling distinctly sorry for herself as she turned back for the house. Unfair criticism was something she was used to. It happened all the time when he wanted an excuse to spank her, and had become a half-joking, half-serious routine. Each of her errors, real or supposed, would compound the points, so that by the evening she would have the five that meant a trip over his knee. She would still pout and kick and snivel, but at base it was a game, and they both knew it. All in all, the use of spanking as discipline was a jolly entertainment for everyone but the victim, and not entirely unpleasurable for her.

This was different. He had not awarded points, and there had been none of the amused looks or meaningful tugs of his moustache that showed he was excited by the prospect of her coming punishment. Instead he had been cold and distant, also distracted.

She passed the Hotbox, which had been driven up by carrier's wagon a couple of days earlier. It was a horrible thing, designed to confine a person in a rigid and painfully cramped position, with no light and very little air. The front of the barrel-like body opened, to expose a bench and a number of adjustable pieces of wood, each with slots to hold the victim's ankles, wrists and neck. The one at neck height was well below the lip, so that the lid could be opened to reveal the victim's head but nothing more. With the lid down, anyone inside it would be in absolute darkness, while the lower portion of the door could be opened to expose their body. A hole in the seat and another door to the rear suggested either a concern for the victim's bodily functions or a way to ensure that yet further cruelties could be inflicted.

It was a device of torture, and seemed horribly out of place, both at Kerslake and in England. Even Sapphie's most elaborate tortures and humiliations had been intensely intimate, and invariably led to the use of a carefully applied tongue, then cuddles and kisses. The Hotbox seemed merely cruel.

Yet it was there.

She pushed in at the back door. It was an hour to lunch, but her breasts were already starting to hurt. By the time the Ministry official left and she could be milked, they would feel fit to burst, and the relief when she finally climbed on to the machine would be ecstatic. Waiting was not easy, and the temptation to milk herself in the kitchen and drink the evidence was considerable. She held back, sure that she would be caught, and contented herself with a glass of water and a quick stroke of her straining flesh through her uniform.

Molly MacCallion walked in at the exact moment Holly would have been milking her breasts. Holly managed a half-hearted salute and a friendly smile. Molly responded with a look of sympathy, tempting Holly to offer to suckle and ask the same favour in return. Again she resisted, and went back outside feeling more than a little proud of herself.

She heard the sound of the Gladiator's engine immediately, and saw that it was coming in to land. Immediately she ran forwards, sure that something had to be wrong if the Squadron Leader had returned so soon. He touched down without difficulty, but even as he swung himself down it was plain that he was angry. As he strode forwards he was already snatching off his helmet and gloves, and she saw that his face was red with rage.

'Bomefield-Mullins!' he yelled, using her last name for the first time in nearly a month. 'What the hell do you think you're playing at?'

'I'm sorry, sir, I . . .' Holly began.

'No excuses!' he roared. 'Twice I nearly cut out up there! You're supposed to be responsible for the engine, are you not?'

'Hazel . . . Aircraftwoman Mullins, and myself, yes, sir.'

'Don't try to put the blame on to other people, Bomefield-Mullins. It was your responsibility this morning, and that's that. I'm been damn decent to you, and I can see it was a mistake. Now you're going to learn some discipline. Corporal MacCallion, place Aircraftwoman Bomefield-Mullins in the Hotbox, until further notice, naked.'

He strode away towards the buildings, anger radiating from every part of his body. Holly was left staring in speechless horror. Molly MacCallion stepped forwards, sympathetic yet determined, to take Holly's wrist. Holly went limp, unable to resist, but fighting back tears as she was led across the grass. It was horribly unfair and, worse, Squadron Leader Gorringe was obviously serious, filling her with a burning self-pity that destroyed all thought of remonstrance.

Molly MacCallion stopped at the Hotbox, to duck down and release one catch, then another. The front of it swung wide, exposing the innards, with the holes and panels designed to trap her legs, arms and head. Holly stood, numb with shock, as Molly slid the partitions out, stacking each neatly to one side. When Molly spoke, there was no command in her voice.

'I'm sorry, Holly. You will have to disrobe, completely.'

Holly nodded and began to strip. As she removed each article, she handed it to Molly, jacket, tie, shoes, blouse, chemise, girdle, stockings and finally knickers,

147

to leave her nude and vulnerable. Molly nodded to the Hotbox.

'Will you be here?' Holly asked. 'Will you talk to me?'

'I can't,' Molly answered. 'I'm supposed to leave you. I'm sorry, Holly, I would.'

She made a wry face and shrugged. Holly bit her lip and came forwards, turning to seat herself in the Hotbox without another word. Molly began to slot the partitions back, locking each in place as she did so. Holly's ankles were trapped, her wrists, her neck and she was helpless. The front of the mechanism swung shut and all she could see was the blue of the sky above her. The lid closed and she was in darkness.

Fear welled up on the instant, and a horrible feeling of confinement, as if she had been buried alive. She forced herself to think clearly, to remind herself that she was in a simple wooden box, that just inches away was light and air and human company. It didn't work, the sense of being trapped growing minute by minute until she was struggling not to scream and thrashing in the cruel embrace of the box.

Finally her will broke. She was calling out, begging to be released, squirming in blind panic, screaming, only for the sound of her own suffering to snap her back to her senses. For a while she sat panting in the dark, with the panic ebbing away as her discomfort rose. It came from the hard wood pressed to her body, from the rapidly rising temperature, from minor physical needs she could do nothing to soothe. Beads of sweat began to form on her skin, and to trickle down, inducing an agonising tickling sensation. Her nose began to itch, and her anus. She tried to rub herself, but could only bring a few areas of her body into contact with the wood, and the effort brought more frustration than relief.

The pain in her breasts was growing too, until it became worse even than the tickling of her sweat and the gradual stiffening of her limbs. Before long her teeth were gritted and her eyes closed, to squeeze out tears of pain and frustration from beneath the lids. Once more the panic began to rise. She began to whimper, and to jerk in her restraints, barely aware that she was doing it, only a sudden sharp pain as a strand of hair caught in her neck hole brought her back from the edge of hysteria.

For a moment she was gasping for breath, before forcing herself to her senses. The pain came back, more sharply than before, her breasts so heavy, so bloated she felt they would surely burst, every inch of her body prickling with sweat, every limb achingly stiff. She began to wonder if the moment of panic had lasted just seconds, as it had seemed to, or minutes. Her bladder had begun to hurt, and she gave a sob of misery as she realised that it was only a matter of time before she wet herself.

She forced herself to think of other things, as she had with her bladder straining during interminable church services at Ashwood and in lectures at Innsworth. A picture of Sapphie came to her, the delicate face full of confidence, the features set in mockery and arrogance. Sapphie, she was sure, would have endured the box, emerging with a glance of contempt for her captors. Even Hazel, she knew, would have managed better than her, taking it with the same stolid resentment she always showed. She could not and, as her efforts at distraction broke in a wave of self-pity, she once more bit down a scream.

When full awareness came back the pain once more began to grow worse. She felt a wet trickle on her breasts and belly, and knew it was more than just her sweat. Her nipples were weeping milk, yet still her breasts ached as badly as before. She shook her torso, struggling to relieve them, but only made it worse, a stinging pain shooting through each fat globe as it slapped on her chest. Her belly hurt too, her bladder now tense with pressure and getting worse. Before long the first pang of real pain came. Her will snapped. Her bladder burst. Pee erupted from her quim.

She was sobbing as she listened to the gentle patter of her urine on to the bare wood beneath her bottom. Fresh tears started, running down her face with the sweat and the saliva trickling from one corner of her mouth. She let her bladder empty completely, vaguely aware that she had done something to be ashamed of, but too far gone to care.

Time passed, her sense of confinement returned, slowly, building to a crescendo that left her screaming and jerking in the box. Clear thought came again, and full awareness of her pain, new panic, new pain, in a cycle entirely beyond her control. When at last she heard voices they brought a relief beyond anything she had experienced, for all that she recognised the tone of her tormentor. There was another too, one she didn't know, asking a question, indistinct. Gorringe replied.

'. . . since eleven hundred hours, more or less.'

'Three hours?' the stranger answered. 'Good. Five hours is normally recommended for the subject to become properly suggestible, but for a woman three should do.'

'I would think so. Now, I've added one or two improvements I'm sure you will approve of. For instance there is the door at the rear should you wish access to her cunt or anus . . .'

'Quiet, it is essential that she hears only my voice. Once she is in the box, she should be cut off from all that she understands as normal.'

'I see.'

There was silence. For a moment nothing happened. Then she heard the rear door open and cool air washed over her sweat-stained bottom and sex. She realised she was not to be released, and that her sex was vulnerable. Her fear rose abruptly, to set her shivering and clutching her fingers, with tears of helpless frustration rolling down her cheeks. Suddenly her thoughts were crystal clear. Her sex tightened by instinct. Her anus began to twitch. Her stomach started to crawl and she could feel a scream starting to bubble up in her throat, fresh and different panic rising up inside her. She tried to fight it, telling herself that for all his cruelties Gorringe liked her, that he at least found her attractive, and yet he deferred to the other man, whose voice held nothing but cruelty, cold, unfeeling sadism . . .

'Holly,' the voice sounded. 'Do you hear me?'

'Yes,' she answered, her voice catching in her fear.

'Good.'

'Who . . . who are you?'

'I am somebody you will come to know very well. You are not to know my name, for now. Think of me as your controller. It is from me that all things derive, both good and bad. When you are punished, it is at my decision. When you are rewarded, it is at my decision.'

'But why? What have I . . .'

She screamed as a sharp pain tore through her quim. Her body jerked, once, then again as the pain struck a second time, to leave her sobbing and whimpering. Even as she struggled to recover herself the voice began again.

'Never ask such questions. There is no why, no reason. This is simply how things are. You have no reason for deeper knowledge, nor are you capable of an understanding. What matters is that I control you, that you may escape pain only through obedience. Understand, Holly, that release from pain comes only with complete obedience to me. I control. My word is absolute. Do you understand?'

'Yes! Yes . . . I understand . . . I'll do as I'm told . . . I promise . . . I will obey!'

'Yes, Holly, you will obey, I am sure of it. But do you want to obey?'

'Yes, yes . . . anything . . .'

'Do not lie to me, Holly.'

Again she screamed as new fire shot through her body, worse than before, to set her jerking and squirming despite the utter futility of her efforts. Her whole quim seemed to be on fire, as if whipped, yet she knew she had not been. Fresh urine burst from her bladder as the voice sounded once more.

'You were punished for your lie, Holly. Do you understand that?'

'Yes,' she managed, her voice weak and breaking to a sob. The merciless voice went on, even as her pee trickled from her quim.

'I do not punish you to be cruel, Holly. I punish you for you own good, that you may learn. Your obedience must be automatic, unquestioning, absolute, and most of all, it must be what you yourself desire. Do you understand?'

'Yes.'

'You are lying.'

She screamed as the pain hit her again, her quim contracting violently to the agonising jolt. Immediately she was babbling uncontrollably.

'No . . . I don't . . . I don't understand. How could I!? Please . . . please . . . not again . . . Mercy! Please!'

Her words broke off in a fresh scream as new pain tore through her. She jerked violently, tossing her head to send tears spraying out into the darkness, kicking and wrenching against the hard wood, writhing her bottom, all in a desperate effort to escape the pain. It came anyway, her body held too tight to let her get the lips of her sex away from the hole. She screamed once more, then again began to babble, willing to say anything in the hope of finding the words that would make it stop.

'I'll obey! I will! I'll do anything! I swear it . . . I do . . . I swear I'll obey . . . anything, anything at all . . . just stop, please . . . I'll be your servant, your slave . . . just stop . . .'

'You will, Holly,' the man said, suddenly. 'You will be all of that, and more. But now you only say it because you fear the pain. Eventually you will come to wish it, to crave for those words to be the truth, and in due time, they will be the truth. Five more.'

'No! No ...' Holly managed, her voice trailing off into a sob of utter despair that broke immediately to a new scream.

Her quim had exploded with pain, to send her whole body into a jerking, spasmodic dance, her limbs wrenching against the unyielding wood, her jaw opening and shutting like a trap, a long fart blowing from her anus as the muscle gave way. Again the pain hit, again her entire body went into violent spasm, a third time, a fourth, a fifth, in quick succession and she was screaming and writhing in helpless, animal reaction, her quim going into frantic contraction, milk spurting from her breasts, air erupting from her anus, liquid squirting out, her vagina closing with a long, burbling grunt.

She collapsed, every muscle limp, barely conscious, yet with a tiny voice of triumph screaming from somewhere in the blackness. She had come.

13

London – June 1940

As he turned into Whitfield Street, Alexander was looking around in a mild surprise that had lasted since he left the train at Waterloo. Very little had changed in the last six months. He had expected the events at Dunkirk to have brought the full realisation of war to the population, but if anything the atmosphere seemed less tense than earlier. Those he had overheard in conversation seemed more concerned about what were seen as unnecessary restrictions by the Government than with the threat of invasion.

He shrugged, sure that his own convictions had, if anything, been an underestimation of the danger. As he walked on he began to consider the possible implications of invasion, only to dismiss the thought. It was impossible to know anything with certainty, and foolish to do anything but get on with life.

At the brothel which had once housed Molly MacCallion he paused to adjust his tie and cap. A glance at his reflection in the tobacconist's window showed him as a clean-cut, dashing RAF officer, elegant, tall and lean, if perhaps a trifle less lean than he had been. He gave his reflection a self-satisfied nod and pressed the doorbell. Tweedie himself answered, his ratlike face working with a mixture of hatred and greed as it appeared around the side of the door.

'Do let me in, Tweedie,' Alexander sighed.

'Let you in?' the pimp answered, although he was already opening the door. 'Why would I be wanting to do that, when you waltzed off with my two best earners?'

'How many girls do you run?' Alexander demanded, his nose wrinkling to the apparently inevitable boiled cabbage smell as he went in.

'Six,' Tweedie answered immediately. 'There's little Vera. She's new . . . only here a couple of months, and a smasher, only –'

'Six?' Alexander interrupted. 'Then shut up. I'm not after girls, Tweedie, I have a business proposition to make.'

'You should have said then, Mr Alexander, sir. I'm your man, anything you want, Scotch, real Seville marmalade, chocolate? I've got some lovely chocolate –'

'So you are a blackmarketeer,' Alexander cut him off. 'I'd guessed as much.'

'Just supply what the gentlefolk need, Mr Alexander, as always. I'm a benefactor to mankind, I am, sir.'

'You're a seedy little pimp who'd sell his own grandmother, given the chance.'

'And you'd buy her, sir, like as –'

'I heard that, Tweedie, damn your impudence. You have a grandmother then? She must be in her nineties!'

'Seventy-two this August, sir!'

'Seventy-two? Your family breed young, I must say.'

They had reached the flat, and Tweedie unlocked the door and pushed inside. It now looked very different, with the curtains closed and boxes piled high against every wall. Most appeared to contain spirits, along with jars of preserves, tins of salmon and shrimp, bales of parachute silk and more. Two racks of clothes occupied a good deal of the space.

'Anything takes your fancy, make me an offer, feel free,' Tweedie stated.

155

'Thank you, no,' Alexander answered, grimacing as he examined the label on a case claiming to contain Champagne but originating in Morocco.

'The real thing,' Tweedie stated proudly. 'And it'll be the last you see until the end of the war.'

'I very much doubt I shall see any after the end of the war,' Alexander replied. 'I must say though, you seem remarkably sanguine. You think we'll win then?'

'We'll win, maybe,' Tweedie said, 'or we'll lose, maybe. People'll need girls just the same, Germans and all.'

'A charming attitude.'

'More like we'll call it a draw, anyway, whatever Winston Churchill has to say. D'you hear his speech last week?'

'Yes. Look, never mind all that, Tweedie. Is there anywhere to sit?'

Tweedie nodded reluctantly and opened the door to the bedroom. Unlike the outer room, it had hardly changed, except that the girl on the bed was blonde. She was also obviously knickerless under an abbreviated school uniform and sucking a lollipop. Tweedie jerked his thumb at the door and she scampered away, bare bottom wiggling beneath the hem of her abbreviated dress.

'Vera,' Tweedie said, 'all yours for just ten shillings . . .'

'Later maybe,' Alexander answered, seating himself in the same chair in which Molly and he had first had sex. 'Now, listen.'

'I'm all ears, Mr Alexander, all ears.'

'Good. Now, this is very simple, but requires absolute discretion . . .'

'Discretion's my middle name, Mr Alexander.'

'Good. What I want you to do is to distribute certain goods for me.'

'Nothing easier, Mr Alexander.'

'Shut up. Each Friday, a case will arrive on the afternoon train from Okehampton to Waterloo, that's LSWR. You are to collect the case and distribute the packages within as addressed, without making a nuisance of yourself. All are within London. Is that clear?'

'Clear as clear is. Valuable goods for select customers. What about the money? I reckon I should send down your share once a month, make out it's rent or –'

'I known you regard everybody who wasn't born within hearing range of Bow Bells as a complete fool, Tweedie, but you are wrong. You have nothing whatever to do with the money. I am paid directly, and you will be paid a flat sum each month, so long as I remain satisfied with your services.'

Tweedie had opened his mouth to remonstrate, but closed it again as Alexander slid a five pound note from his billfold.

'This is on account, Tweedie,' Alexander stated, holding it out, 'and to confirm my end of the bargain. To confirm yours, you can get out, and send little Vera in.'

Tweedie obeyed promptly, and Alexander had barely opened his fly before Vera was standing in front of him, the lollipop still in her mouth, her face set in an expression of insolent challenge. Alexander nodded thoughtfully.

'Turn around, my dear, and bend across the bed.'

As Vera's neat little buttocks came on view he had already began to massage his cock.

14

Kerslake Manor, Devon – July 1940

Alexander Gorringe struggled to hide his grin as he strode across the rough grass of the moor. The figures looked very good indeed. Those clients who had come to rely on Jervis Maray's services seemed actively keen to throw their money at him. There were also some impressive offers for girls in milk to suckle from, punish in various ways or simply have sex with, all services that Jervis Maray seemed to have provided at one time or another. Cora at least could be guaranteed to oblige, Molly would do as she was told, and it even seemed possible that some of the others might be tempted.

Another plus point was that Reginald Thann had been too busy again, while Holly had so hated the Hotbox that her behaviour had been immaculate ever since. Nothing seemed to be too much trouble for her, or too rude. Just the previous evening he had had her stripped nude and passed between them for spanking. She had gone over Molly, Hazel and even Cora's laps without a murmur of complaint and used her mouth to good effect on all five of them afterwards.

He had reached a low stone wall, and vaulted it in sheer exuberance. He had his safe place for the war, a comfortable lifestyle, plenty of sex and an excellent money-making scheme to keep him amused. The future, it was true, might hold all sorts of horrors, even invasion, although for all Churchill's words he felt it likely that the fighting would stop short of Devon. Rather than mope, he was determined to get as much out of life as possible while he could. The immediate future held a much more appealing prospect.

A minor irritation was the unexpected efficiency and lack of pliability of the village girls. He had supposed they would come up alone or in small groups as convenience suited them, and as their milk came in. Given the reaction the milking machines brought on, and how absolutely helpless a girl was once in the straps, it should have been easy to slip himself into a convenient quim, or even up a bottom. Unfortunately the girls came in groups, each led by a 'Nurse' and chaperoned by one or more formidable 'Matrons' who never let the girls out of their sight. In the circumstances it was hardly practical to even watch, the Matrons hustling him or Herbert away, so that they were forced to peer through chinks in the door, which he found demeaning.

The girls were milked nude, and according to a strict regime. They would strip, wash and allow themselves to be fixed in place. The Matron would control the milking, mix the yield, oversee the measurement and take the money at the half-crown a pint agreed on. The girls' figures varied from impressive to magnificent, and their reaction to being milked from coy to openly lewd. Herbert in particular found their inaccessibility frustrating, despite Cora's availability. Initially, Alexander had contented himself with what he had, reasoning that it was worth putting up with when daily production was in excess of four gallons and rising. The money had begun to roll in, and even after expenses the operation looked like being very profitable indeed.

Yet it had proved difficult not to at least consider ways to avoid the Matron's attentions. It was a

159

challenge, and one he found it impossible not to rise to, even if only as idle speculation. The speculation had rapidly become anything but idle.

The younger girls were clearly game, especially those who were unmarried. Of the more sensible ones and the Nurses, he was sure all could be cajoled or bribed into silence or playfulness, as need demanded. Once a girl had indulged herself, she could be guaranteed to keep silent, as it was clear that the Matron's influence rested on a threat of some kind, or in many cases on maternal authority.

If the obvious solution was to get rid of the Matrons then that was not so simple in practice. They were sisters, and seemed to have plenty of spare time to chaperone the girls, certainly more spare time than the girls themselves had. Of the fourteen girls, nine were the daughters of one or another Matron. Two more were daughters-in-law, while Alice Barracombe and Jenny Penrose were equally under the Matrons' thumbs. Only Roberta Slater seemed to have the courage to challenge the older women's authority.

He had considered Roberta. She was a fine, buxom girl in her mid-thirties, dark and curly as so many of the local girls were, but originally from South Brent on the far side of the moor. She was one of the Nurses, which he was fairly sure meant she had been one of Jervis's milkers, possibly even one of the girls hired out to wealthy clients. There was a knowing look in her eye, almost of mockery, that reminded him of Cora and made him pretty well certain that she was not only willing, but eager for sex. Better still, she lived on the edge of the moor a good quarter-mile out of Kerslake Village. Once she was corrupted, he would at the least be able to communicate to the others, hopefully more. A visit to her cottage was clearly in order, and it was now his destination.

It was directly ahead, a low, whitewashed building among trees. He was not entirely sure what she did. It seemed to involve animals, as the garden was full of chickens and goats, and also sewing, as when he rounded the garden wall it was to find her sitting in front of her door, mending a pair of men's trousers.

'Good afternoon, Miss Slater,' he greeted her, trying not to stare too obviously as the impressive spread of her bosom. 'A beautiful day, is it not? Ideal for a stroll on the moor, I thought . . .'

He stopped. She had looked up as he appeared, in surprise, then with a coquettish smile. As he spoke, she had glanced quickly to either side, where the lane disappeared between high hedges, then nipped smartly inside, beckoning him to follow.

'Make yourself comfortable in the back parlour here, Mr Gorringe,' she said as he entered the house.

Somewhat nonplussed, he made for the door she had indicated, to find a small, comfortably furnished room. There was an enormous and well-padded sofa against one wall, what appeared to be a genuine tiger skin on the floor in front of the fireplace and an extremely fine clock on the mantelpiece. A selection of extraordinarily lewd hunting prints decorated the wall. For a moment he stared in astonishment before it dawned on him that she was clearly the local tart, and highly successful.

She had not followed, but gone into a different room. Alexander waited, admiring a print of a busty, fat-bottomed girl with perfectly white skin being chased by hounds to the direction of a group of huntsmen. So closely did the girl resemble Hazel Mullins that it might have been painted from life, and he found his mouth curving up into a grin and his cock stiffening in his trousers.

He turned as he heard a footstep outside the door, and stopped dead, staring. Roberta was no longer in the plain blue dress she had been wearing. In its place was a corset, a huge whaleboned thing in crimson satin which gave an elegant curve to her waist and made her naked breasts and hips seem simply enormous. Alexander could only stare, letting his eyes travel slowly down from the mass of brown curls that now framed her face, to the swell of the magnificent chest, and lower, to the plump, furry bulge of her quim and her long, shapely legs. Her skin was pale and creamy smooth, her flesh firm yet more than ample. She was clearly in milk, white beads showing on both large, erect nipples.

She smiled and came forwards, her hands going directly to his fly, to pop the buttons open with deft, practised movements. He made no effort to resist, more than happy to take what was so clearly on offer. Soon his cock was out, and she went down, squatting with her bottom pushed well out, to use her mouth and boobs on his penis. She was skilled, using her tongue, her lips and her throat with an expert understanding of all the most sensitive parts of his cock. The sucking alternated with being rubbed between her magnificent breasts, and in no time he felt fit to burst.

He determined to fuck her, and pulled her up by the hair. She came, giggling, and made no resistance as he pushed her into a kneeling position on the sofa with the glorious, meaty globes of her bottom spread to offer her quim, fat and soft, the lips swollen, the centre a puffy, moist tart of flesh. He put his cock to her and slid in, moaning in delight as his erection was engulfed in hot flesh. She was moaning too as he began to fuck, and wiggling her bottom on his cock. He climbed on to her back, all the while jabbing his cock in and out of the mouth of her sex as he took her vast, milky boobs in hand. They felt tight with pressure, and immensely heavy, while the nipples were slick with spilled milk. He clung on, pumping faster and faster as he revelled in the sheer volume of soft female flesh beneath him, pushing himself against her great cushion of a bottom, kneading her enormous breasts, and coming deep up her with a great jolt of ecstasy that left him trembling and weak at the knees.

Roberta stayed still as he finished himself inside her, moving only when he had dismounted, to quickly take his cock into her mouth and suck away his juices and her own.

'Too many of them wipe it on the furniture,' she explained casually as she pulled back.

'I wouldn't dream of doing any such thing,' Alexander assured her as he sank down into the corner of the sofa.

'You're a naughty boy anyways,' Roberta chided gently. 'You should have done that over my bottom. Now I'll have to douche.'

She left the room. Alexander blew his breath out and began to tidy himself up. It was better even than he had expected, Roberta clearly serving as the local tart in addition to her other work and so presumably willing to do anything so long as she was paid. There were already several offers.

Realising that it would only be polite to pay himself, he withdrew a crown from his pocket. Roberta returned as he was placing it on the mantelpiece, now dressed once more.

'Don't worry with that,' she assured him quickly. 'You may not be Squire, but I dare say you're entitled.'

'Yes, quite,' Alexander answered, wondering if it was normal for West Country prostitutes to provide free service to the local squires. 'You were a friend of Jervis Maray then?'

'His favourite,' she answered, 'towards the end, and of the Lady Genevieve too. She was a cruel one, she was, little wonder they locked her up.'

'She was . . . is, yes, a touch unstable,' he said. 'You provided milk then, for Jervis?'

'Milk, yes,' she answered. 'Me, and Lucy and Alice and Anna Wescott, Eliza's eldest, it was, last off. Twelve of us there was, at one time.'

'This was when?'

'Thirty-two, Mr Jervis died. Not old, he wasn't. Too much drink and too many girls, that's what did for him. Same with his father. Drowned in a bath of girls' milk, did Archibald Maray. Now, Mr Herbert, he seems a nice young man.'

'Puffer? Yes, fine fellow, and he'd be keen for a go at those bubbies of yours, I can tell you. So you stopped in thirty-two?'

'Not altogether, no. There was still the lady, but she was too cruel, and with him gone, she went altogether too far.'

'Oh yes?'

'Indeed, yes. She put a pig ring though Lucy's nose, she did, and used to fix it with a chain to keep her in place during milking. You could hear Lucy's cries to Ermecombe, I'm told, and I wouldn't be surprised if it wasn't the truth. She had these awful gloves too, with them curved sacking needles sewn into the fingers, like claws. A real devil she was. I wasn't having it, and nor would the others, and when we told her, she went into a rage. So that was that.'

'I see . . . a nose ring . . . like a pig . . . extraordinary. So, did you do any other work for Jervis? Did you visit any gentlemen elsewhere in England?'

'I did, and Lucy too, before she married Jan Linnel. Handy that was, and did me proud, presents and all.'

She nodded to the rug, then to the clock.

'The prints?' Alexander queried.

'Oh, no, them's by a regular of mine. Used to paint the moor he did, and famous for it. That's me, that is, in the one you were so admiring.'

'With the hounds! You didn't?'

'No, don't be foolish. That's supposed to be Devil John Truscott, two centuries gone, when he used to hunt his servant girls across the moor.'

'Quite,' Alexander answered weakly, his view of himself as cruel and masterful taking a sharp nosedive.

'So, ah ... would you perhaps be prepared to take on new assignments ... er ... new assignations of the sort you used to for Jervis?'

'I'd be that, sir. It's not been so easy, these last few years, and worse still now there's war again.'

'I can imagine. So, er ... you are not concerned by Eliza Grant then? She seems to have something of a hold over the girls?'

'Only because they know she'll wallop their backsides for them if they stray. Spanked Lucy, she did, in the church hall if you please, in front of everyone, just to show she meant it. She doesn't frighten me.'

'I can well imagine it. Splendid, splendid. Well then, I need to get in touch with certain gentlemen and I would hope to have something for you within a few days.'

'Thank you kindly, sir.'

'Please don't mention it. And, ah ... what of the other girls, Lucy perhaps?'

'She would, if she dared. Jenny Penrose is a flighty little baggage, and would do it for sport, but for her father and Eliza. Takes after her mother, they say. Otherwise, I wouldn't like to say.'

'No matter, my dear, you have been very helpful. I had better be getting back, but I'll drop in again soon.'

Ten minutes later he had gone, taking care to leave the crown piece behind as if by accident.

15

Kerslake Manor, Devon – August 1940

Alexander Gorringe shook his head as he scanned the letter in his hand. As before, it was a single sheet of text, typed and unsigned. Unlike before, a large crate had arrived with it.

'What is it this time?' Herbert queried.

'Another one of Thann's infernal devices,' Alexander answered, 'some sort of head cage ... dum de dum ... yes, apparently a heavy chair has to be bolted to the floor and fitted with straps, heavy duty straps, he specifies. The cage thingy is then fitted over her head ... Good God! He wants me to put rats in it!'

'Rats? The man's insane!'

'Absolutely, I'm an officer in the RAF, damn him, not a ruddy rat catcher!'

'So, these rats can get at her face, and she's helpless? That's barbarous!'

'Well, no ... yes and no. There are partitions, wire mesh so that she can see the rats. The rats can only get at her if both partitions are lifted. Judging from his letter the idea is to get her into a state of stark terror, then not do it, which is apparently supposed to induce in her a feeling of intense gratitude ... I wouldn't have thought so. I'm sure I'd develop an undying hatred for anyone who did that to me, wouldn't you?'

'Yes, absolutely.'

'He seems to think otherwise. Apparently it will allow us to reinforce her dependence on us, and therefore him, to the point where it becomes absolute.'

'What a load of tommyrot!'

'Yes, you'd have thought so, wouldn't you? On the other hand, look at little Molly. She seems to become more and more devoted, regardless of what I do to her.'

'Well, yes . . . Speaking of which, isn't it about time you gave her that spanking?'

'Yes, undoubtedly, but I don't want to spoil her authority over the other girls, which is damned useful. It's hard to respect someone when you've seen them bare-arsed and blubbering over a man's lap. She hates pain, too, and she'll howl likes the blazes. So what shall we do with the head cage?'

'Get rid of the horrid thing. Cut it up into pieces.'

'We can't do that. He's sure to want to see it when he comes down.'

'You wouldn't actually use it, would you?'

'Good heavens, no! Not with rats, anyway. I wonder if Thann would recognise a vole if he saw one.'

Holly placed a hand to her stomach. There was no doubting it. Her flesh felt firmer, and rounder. It was not simply the extra fat she had put on since coming into milk. She was pregnant.

Being illegitimate herself, she had been warned time and time again about the dangers of allowing herself to get carried away with her feelings. Not only her own mother, but Cicely Yates and even Kitty Mullins had lectured her repeatedly. It had happened anyway, and in the most embarrassing of circumstances.

She had felt the changes in her body a while before, a sick feeling every morning first, then a growing sense of weight in her belly. Compared with the changes due to being in milk they had been minor, with her breasts now weighing over eight pounds each and her overall weight at over twelve stone. Yet the effect of the milking regime had begun to stabilise, and the feeling in her belly had not.

The father could be one of two men, but she had no way of telling which. Both Alexander Gorringe and Herbert Maray had fucked her and come in her quim the night she had lost her virginity. Both had also fucked her since and, despite their best efforts to spend over her bottom or in her mouth, she was not at all sure that some semen had not gone inside her.

She was biting her lip as she began to dress. They had just been milked, and the relief to her breasts had made her more aware than ever of her swollen belly. Now, with the four of them off the machines, they had to tidy up quickly and make way for a group of village girls. Already Judy Draycott was waiting in the dairy door, great, heavy arms folded across her chest as she watched the four girls struggle into their uniforms.

A thought came to Holly that, while she could expect sympathy from her friends, for any worthwhile advice it would be better to speak to an older woman. Judy Draycott looked to be in her fifties, and had three daughters among the village girls in milk alone, so at the very least would know about childbirth. It was not easy. Judy Draycott gave the impression that she disapproved of just about everything, as did her sisters, overseeing the milking process with stern efficiency and making very sure that the men were kept well away. On the other hand, she had never seen Judy loose her temper, even when Roberta Slater had been lured away on some mysterious but undoubtedly perverse visit to somewhere up country.

She began to slow down in her dressing, deliberately taking her time with her stockings and the catches of her suspenders and pausing to rub margarine into her nipples before putting on her chemise. Hazel was already fully dressed by the time Holly was pulling up her skirt.

'Hurry up,' Hazel chided, 'we'll be needed on the balloons in ten minutes.'

'I'll catch up,' Holly promised. 'I . . . I need . . . never mind, I'll talk to you later.'

Hazel threw her a concerned look, but hurried to get into line behind Cora at the door. Molly MacCallion turned Holly an officious scowl.

'Black point, Bomefield-Mullins,' Molly snapped.

No more needed to be said. The black point was Holly's fifth and meant a bare-bottom spanking that evening. She had come to treat the punishment system as a game, enjoying the sense of anticipation and even the fear that came with it. Usually the award of her fifth point left her in a state of confused excitement, as scared as she was aroused by the prospect of what was coming to her. Now it seemed insignificant.

As she finished dressing, the village girls were already trooping into the room. There were three, the two blonde sisters, Alice Barracombe and Jenny Penrose, and one of Judy's daughters, Nellie Causey. She greeted each with a smile as she made for the door, stopping as she reached Judy Draycott and speaking after only a moment to get her courage up.

'Excuse me, Mrs Draycott, but might I have a word?'

'Certain sure, you may, just as soon as you've helped me get these three little baggages into order.'

Holly turned, reflecting that 'little' was hardly an accurate description of the girls. All three had begun to undress, and with only light summer frocks on in the first place, they were already showing just about everything. Alice Barracombe was the tallest, and the least meaty, blonde and lithe, her body muscular and heavy only at the chest and bottom cheeks. Her little sister Jenny was very different, also blonde, but a head shorter, a smiling, rosy-cheeked butterball of a girl, with breasts so enormous they made her fleshy midriff seem small and a big, wobbling bottom. Nellie was more typical of the local girls, voluptuous without being really fat, with smooth skin and a great mass of thick, curly brown hair.

Judy had gone to see to her daughter, so Holly took the closest machine, in front of which Jenny was stripping out of her knickers. They exchanged a warm but somewhat embarrassed smile as Jenny stepped forwards to lay herself on the bench. Holly took the waist strap, her hands brushing Jenny's warm, soft flesh as she buckled it into place. It was hard not to giggle as the way the machine lifted and spread the fat girl's bottom, despite Holly's knowledge that she looked much the same herself during milking. She held back, though, trying to be calm and efficient as she fixed the remaining straps into place and adjusted the suction cups that had so recently been on her own breasts to fit. As she worked she could smell Jenny's milk, and her quim too, filling her with both embarrassment and desire.

By the time she had finished, Judy was already working on Alice's breast cups, and Holly stood back to wait, thinking of sex and wondering how it would feel to have her face smothered in Jenny's more than ample bottom. Only when Judy stood up was her mind brought sharply back to the consequences of her lewdness. She turned the machine on, almost absently, starting the suck and gurgle of the pumps. Judy approached, took her arm and drew her to the side, leaning close to talk.

'So you've a mind for advice over the child in your belly?'

'How did you know?' Holly demanded.

'After seven of my own, and all my sisters' children? How could I not know?'

'I suppose so. Yes, I thought, as you . . . as you have

so much experience, you might be able to provide some advice.'

'I can. Marry the father and see he looks after you. Don't take no for an answer.'

'How am I to do that? And . . . and . . . I'm not even certain who the father is!'

'Well, you wouldn't be the first,' Judy answered, her eyes flicking momentarily to the girls on the machines. 'Young Squire Maray, is it, and Mr Gorringe?'

'Yes,' Holly admitted.

'Had you on a milking machine, I'll be bound,' Judy went on. 'Mr Jervis was the same . . .'

'I was willing,' Holly said hastily. 'He didn't rape me or anything . . .'

'I'm sure he didn't,' Judy answered. 'He wouldn't need to, would he? Not after a half-hour of milking, then a fine dinner I dare say, and wine, and some dirty talk or making girls do disgusting things to one another.'

'Well, yes,' Holly admitted, now blushing furiously and wondering if they had been spied on, or if one of the other girls had been letting out their secrets.

'It was much the same with Mr Jervis,' Judy went on, 'and his father before him, the real Squire, old Archibald Maray.'

'What should I do then?' Holly asked.

'Choose one or the other,' Judy stated, 'and tell him he's to make an honest woman of you, here and now. Don't make no threats, but they're not stupid, and I don't suppose the bigwigs up London would take too kindly to their officers getting their own girls pregnant, nor to what's going on here.'

'No, I suppose not,' Holly answered. 'But it's not so easy. Squadron Leader Gorringe is very attached to Corporal MacCallion. I think he means to marry her. Likewise with Flight Officer Maray and Cora . . . Aircraftwoman Jackson.'

'They're pregnant, are they, either of them?'

'Well, no . . .'

'Then it's no matter. Choose the Squire, that's my advice. He may not be so straight and handsome as Mr Gorringe, but he's as soft as butter, and he'll do as he's told, I'll warrant, once you're man and wife. You'll find that's important, once you're older. Why, I have enough trouble getting my Jan to take his feet off the furniture, and that's after thirty and more years of marriage.'

Holly pursed her lips, considering the prospect of marriage to Herbert Maray. Her feelings towards him had always been odd, and hard to reconcile. She had despised him initially, and been disgusted by his soft, bulbous body. His friendliness and lack of any real malice had improved her opinion of him, but the disgust had remained. Then there was the desire she could never overcome, to have him inflict every perverse sexual act she could think of on her body, preferably while she was helpless. It only made her disgust worse.

'I don't know . . .' she said.

'Make your choice, and don't linger,' Judy advised. 'Remember, nobody gets all they want out of this life, and if you take too long about making your choices, you'll likely get nothing at all.'

Holly nodded.

'Thank you, Mrs Draycott. I'd better go now. Thank you.'

'That's Judy, no call for formality, and glad to be of service. You run along then.'

Holly left, pondering the advice as she walked out on to the field. Hazel was nowhere to be seen, but Alexander Gorringe was, standing by the accumulator with an impatient scowl on his face. She hurried towards him, glancing in sudden fear at the Hotbox as she passed it.

She was already stammering out apologies as she reached him, only to stop and turn to the west as she caught the drone of an aircraft engine. She saw it immediately, the neat form of a single-seater fighter coming in over Kerslake woods at speed. A jolt of raw terror hit her, fading only slowly with her recognition of the outline of a Hurricane. Her hand went to her stomach and she blew her breath out as the plane roared past, going into a spectacular victory roll as it came over the airstrip and rising beyond into a high loop.

'Damn show off!' Gorringe commented.

Holly put her hand to her tummy, unable to speak for a moment as she watched the aeroplane rise to the top of its loop and swing down once more towards the airstrip. This time it came in, landing neatly and turning to taxi back to stop beside the Gloster Gladiator. Gorringe began to walk forwards, Holly following a pace behind.

The pilot had jumped down long before they had reached the plane. He was a slim young man, carrying a riding crop. He seemed elegant to a fault, especially in his tight leather boots, effeminate almost, and as he shrugged off his flying jacket Holly realised that it was not a man at all, but a woman. Two pert tits were pushing out the front of her uniform jacket, and her hips, while slim, had an unquestionably feminine curve to them. Helmet and goggles followed the jacket, revealing yellow hair cropped short and a delicate, oval face. Holly's mouth came open in a delighted yell.

'Sapphie!'

'Sapphie? Sappho Yates?' Gorringe demanded.

'Yes, she's my oldest friend,' Holly answered. 'Hazel! Hazel! It's Sapphie!'

Hazel appeared from one of the sheds, wiping oil on her overalls, her face set in surprise, then delight. Sapphie was smiling broadly as she stepped forwards, and caught Holly in her arms as they came together.

'Steady on!' Sapphie managed, whispering. 'Not in front of your CO! Heavens, girl!'

173

Holly ignored the protest and hugged her friend. Sapphie disengaged herself gently and threw Gorringe a salute, then another to Herbert Maray, who was walking from the buildings.

'Squadron Leader Gorringe?' she asked, extending her hand. 'Section Officer Yates. I'm your relief.'

'My relief? I'm not due to be relieved.'

'No bumph come through? Typical! Never mind, I've all the papers for your new posting,' she announced breezily. 'Kenley.'

'Kenley?' he answered. 'But that's . . .'

'Surrey. Everything you need to know is here.'

She had drawn a sheaf of papers from her flying jacket, and passed some of them across. Gorringe took them, to stare at the top sheet as if unable to believe that it was real.

'We need every experienced man we can get,' Sapphie went on, 'and we girls are needed for the lazy jobs. With you two down here I thought I'd apply for the posting. They even let me fly your Hurc down, sir. I'm on the Gladiator, am I? A conversion, is it?'

'And me?' Herbert Maray quavered.

'You stay here as a ground wallah,' she answered, not troubling to hide her contempt. 'AOC too, with the rank of Flight Lieutenant.'

Maray's face brightened immediately as he took the papers. Alexander Gorringe was still staring at his papers. His face had turned green.

16

Meadway Hall, Yorkshire – August 1940

Roberta Slater stifled a sigh and began to crawl forwards. She was nude, on her hands and knees in a great open barn strewn with straw. Her head had been shaved and her body painted with irregular black patches. Her breasts hung heavy beneath her, swinging to her motions as she crawled. Her bottom was a mess of deep purple welts, sore and swollen. On her back sat the diminutive Lord Farthinghurst, also naked, save for a red hunting coat and a top hat, his outsize genitals spread warm and flaccid on Roberta's back. In one hand he held a pint mug of fresh milk, her milk, mixed with a shot of brandy. In the other hand he held a riding whip.

'Faster!' he demanded and brought the thick leather sting down on Roberta's naked bottom with a vicious flick.

'Ow!' she protested.

'Not "Ow", you silly girl!' he snapped. 'Whoever heard of a cow that went "Ow". Cows go "Moo", everyone knows that.'

'Moo,' Roberta managed sulkily.

'Put some spirit into it, girl!' Farthinghurst demanded.

'Moo!' Roberta repeated.

'Better, but you've still a long way to go. I don't think you're really trying at all. I think you're being deliberately naughty! Now you know what happens to naughty cows, don't you? To naughty cows who won't do as Master tells them?'

'Yes,' Roberta answered miserably.

'And what is it?' he demanded.

'They have to go . . . to go plop-plops in front of their Master,' Roberta sighed.

'Yes!' he crowed. 'They have to go plop-plops in front of their Master! And have you been a naughty cow?'

'Yes,' Roberta sighed.

'And is naughty Roberta cow ready for plop-plops?' he asked. 'She should be, I think, after all the yummy mangels she ate up this morning.'

'Yes, I'm ready,' Roberta admitted.

He climbed off immediately, cackling with mirth. Roberta set her knees apart, flaunting herself.

'Stick it up, stick it up!' he whined. 'I want to see properly!'

Roberta obeyed, pushing her bottom high to spread her big cheeks to his gaze, with her anus pointing up and out. He was right, she needed to go, but the strain in her bladder was even more urgent than in her rectum. For a moment she held on, knowing he liked a good strong gush. Then she let go.

Farthinghurst gave a delighted squeal as piddle erupted from her quim to splash in the straw beneath her. With the pee gushing out, her rectum began to contract. She felt her anus start to pout and a shame-filled sob burst from her lips.

'Not yet! Not yet!' he screamed.

The riding whip cracked down on her bottom.

'Ow . . . Moo . . . No!' she cried. 'I can't do it while you beat me, you know I can't!'

'Good!' he cackled.

'No . . . please . . . please, Master . . . I'm so sore! Ow! Moo . . . moo . . . moo! Please stop!'

176

He paid no attention, belabouring her bottom with cut after cut as he wrenched at his rapidly stiffening cock. Roberta struggled to moo, and to contain the huge load threatening to explode from her rectum and give the lie to her claims to be unable to perform while under the lash. Not that Farthinghurst seemed to care any more, jerking at his cock and lashing away at her agonised bottom until she wasn't sure if she would soil herself or faint. Only when he was forced to change to wanking right-handed did it stop, the peer hurling the whip away and fixing his eyes to her open bottom.

Roberta blew her breath out. It was going to happen, at any moment, whether she liked it or not, whether he was ready or not. Her face screwed up with effort as she pulled her load back, and she turned to look at him. He was masturbating furiously, his face set in maniacal glee as he jerked at his enormous cock.

'Do it!' he grunted. 'Do it, my lovely fat cow! Do plop-plops! Push!'

Roberta groaned deep in her throat as she let her bottom hole open, her ring spreading wide to the pressure in her rectum, until she could feel the head of what was in her pushing out. Farthinghurst gave an ecstatic cry. Spunk erupted from his cock, to patter down on her back and buttocks. More came, catching her between her cheeks and on her quim. A third explosion landed full across the width of her bottom cheeks, even as she struggled to stop what she was doing now he had come.

It was too late. Roberta closed her eyes in exhausted resignation as the turds began to roll slowly down over her quim to make a fat, steaming pile beneath her.

17

Kerslake Manor, Devon –
August 1940

Holly put her back to the sideboard, trying desperately to seem relaxed as Sapphie worked on the venison tornedos that formed the centrepiece of dinner. They had been flamed in brandy at the table, and were topped with soured girls' milk cream.

It had been a long and trying day and a half. Her first instinct had been to hide what they were doing from her friend. It had also been Alexander Gorringe's order. By leading Sapphie straight into the house, they had managed to get Judy Draycott and the three girls out of the milking shed and away across the moor without being noticed.

The deception had been maintained all afternoon and all night, but had collapsed in the morning. Unmilked, the girls' breasts had become ever more swollen and painful. By dinner time Holly had been in an agony of need, both boobs straining fit to burst and the milk soaking into her blouse. The other girls had been as bad, their discomfort evident in their faces. The two officers had done their best, insisting on going through the station paperwork in detail and on entertaining Sapphie themselves, although she was clearly keen to talk to Hazel and Holly.

They had finally managed to relieve themselves as they prepared dinner, taking turns to suckle or express their milk into jugs while the others cooked and Sapphie drank Champagne with the men in the drawing room. Dinner had been easier, although more than once Sapphie had made teasing remarks about the weight Holly and Hazel had put on when the men were out of earshot.

Fortunately Sapphie had been tired and gone to bed early, with Holly, Hazel and Cora following not long after, to leave the officers and Molly MacCallion in heated discussion over how to keep their secret from getting out. Alexander Gorringe had been feeding letters into a roaring fire as Holly left.

In the morning she had woken with stiff breasts and wet nipples. Hazel had provided hurried relief and Holly had returned the favour, but it left her flustered and hot as they came down to help prepare breakfast. No sooner had she finished than she was ordered to run out across the moor and turn back the group of Ermecombe girls due to be milked that morning. Becky Apcott, the second of Eliza Grant's sisters, was with them.

By the time Holly had managed to persuade the Matron and four girls to turn back and milk themselves by hand, it was mid-morning. She had watched the Squadron Leader's Hurricane rise into the sky from the ridge above the airstrip with a vague sense of loss. Back at the Manor, Sapphie had cornered her and demanded to know what was going on. She had protested innocence, denying that anything was amiss. Sapphie had twisted her arm into the small of her back. Still she had held out, gritting her teeth against the pain as she begged for mercy, only for Lucy Linnel to walk into the kitchen with a milk churn and her breasts already bare for milking.

There had been no choice but to explain. Herbert Maray had made one pathetic attempt to pull rank, then caved in completely, babbling out an incoherent string of apologies and admissions. Sapphie had listened in growing astonishment, then demanded to inspect the premises. Molly MacCallion had shown her around, and while they were in the dairy the group of girls from the moor farms had arrived. Eliza Grant herself was with them as Matron and had taken over, explaining the situation to Sapphie in her usual forthright manner, without so much as a twinge of guilt or remorse.

Sapphie had said very little, and watched the milking in amazement, then walked out on to the moor, saying she need to think. A hasty conference had been held, with Eliza Grant firmly in charge, and by lunchtime it had been agreed to try to persuade Sapphie to join them.

Holly had spent the afternoon in a state of nervous anxiety, alternately reminding herself how close she had always been to Sapphie and worrying about her friend's dedication to duty. Among the others, Molly had seemed listless. Herbert Maray had spent his time biting his fingernails and muttering to himself. Hazel and Cora had been more practical, preparing an exceptional dinner that included as many girls' milk products as possible.

The shadows had begun to lengthen on the moor by the time Sapphie returned. She had taken her seat at the table without a word and accepted a Welsh rarebit and a glass of ale, eating with a faraway look in her eyes as Herbert Maray struggled to make polite conversation from the opposite end of the table. Cora's speciality of trout in hazelnut butter had followed, accompanied by a Meursault, then the venison, but still Sapphie had declined to let herself be engaged in anything but casual conversation.

Holly was biting her lip as Sapphie swallowed the last of her wine and put the glass down on the table and dabbed her lips with a napkin.

'I must say, you certainly eat well,' Sapphie remarked. 'This is very cosy all round, in fact.'

Holly hastened forward to fill her friend's glass from the decanter.

'We've rather a good cellar,' Herbert Maray said, his tone timid, almost awestruck.

'So I notice,' Sapphie replied, holding her glass up to catch the gleam of the candlelight in her wine. 'This is excellent claret, certainly.'

'Langoa-Barton ninety-nine,' Herbert supplied hastily. 'An exceptional year.'

'Yes,' Sapphie agreed, 'venison too, and the cream is delicious.'

'Girls' milk cream,' Hazel stated, finally breaking the tension.

'I had guessed as much,' Sapphie answered. 'The butter?'

'The butter too,' Hazel confirmed. 'The butter, the cheese for your Welsh rarebit, the sour cream, everything.'

'I see. Let me get this straight then. You and various local girls are milked each day . . .'

'Twice, usually. There are eighteen girls in milk, including the four of us.'

'Which produces?'

'Four gallons at least, nearer five.'

'And the spare girls' milk goes to the dairy in the village, where it's made into cream, butter and cheese –'

'Two sorts of cheese,' Hazel interrupted. 'There's Erme Head, which is a hard cheese a bit like cheddar, and Dartmoor Blue, which is simply delicious and fetches . . .'

'Two cheeses then,' Sapphie went on, 'which are sent up to London once a week and distributed to the customers by a pimp turned racketeer.'

'That's is, more or less,' Herbert admitted.

'Don't give us away, Sapphie, please,' Holly blurted out. 'We'd be in terrible trouble, I'm sure, and –'

'I have no intention of doing anything of the sort,' Sapphie answered. 'After all, while I can certainly imagine some raised eyebrows at the Ministry, I am absolutely certain that human milk is not on the ration. I wouldn't like to put it to the test, true – but, so far as I can see, you're doing nothing illegal.'

'No?' Herbert asked. 'Really?'

'Immoral, yes,' Sapphie answered him, 'or at least I expect your average, decent, godfearing Ministry wallah would think so. They'd probably assume it was illegal too, simply because that sort always assumes anything they find offensive is either illegal or ought to be. Personally, while I admit to being a little surprised, I'm perfectly happy, especially if this is an example of the way you eat. But I shall certainly expect a cut.'

'Absolutely . . . of course,' Herbert Maray hastened to reassure her. 'And . . . and will you be adding to the production yourself?'

Sapphie turned him a hard look, immediately quelling the lecherous gleam that had appeared in his eyes.

'No,' she answered firmly. 'Not my style, as Holly and Hazel here will tell you. I prefer, shall we say, a more commanding role. Don't I, girls?'

'Yes,' Hazel sighed. Holly nodded.

'You do?' Herbert asked, his eyes shining again.

Sapphie gave him a look of utter contempt and turned to Hazel.

'Do I sense rebellion, Hazel Mullins?'

Hazel shook her head.

'Good,' Sapphie went on, 'then I can see we will all get along famously. Now, what's for pudding?'

'Custard tart,' Holly answered, 'made with –'

'I know, girls' milk,' Sapphie cut her off. 'And that's "custard tart, Ma'am" unless I say otherwise.'

She was smiling as she took another swallow from her glass. Holly felt her tension start to drain away, a blissful feeling that left her weak and close to tears of sheer gratitude. The WAAF had not changed Sapphie. Her friend was still the calm, cruel and fiercely independent girl she had worshipped and followed her entire life. Even Hazel was smiling as she went to fetch the pudding.

Holly busied herself with the Sauternes, wondering if she dared take some for herself while Sapphie was distracted, and if she did and was caught, whether Sapphie would dare to give her a punishment spanking in front of Herbert Maray and the other girls. Just the thought was enough to set her stomach fluttering, but her courage failed her and she found herself serving the wine without stealing any.

Sapphie talked brightly as she ate, addressing Herbert and ignoring the girls. It was very different to her behaviour the day before, as if she was determined to show off her authority. Holly found herself responding, and thinking back to Ashwood, and spanking, and being tied up, and made to utterly humiliate herself. She also wanted to tell Sapphie she was pregnant, and to be punished. Both things she knew would leave her feeling much better about her condition. Also, from the way Herbert Maray seemed to look up to Sapphie, it was plain that he would not dare gainsay her if Holly decided to demand marriage.

The pudding taken care of, Sapphie and Herbert were served cheese and port, Holly waiting patiently until they were done, and wondering what was going to happen later. At last the dinner came to an end.

'Delicious,' Sapphie remarked. 'Now, Herbert, what do you do for after dinner entertainment here? Bridge, a little backgammon?'

'We, ah ... tend to gather in the drawing room,' Herbert answered. 'All ranks, very informal, I'm afraid.'

'I have nothing against informality,' Sapphie answered, 'so long as it doesn't lead to a lack of proper respect. The drawing room it is then, and Corporal MacCallion and Aircraftwoman Jackson may join us. You can bring the decanter, Holly.'

Herbert Maray hastened to help her with her chair, but she had already risen by the time he reached her. He followed her from the room, bobbing in her wake like a tethered barrage balloon. Holly went to the kitchen, where the other two girls greeted her with anxious looks.

'Well?' Molly MacCallion demanded.

'She's definitely OK?' Cora added.

'Definitely,' Holly confirmed. 'She even says we're all to come and have a glass of port in the drawing room.'

'Money talks, like I said,' Cora stated.

'I'm still not sure . . .' Molly began.

'A week and she'll be in it up to her neck,' Cora insisted. 'She's human, ain't she? And from what you say, Holly, she's one evil bitch.'

'She's not evil,' Holly protested. 'Just cruel . . . in a playful sort of way. She's no worse than Gorringe, anyway.'

'He's a man,' Cora pointed out.

'I don't see . . .' Holly began and broke off.

Hazel had opened the door, bringing in the pudding bowl. Beyond, Sapphie could be seen standing at the noticeboard, talking to Herbert, who looked more flustered than ever.

'What is this?' Sapphie demanded, nodding to the punishment sheet as the girls came near. 'And no nonsense.'

'Squadron Leader Gorringe liked to keep tight discipline,' Hazel explained. 'We get a black point if we do something wrong, and when we get five –'

'He spanks your fat bottoms for you, I expect,' Sapphie cut in.

Holly went scarlet. Sapphie laughed.

'I guessed as much. I recognised the expression on your face, and Holly's too. Mark you, a pound to five says you put him up to it.'

'We did not!' Holly exclaimed.

Sapphie merely sniffed and passed on from the notice-board.

'I'll keep the system,' she announced as she entered the drawing room. 'It sounds rather fun. So the four of you –'

'Three, Ma'am,' Molly MacCallion put in quickly. 'I'm exempt.'

'Why?' Sapphie queried.

'As a corporal,' Molly answered. 'Squadron Leader Gorringe said it would destroy my authority if the others saw me sp– saw me punished that way.'

'Sadly, Corporal MacCallion, Squadron Leader Gorringe is no longer your AOC.'

'With respect, Ma'am, Flight Lieutenant Maray is AOC. I am sure he'll agree that physical discipline would be inappropriate for me.'

'Er ... yes, absolutely,' Herbert put in.

Sapphie sat down, at the exact centre of the sofa.

'I think I shall spank you anyway,' she announced. 'Personally, I don't think corporals should be allowed to get too uppity. Over my knees, Molly.'

'No,' Molly answered, backing towards Herbert.

'Over my knees,' Sapphie ordered, patting the lap of her uniform skirt. 'Right now, or I shall have Hazel and Holly hold you down.'

'I forbid it, it's not to be done!' Herbert squeaked. 'Alexander ... Squadron Leader Gorringe was adamant she should not be spanked.'

'To save her dignity? I don't believe it, not from what I've heard of Gorringe, and, after all, being milked is hardly dignified, is it?'

'Er ... no,' Herbert admitted, blustering, 'but it won't do ... it won't do at all. You must respect my authority, Section Officer Yates!'

'Your authority?' Sapphie queried, cocking one eyebrow up. 'You're not fit to wear the uniform, Maray. You shouldn't be in the RAF at all, you should be ... be a butler, yes.'

'I . . . I have never . . . you . . .' Maray blustered.

'Do be quiet,' Sapphie cut in, 'or I won't let you watch. No, don't be quiet. Tell me why Gorringe wanted Molly in milk but wouldn't spank her?'

'It's . . . it's . . . it's different,' he stammered. 'Spanking is demeaning, for a grown woman . . .'

'Rubbish! Well . . . not for common women, anyway. Spit it out, Herbert!'

'He . . . he was saving it up for a special occasion,' Herbert muttered.

'Saving it up for a special occasion?' Sapphie echoed.

'Yes,' Herbert went on, now looking absolutely miserable. 'He . . . he thought the longer he waited the worse it would be for her when she did get it, and . . . and he kept postponing it, and . . . and he said he'd do it when she was made a Corporal, and . . .'

'I see,' Sapphie cut in. 'So there we are, Molly, he was just building you up for a fall. I had guessed as much. Nice fellow, your boyfriend. I, on the other hand, will be honest. You're a pretty girl, you have a lovely bottom, and I think you ought to be punished.'

'Why?' Molly demanded brokenly.

'A dozen reasons,' Sapphie answered. 'For a start, to make sure you appreciate my authority . . .'

'I do!'

'Then come over my lap.'

Molly MacCallion was close to tears, her air of command gone completely.

'You can't!' she wailed. 'You just can't!'

'Hazel, Holly,' Sapphie ordered. 'Tie her hands behind her back and put her into a chair, you know how. I'm going to cane her instead.'

'No!' Molly squealed. 'Cora! Someone!'

She dashed for the door, only to find it blocked by Hazel.

'Cora, please!' she begged, turning to the black girl, who taken one of the more comfortable chairs.

Cora shook her head. 'No, Molly. It's about time you got yours.'

Molly glanced frantically around the room. Herbert Maray was pretending to study a picture. Everybody else was looking at her. Hazel was already starting forward, and Holly rose to help.

'I'll come,' Molly said suddenly, raising her hands in defence, 'but not hard, please. I hate pain!'

Once more Sapphie patted her lap. Molly came forwards, her face set in fear and misery, to lay herself down over Sapphie's knees, already snivelling.

'There we are,' Sapphie said. 'Now there's no need to make such a fuss over a little spanking.'

Molly said nothing. Her body was trembling, and she had taken hold of a cushion, clutching it to her chest as if it were a doll.

'You see,' Sapphie went on. 'It's not the pain that matters, it's that you accept my right to spank you. If you don't fight, I shan't have to hurt you. Now, let's have that pretty bottom bare, shall we?'

Molly gave a miserable nod.

'Good girl,' Sapphie said, taking hold of the base of Molly's uniform skirt. 'Now, lift up a little, please.'

The skirt started to come up as Molly raised her hips. Neat, stocking-clad calves were revealed, lower thighs, a bulging slice of pale flesh, the lacy fringe of her knickers, then the full seat, the cotton stretched tight over the pert cheeks. Sapphie tucked the skirt up high, then rummaged beneath it to tug out Molly's waistband. The knickers were peeled down, Molly's buttocks casually exposed as they came away, and inverted around her thighs.

Sapphie put her hand to Molly's now bare bottom, cupping one quivering pink cheek. Holly watched, trying to hide her delight, then gave in, letting her mouth curve up into a broad smile as Sapphie planted a gentle pat on Molly's flesh. So many times she had

187

had her own bottom stripped bare in front of the little Corporal, for spanking, to have a hose inserted in her anus, or as she was tied on to the milking machine. Even when in line beside them, Molly had managed to retain an air of superiority, and had always enjoyed the punishments. Worse still had been those occasions she had been passed round for spanking. Molly had always taken immense pleasure in it, and in having her quim licked afterwards.

Now the tables were turned, and as the small girl's bottom began to bounce to harder slaps, Holly was grinning. So were the others, Herbert Maray included, everyone thoroughly enjoying the punishment. Molly was not, whimpering and snivelling across Sapphie's lap, with the cushion clutched tight to her chest. Sapphie's slaps were still light, yet already Molly had begun to kick her legs and jerk about, her loss of control providing peeps of red pussy-fur and little plump sex-lips.

It stopped, suddenly. Molly sighed in relief, only to squeal in surprise as her knickers were whipped smartly off her legs. Sapphie laughed at her victim's distress as she went back to spanking, harder now, to leave pink imprints on Molly's pale flesh and turn the little whimpering noises to cries of shock and pain.

'What an absolute baby!' Sapphie crowed, and laughed again, a cool, clear sound of pure joy as she pulled Molly's squirming body tighter in.

Molly burst into tears, burying her face in the cushion in utter misery. The spanking immediately grew harder, to a steady, fast rhythm, the smacks now hard enough to send ripples through the soft bottom flesh. Molly's crying grew broken, her yelps of pain sharper. Her legs, already kicking, began to come apart, showing off the neatly split fig of her quim and the brownish-pink spot of her anus.

'Uh, uh, cunt's on show!' Sapphie called. 'She'll be getting warm.'

'No!' Molly wailed, kicking violently but only succeeding in making a yet ruder display of herself.

Again Sapphie laughed, and began to lay in properly, really spanking now, hard, deliberate swats laid full across Molly's cheeks. The flesh had started to go red across the crests, and her quim and bumhole were now on full show, with her legs pistoning up and down in desperation and her head shaking from side to side. Her hair burst free in a cloud of red. One shoe kicked off, to sail across the room and hit the wall. Her howls grew to a pitiful wailing punctuated by gasps and yells of pain.

Still Sapphie spanked, harder and harder, her face now set in grim determination. Molly lost herself completely, flying into a wild, uncontrolled tantrum of flailing legs and bouncing bottom cheeks, of flying hair and pumping fists, her face red and wet with tears, her bottom redder still, her bumhole pulsing, her fanny wet and puffy. She began to scream, high-pitched shrieks of raw, uncontrolled panic. She farted, the noise loud in the room despite the crescendo of fleshy slaps and agonised wails.

Sapphie stopped and pinched her nose with a delicate gesture.

'I say, really.'

Molly collapsed, blubbering, desperate pleas tumbling from her lips as she lay broken and sweaty across Sapphie's lap, her bottom now the colour of a ripe cherry, her face red and streaked with tears and the ruins of her make-up, her legs open in heedless display of her wet sex and still twitching bumhole.

'Oh very well,' Sapphie said, 'as you're such a baby. But really, I don't think I've heard a girl make so much fuss over a little spanking in my entire life. I need a drink. Fatso, the port ... no, a little milk would be more refreshing, I think. Hazel, bring a glass.'

Hazel obeyed immediately, fumbling with the buttons on her blouse as she went to fetch a glass.

'Not yours, you silly tart,' Sapphie chided. 'Molly's.'

Relief showed in Hazel's face as she knelt down. Molly gave no resistance, propping herself up to allow Hazel to get at her front. Her jacket was unfastened, her blouse and bra rearranged, to leave one pale little tit hanging down. Hazel took hold, to press Molly's nipple into the glass and squeeze. There were still tears running down Molly's face as she was milked, but she said nothing. When the glass was half full Hazel stopped and took it away. Molly stayed down, not troubling to cover her breast.

'Milk, er . . . Section Officer Yates,' Hazel offered.

'Miss Sappho will do at present,' Sapphie answered and took the glass, to drain the contents at a gulp. 'Hmm . . . very pleasant, rich but with an interesting tang. Yes, excellent. Now my port.'

Herbert Maray went to the sideboard without an instant's hesitation. Holly had been leaning forwards in rapt fascination as she watched Molly MacCallion punished, and now leaned back. She was shaking with excitement, and unsure whether she wanted her own bottom given the same treatment, or have Molly's face pressed to her urgent quim. Her hand was shaking as she accepted a glass of port from Herbert, but she said nothing, waiting for Sapphie's decision.

Molly had closed her legs, but made no effort to get up, lying limp over Sapphie's lap, the big, oily tears still rolling slowly down her cheeks. Sapphie put her hand back to the rosy-skinned bottom, not to spank, but to stroke. Still Molly gave no resistance, even as Sapphie's fingers began to work down into the groove between her buttocks. Only when her legs were eased gently apart to show off her quim once more did she react, a weak sob as she tried to close up.

'Tut, tut,' Sapphie said and planted a firm pat on the inside of Molly's thigh.

The redhead's legs stayed open. Sapphie was smiling as she began to explore again, running her fingers along the crease of Molly's bottom, and deeper, briefly spreading the little cheeks to show off the pink star of the anus. Sapphie extended a finger to tickle the little hole. Molly jerked. Sapphie's finger went lower, to slide up into Molly's quim.

'My, you are excited. I suppose you want me to do something about it?'

'No, not that ... no ...' Molly sobbed, her body lurching as she made a sudden effort to get up, only to be pulled gently but firmly back into place.

Sapphie laughed. Her finger came out, to slide along the wet groove of Molly's sex, starting to rub even as her thumb forced the neat anal ring. Molly groaned as her bumhole opened, still shaking her head, but no longer trying to get away. Sapphie was smiling as her fingers worked in Molly's sex, a firm, regular rubbing motion as her thumb moved in the straining bumhole.

Molly gave a sob, ecstasy or despair, and suddenly she was pushing her bottom up to meet the pressure of Sapphie's fingers. Sapphie laughed louder still, eyes sparkling in delight as she masturbated the now writhing Molly, faster and firmer, digging deeper into the now sloppy bumhole, working the juice-smeared cunt hard beneath her fingers. Molly's whole body went tight as she came. She screamed, louder than before, and went into a frantic, lewd bucking motion as Sapphie tightened her grip, forcing Molly to bear the consequences of her spanking to the last.

Only when Molly collapsed once more did Sapphie stop. Casually, her face set in a knowing and thoroughly superior smile, she removed her hand and put it to Molly's mouth. Molly sucked obediently, each finger, then the thumb which had been up her bottom.

'Good girl,' Sapphie said happily. 'There we are, not so bad at all, was it?'

Molly didn't reply, or make any effort to move.

'All women of the lower classes should be spanked on a regular basis,' Sapphie stated. 'It does them no end of good.'

Nobody contradicted her. Hazel was biting her nails. Cora was staring, her mouth a little open. Herbert was red faced, his cock quite clearly at full erection. Sapphie took a sip of port and went on, gently stroking Molly's bottom as she talked.

'Yes, we shall keep the punishment system but, from now on, I do the spanking. After all, it would be terribly improper for a male officer to do any such thing.'

'Oh I say!' Herbert managed.

'Yes?' Sapphie asked.

'Well it's just . . . I mean to say . . . Damn it, Sapphie, I enjoy dishing out a good spanking, and . . . afterwards . . .'

'Afterwards?'

'Yes, we . . . that is, the girls who'd been spanked would . . . you know, provide little favours . . .'

'Cock-sucking, he means,' Cora stated flatly.

'Yes,' Herbert admitted.

'Oh I don't think so,' Sapphie said. 'Certainly I have no desire to see your dirty little winkle.'

Herbert looked as if he was about to burst into tears, but said nothing, instead taking a seat with a sulky expression on his face. Holly swallowed her port and refilled her glass, wondering if she dared ask to have Molly crawl to her and lick. It was a delicious thought, but she knew full well that Sapphie was as likely to make an issue of it as to acquiesce. If that happened, she was likely to end up across Sapphie's lap herself, in the same sorry state as Molly, and it might well be her who ended up doing the licking. It tempted anyway, and she was going to speak when Sapphie suddenly drained her glass.

'Bedtime, I think,' Sapphie stated, planting a last resounding slap on Molly's bottom. 'Bed, and Champagne, the best you have, Herbert, two bottles and a glass, chop, chop.'

Herbert left the room, looking more downcast than ever. The others followed, trooping upstairs behind

Sapphie with Molly at the rear, still with her skirt bunched up and no knickers, rubbing ruefully at one smarting buttock. It seemed that a halt had been called to the evening's sex, and they dispersed, taking turns to use the bathroom, with Sapphie going first without dispute. Only when Holly was propped up in her bed waiting for Hazel and urgently needing relief for both her boobs and quim did Sapphie appear, in a black silk negligee with a bottle of Champagne in one hand and a glass in the other.

'What are you doing?' she demanded.

'Nothing, really . . .' Holly said quickly.

'Why? You ought to be in my bed.'

'Oh . . . I thought you'd had enough.'

'No, now get out of bed and pour me a glass of Champagne.'

Holly hastened to obey, taking both bottle and glass to her bedside table. Sapphie crossed the room, swaying her slender hips gently as she walked, to get into Hazel's bed. As Holly popped the cork, Sapphie adjusted herself, propped up against the pillows with knees up, her nightie up and her legs wide open. The dark blonde puff of her pubic hair and the neat pink lips of her sex were both on plain show. Her bottom crease was a dark shadow beneath the hard bar of flesh separating quim from anus, with the brown, butterfly-shaped marking that had given her the play name of 'Swallowtail' just showing. Memories came flooding back to Holly, along with a wonderful sense of intimacy, then more, of punishments dished out and cruelties inflicted, of deep humiliation and exquisite ecstasy. She found herself biting her lip, and her hand was trembling as she filled the glass.

'Come here, you. Kneel between my legs,' Sapphie instructed.

'Yes,' Holly answered.

'Not you, you little slut,' Sapphie answered. 'Come here, Hazel.'

Holly turned, to find Hazel in the doorway. She felt a rush of relief immediately followed by one of jealousy. Hazel had her normal resentful pout on her face, but was crossing to the bed.

'Nightie up,' Sapphie ordered.

Hazel obediently lifted her nightie. She was naked beneath, her lush curves appearing fuller still in the dim light, her flesh showing a rich pink yellow set off by dark shadows. Her breasts in particular seemed enormous, the skin glossy with pressure, the nipples taut in erection and spotted with glistening milk.

'My, you have grown,' Sapphie remarked. 'I do like fat girls, they look so helpless.'

'I'm not fat!' Hazel protested.

Sapphie merely raised her eyebrows and pointed to her quim. Hazel came forward without hesitation, to climb on to the bed and bury her face between Sapphie's thighs. Sapphie's face set in bliss as the wet slurping sounds of Hazel's vigorous licking began. Holly approached. Sapphie took the glass of Champagne and adjusted her position slightly, then reached down to tousle Hazel's hair.

'Just gently,' she instructed. 'There's no hurry. Concentrate on my butterfly until I tell you otherwise.'

Hazel gave a muffled assent and her head bobbed lower, her nose going to Sapphie's quim as her tongue began to flick over the dun-coloured flesh around her friend's anus.

'Good girl,' Sapphie said. 'You can put the bottle down now, Holly, or have a drink yourself, unless you'd rather amuse yourself with Hazel's rear end. And do get that silly nightie off.'

Holly put the bottle down and quickly pulled her nightie off over her head. Hazel was effectively in the nude, her own nightie rucked up so high that the full mass of her naked breasts was squashed out on the bed beneath her, while her bottom was high, wide and quite bare. Holly hesitated, weighing the pleasure of spanking her friend against the pain of the revenge that would undoubtedly come in due time.

Reluctant to risk punishment, she contented herself with sitting down on the bed and stroking Hazel's bottom. Sapphie chuckled and twisted her hand into Hazel's curls, pulling. Hazel burrowed her face in, eager now, as she gave a wiggle for Holly's attention. Holly slipped her fingers into the soft, deep crease of her friend's bottom, to tease the furry sex-lips and tickle the puckered anus. Hazel's body began to quiver with the fervour of her licking.

'That's right,' Sapphie sighed. 'Now do my bottom hole again. Yes, lovely . . . put your tongue well in . . . oh, that is beautiful . . . Can you taste me, Hazel, darling, can you taste my dirt? Oh, I have missed you two. Do you know, I haven't had my bottom hole licked since that last day in the nursery? My quim, yes, there was this pretty little blonde in the canteen, but she wasn't really dirty, not like you two. Oh, yes . . . lovely, and I need to pee too . . . I'm going to do it in your mouth, darling, open wide.'

Holly leaned close to watch. Hazel gasped in protest even as Sapphie gave a low moan. Urine exploded from the tiny hole at the centre of Sapphie's sex, full in Hazel's face. Holly stifled a giggle, then gave in, laughing openly as Hazel struggled to swallow the hot yellow piss filling her mouth. Not all had gone in her mouth either. Some had hit her nose, splashing liberally over her face and into her hair. It was over Sapphie's belly and thighs too, with a little pool already formed in her belly button.

Holly watched in delight, her own lewd feelings growing as Sapphie's urine splashed in Hazel's mouth and ran down over the bed. On sudden impulse she bent down to suck the pee from Sapphie's tummy button and rose, smiling in pleasure for what she'd done. Suddenly

Hazel began to cough, then came up, gagging and spluttering, with bubbles coming out of her nostrils and sprays of fluid bursting out from around her lips as her face turned crimson.

'What's the matter?' Sapphie demanded, her pee spray cutting off abruptly

'I . . . I was choking!' Hazel gasped. 'And anyway, it's not fair to do it all over my bed!'

'Oh, don't whine so,' Sapphie answered. 'Damn it, girl, that must be just about pure wine by now, and we had some excellent bottles. Now get on with it, or I'll have the girls drop their morning curtsies in your face tomorrow, all three of them.'

Hazel quickly went back to her task, more pee froth erupting from her nose as she began to breathe through it. Sapphie's belly relaxed once more.

'Glorious,' she sighed as the last of her piddle bubbled out over Hazel's nose. 'Now make me come.'

Piddle was still running from the corners of Hazel's mouth as she transferred her attentions to Sapphie's clit. As Sapphie's face went slack with pleasure, Holly took the glass, then leaned in to kiss her friend. Sapphie responded, their mouths opening together, hands finding each other's breasts. Holly felt the warm, wet of milk on her skin as Sapphie squeezed her breast. Then Sapphie had moved, taking the swollen teat into her mouth to suckle, urgently, mouthing on Holly's boob. Holly's mouth came open in a blissful sigh. She held her breasts out and cradled Sapphie's head to her chest, feeding from the nipple. It felt glorious, sensuous and loving, making her want to yield utterly.

Sapphie's body went tight, her mouth clamping on Holly's nipple, to suck it in hard. Holly cried out in pained ecstasy, cuddling Sapphie's head closer as her friend went into orgasm, suckling fiercely and kneading as her quim was licked, on and on until she had had her fill.

Holly stood, unsteady as she was finally released. Sapphie lay back, eyes closed in bliss, mouth open, with a trickle of white running from one corner. Hazel came up too, pouting slightly, her face and breasts wet with piddle, but with her knees well parted and her hand still down between her thighs.

'You should have waited for me!' Holly protested. 'Greedy pig!'

'Don't squabble, you two,' Sapphie sighed. 'That was adorable, thank you. I thought the milk thing was just a bit of a lark until now. It's not, it's wonderful.'

'My bed is soaking, Sapphie,' Hazel pointed out.

'I know, I'm sitting in it,' Sapphie answered. 'You'll just have to sleep with Holly.'

'We do anyway,' Holly admitted. 'Now can I have some attention, please?'

'Of course you may,' Sapphie said immediately, swinging her legs off the bed. 'How thoughtless of me.'

Sapphie had her nightie up, showing off her lower back and the neatly formed cheeks of her bottom, which were wet with piddle.

'You can clean me up,' she offered. 'Squat in Hazel's face while you do it, and she can lick you.'

Holly opened her mouth to protest but thought better of it. Sapphie had never understood that her ideas were not necessarily perfect for everybody else. She exchanged a knowing glance with Hazel as she rounded the bed. Sapphie set her feet apart, presenting her bare bottom. Hazel went down quickly, sliding her body between Sapphie's open feet, and Holly climbed on, in a squat, bottom to face over Hazel, face to bottom with Sapphie. As Hazel's tongue found her sex, Holly began to lick up the already sticky pee from Sapphie's bottom cheeks.

Everything bad, even the nagging fact of her pregnancy, faded as she licked at Sapphie's bottom. She closed her eyes in bliss, lapping up the piddle in the sure knowledge that it was right for her, what she should be doing. Below her, Hazel was doing wonderful things with her tongue, both on quim and bottom hole, and she knew she would soon come. When she did, she knew it would be in more than simple physical pleasure, but in deep love for Sapphie, a love she realised had always been there.

Eager to express her devotion, she buried her face between Sapphie's bottom cheeks, burrowing her tongue into the sloppy, sticky bumhole. Sapphie moaned and pushed her bottom back; Hazel found her clit. In the next instant Holly was coming, in a great rush of overwhelming ecstasy as she feasted on Sapphie's bottom hole and squirmed her own rear end into Hazel's face.

'Happy now?' Sapphie asked.

Holly was still coming, and responded by sticking her tongue as far up Sapphie's bottom as it would go. Sapphie gave a little gasp, Holly swallowed and it was over, leaving her to settle on Hazel's face with a contented sigh. Hazel made a muffled complaint and slapped Holly's bottom. Holly lifted, giggling as she cocked her leg up, only to freeze as a knock sounded at the door.

'Do come in,' Sapphie called.

'Sapphie!' Holly squeaked.

It was too late. Already the door was swinging open, to reveal Molly and Cora, both in their nighties. Holly managed a smile.

'And I suppose you two want to join in?' Sapphie asked. 'Come on then, and you can both kiss my arse, which is what these two have been doing.'

Holly found herself blushing. Cora didn't hesitate, but pulled her nightie up and off as she came forwards, exposing her dark, voluptuous curves. Her nipples were already milky, slick and shiny, white spots appearing as she caught her breasts up in her hands. She knelt down beside Holly, leaned forwards to give Sapphie a perfunctory peck on one bottom cheek and pushed her breasts into Holly's face. Holly responded, taking one huge black nipple into her mouth to suckle, only to be pulled sideways as Sapphie reached down to take Cora firmly by the hair.

Cora squeaked as her head was dragged around, then again, this time muffled by Sapphie's bottom as it was pushed firmly into her face. There was a wet sound as she kissed Sapphie's anus and she was released.

'That's better,' Sapphie stated. 'You too, Molly.'

Molly had stayed in the doorway, but she came forwards at the order. She was biting her lip and looked more than a little uncertain. Her red bottom cheeks showed beneath the hem of the ridiculously short nightie Alexander had been making her wear.

'Nightie off,' Sapphie ordered.

Molly shook her head, then abruptly changed her mind. Her nightie came off as she reached the others, to kneel, looking expectantly up at Sapphie.

'You need to be made to do it?' Sapphie queried. 'Fine.'

She took Molly by the hair and gave her the same rough treatment as she had Cora, bottom in the face, head dragged in and held tight until Molly had kissed her anus. Sapphie then let go, but Molly stayed where she was, eyes closed as she licked Sapphie's bumhole. Holly went back to suckling as she climbed off Hazel's head, watching Molly lick all the while. Hazel clambered up, to fix her mouth to Cora's spare teat.

Holly's mouth was full of warm girl's milk, and she swallowed as she cuddled up to both Cora and Hazel. Cora squeezed her breast and Holly felt new milk squirt into her mouth, quickly filling it once more. Sapphie gently detached Molly from her bottom and stepped back, letting the Irish girl join the others.

The four of them came together, cuddling, their breasts squashed out on one another's bodies, milk weeping from their nipples. They sank down to the floor in a tangle of limbs, hands groping for bottoms and boobs, mouths seeking other mouths, nipples and quims. Holly found Cora's plump black sex close to her head and buried her face in it, even as fingers slid into her quim and bumhole. Someone's mouth attached to one of her nipples and she was being suckled. Her left hand was on a small bottom, Molly's, and she slid her fingers into the crease to tickle the anus, at the same time squeezing a fat breast with the other.

She could see nothing, her face smothered in Cora's bottom flesh. She could hear only the wet sucking and smacking sounds of the four of them as they groped and fondled, licked and sucked. She was soaked in milk, their bodies slithering in it as they writhed together, and more was coming, spurting from squashed breasts as they moved.

Cora came, full in Holly's face, wriggling and squirming her fat black bottom. Holly tried to rise as Cora dismounted. She caught a brief glimpse of Sapphie standing over them with the Champagne bottle upended over her mouth, and then Molly had taken Cora's place and was wiggling her neat white bottom for a lick. Holly obliged, sticking her tongue up Molly's anus even as someone's face was pressed between her own thighs. A mouth found her nipple, and she was being suckled too.

She knew she was going to come immediately, and as before, with her tongue up one girl's bottom while she was licked by another. It seemed right for her, the perfect way to treat her, making her lick bumhole for her pleasure as she lay at the bottom of a pile of milk-soaked girls.

In seconds she was coming, and as her body went tight in orgasm she felt the splash of warm fluid on her belly and breasts. She heard laughter, from Sapphie, and Molly's squeak of shock. She realised that Sapphie was pissing on them, standing tall above them and urinating on their squirming bodies. It was the perfect thing to do, a gesture of absolute dominance. Holly felt the force of her orgasm double, and redouble, to hit a near unbearable climax as she writhed in a welter of milk and piss and cunt-juice . . .

Even when it had finished she went on licking Molly, happy to provide her face as a mount until the Irish girl also reached orgasm a few moment's later. Only when they finally came apart did she realise it was Hazel who had licked her and Cora who had suckled her. She also realised that Herbert Maray was watching from the open door, his face crimson with lust and jealousy, his cock a blatant bulge in the crotch of his pyjamas.

Sapphie realised at the same moment, and laughed.

'Be nice to the poor boy, someone,' she ordered. 'You can see he's desperate.'

'Please, yes,' Herbert croaked.

Cora responded, climbing shakily to her feet. Herbert immediately lay down, even as he pulled his stubby cock from his pyjamas. Cora, clearly knowing exactly what was expected of her, straddled him and dropped a neat curtsey on to his head. As his face disappeared beneath the fleshy black bottom, she reached back, spreading her big cheeks to show off the wrinkled, jet-black star of her anus, directly over his mouth. His tongue came out to lick at her bottom as he began to masturbate.

'A piece of cake,' Sapphie stated as she handed her gloves and helmet to Cora. 'She's a bit slow, but she handles well enough.'

She patted the flank of the Gladiator and began to walk across the field, to where the others were gathered. Reaching them, she put her arm around Holly's shoulders.

'So,' she asked, 'aside from spankings and this milking business, what's been going on around here? Anything juicy?'

Holly exchanged a glance with Hazel, then Cora. Both looked worried. Sapphie gave Holly's bottom a purposeful smack.

'Well?'

'We get enemas sometimes,' Holly admitted, the blood rushing immediately to her cheeks. 'There's a special machine.'

'Amusing, if a little messy,' Sapphie replied. 'And?'

'If we do something really awful we go in the Hotbox, but that doesn't happen very often. It's for show, mainly.'

'The Hotbox?'

'That thing,' Holly answered, pointing.

'The thing like a giant barrel? Yes, I was going to ask what that was.'

'You've seen them, surely?'

'No I have not!'

'But, I thought they . . . that all stations had them.'

'What, torture devices for recalcitrant WAAFs? You must be joking! They don't have regular spankings and the girls aren't milked either, come to that.'

'Well, no . . . but . . .'

'For goodness' sake, can't you see that this Gorringe fellow and fat Herbert here have had you over a barrel? Well, in it, even.'

She laughed. Holly found herself biting her lip.

'You . . . you won't put us in it, will you?'

'Probably not,' Sapphie answered. 'It seems a little impersonal, really. After all, where's the fun in it if you're just sitting in the box? I can't even see you.'

'You can,' Hazel put in. 'There are doors, front and back. The Squadron Leader and some man from the Ministry torture Holly's quim.'

'A man from the Ministry?' Sapphie queried. 'Are you sure?'

'That's what he said,' Hazel confirmed. 'I think he was an MP.'

'An MP?'

'I think so.'

'That's highly peculiar . . . or is it? You don't suppose it could have been Reginald Thann, do you?'

'I don't know.'

'Well, I'm going to find out. I smell a rat here, a dirty big one.'

'How do you mean?'

Sapphie didn't answer. She was looking at Herbert Maray.

'Out with it, Fatso.'

'I . . . I don't know what you're talking about,' he blustered.

'Oh yes you do,' she answered, 'and you're going to tell us, in detail.'

'I shan't!' Herbert squeaked.

'Very well,' Sapphie answered. 'I dare say the Hotbox works as well for a man as for a woman. Stick him in it, girls.'

'You can't do that!' he squealed, backing away. 'You just can't! I'm your commanding officer, damn you!'

'Maybe,' Sapphie answered him, 'but I think you'll find they do as I say, and in the circumstances, I don't think there's much you can do about it. You can hardly report us for insubordination, after all.'

'I . . . I won't allow this!' he blustered as Holly and Hazel stepped forwards. 'Cora, Molly, help me!'

Molly just looked at the ground. Cora made to move forwards, then shook her head.

'I'll tell you! I'll tell you!' Herbert squeaked. 'It's nothing to do with me anyway . . . Alexander's the man you want. Thann's his uncle. He made the deal!'

'What deal?' Sapphie demanded.

'To . . . to get this . . . this posting,' Herbert stammered. 'You see, we . . . he wanted a cushy billet for the war, and I thought I'd tag along, and . . . and Reginald Thann at the Ministry said he would arrange it all, if . . . if we did him a favour.'

'So it was Thann. And the favour?'

'Ah, yes, well, he has a bit of a bee in his bonnet, as it were, about your mothers . . .'

'Our mothers?'

'Yes. He seems to, er . . . blame your mother, Sapphie, for the behaviour of Holly's mother . . . that's Lady Cary, isn't it, Holly? For Holly's mother rejecting him. And so, he wanted you here . . . Sapphie first, then Holly when he found out about you from Alexander. The idea was to have one of you devoted to him . . . no, more than devoted, enslaved really, I suppose, not physically, mentally.'

'Why, in God's name? And how?'

'I, er . . . think your mother rather wounded his pride, Holly.'

'Wounded his pride? She must have done!'

'He's terribly jealous, you know. Alexander says he remembers every slight, right back to his school days, and he ticks them off in a little black book when he feels he's had his revenge . . .'

'Mother said he was a nasty piece, pompous too, always preaching at her for being an invert, the hypocrite! So you went along with this, did you, Fatso?'

'We didn't know! Not at first! We thought he'd just want her humiliated, made to do her exercises in the nude, spanked on the bare bottom, that sort of thing . . . you know, just a bit of fun, really . . .'

'And the milk?'

'No, no, that was nothing to do with him. My cousin Jervis used to like to milk girls, and when I found out, I couldn't resist it. I've always liked nice, chesty girls, you see . . .'

'Never mind your perverted habits. So he had the Hotbox sent down here to use on Holly, to break her?'

'Yes, more or less. He had all these strange ideas, Russian, I think, about how one person can be made totally dependent on another, by being under control . . . complete control . . .'

'By torture?'

'Yes. We didn't want anything to do with it! He wanted us to starve her, and all sorts of beastly things, but we wouldn't, we . . .'

'And how about you two?' Sapphie demanded of Molly and Cora.

'We knew a bit, not everything,' Cora admitted. 'Mainly we made it seem OK for Holly and Hazel to do dirty things.'

'You did, did you?' Hazel cut in. 'The enemas? The exercises in our undies?'

'Yes,' Cora admitted.

'Never mind that,' Sapphie snapped. 'I want to know about this beastly man Thann.'

'That's all there is to tell, really,' Herbert said limply. 'It's not my fault, honestly. I wouldn't want to do things like that, I'm not that sort of person –'

'You just like to fatten girls up and bring them into milk?' Sapphie broke in.

Herbert made a face and looked down at his shoes.

'You are a sorry piece of work,' Sapphie addressed him. 'And as for Thann, by God I'd like to give him a dose of his own medicine. I suppose he'll expect you to add me to his scheme now, eh? Well he's got another thought coming!'

'It's all gone wrong anyway,' Herbert whined. 'Thann expected Holly to be pure, so he'd be the first, and, well, we all got a little tipsy one night, the first night the girls came into milk, and . . . and things went a bit far. Holly and I . . . well, we fucked.'

'And I'm pregnant,' Holly admitted.

18

Meadway Hall, Yorkshire – September 1940

Roberta's knees sank slowly into the thick slurry. It was a greenish brown, and it stank. She looked back to where Lord Farthinghurst was seated on a stump, watching her. His cock and balls hung out of his trousers, grotesque in proportion to his tiny body.

'Deeper,' he demanded, 'and put your titties in it, have a good wallow.'

'I thought you said I should be a cow,' she protested. 'Cows don't wallow, pigs wallow.'

'Nonsense!' he snorted. 'Cows like a spot of mud. You should see mine down by the stream on a hot day, they adore a good roll.'

'It's not hot, it's cold!' Roberta answered.

'Oh, stop carping, girl. Get in there and get on with it!'

She didn't answer, but heaved a deep sigh as she began to crawl. Her leg came up with a disgusting sucking noise as she pulled it free, then sank once more into the thick muck, deeper this time, halfway up her thigh. She moved an arm, which sank in deeper still, to leave one fat breast dangling in the cold mud. Behind her, she caught the slapping noise of Lord Farthinghurst's cock being brought to erection. Again she moved forwards, almost losing her balance as she pulled her leg free of its sticky embrace. Her other breast went in, then both of them as her hand slipped on something especially slimy deep in the muck. Her face screwed up in disgust as she lifted herself, her breasts sticking and pulling at the surface. Both were filthy, half of each fat orb caked with slurry, which ran slowly down them in lumps.

'Play with them,' Lord Farthinghurst demanded. 'Rub it in! Show me!'

Roberta glanced back. He was nearly erect, his cock sprouting up from his open trousers above his bulging scrotum. His face was red, his eyes staring.

'Get that sulky look off your face!' he demanded. 'Enjoy it!'

She forced a smile. Turning a little, she took a boob in each hand, squeezing gently and rubbing her fingers over her nipples. Her skin felt slimy and taut, her nipples sensitive, her touch soothing despite everything. Shutting her eyes, she began to play with herself, trying to ignore the rich scent of cow dung and rot.

'That's my girl!' Farthinghurst called. 'Squeeze 'em tight. Go on, squeeze those fine udders . . . squeeze 'em until the milk comes!'

Roberta did her best, letting her mouth go slack in apparent pleasure as she cupped and kneaded her breasts. The milk came quickly and she pinched her nipples to make it spurt, drawing a low cry from Farthinghurst. Thinking he was going to come, she began to show more excitement, wiggling her bottom in the muck, then starting to bounce in it, filthy water and bits of slurry splashing from beneath her heavy buttocks. Farthinghurst groaned again, and she opened her eyes to look.

His face was crimson, his cock a solid bar of pale flesh, with his hand jerking furiously up and down on the shaft. She looked down, to her breasts, to find her flesh filthy with brown-green muck and streaked white where her milk had run down. Twisting her body to give him a full view of her chest, she bounced her breasts in her hands. He began to jerk harder still, his eyes fixed on her slime-covered chest as she once more began to make the milk squirt.

'On your knees!' he gasped. 'Like a cow . . . be my cow . . . flaunt that big arse . . . show your cunt-lips . . . let your udders hang . . .'

Roberta rocked forwards, back on to all fours, her bottom pulling from the muck. She wiggled it, dislodging bits of filth from her skin. Her knees came apart, she felt her quim peel open, her boobs went back into the slurry.

'Rub it!' he demanded, his voice a shriek. 'Rub your dirty cunt, you fat heifer . . . rub!'

Roberta grimaced as she reached back, to scoop up a big handful of the muck beneath her. Slapping the mess to her quim, she began to masturbate, full of shame and consternation at what she was being made to do, but unable to deny the physical responses of her body as her clit twinged beneath her fingers. She let out a sob as she realised she was really going to do it, and she was masturbating in earnest, rubbing the slimy filth into her quim as her boobs bounced and slapped at the sticky surface.

She cried out in mingled ecstasy and shame as the orgasm hit her, wiggling her bottom and boobs, rubbing hard, and at the very peak, calling out to be fucked. Suddenly he was on her, mounting her bottom, his cock rubbing in the slimy valley between her cheeks, prodding her quim, and in. Mess squirted from her hole as his cock was pushed home, then a filthy mixture of spunk and dirt as he came on the second push.

19

Kerslake Manor, Devon –
October 1940

'Hell!' Sapphie swore, throwing the letter down on the table. 'Thann's managed to foist himself on Bristol, something to do with "overseeing the production of vital aircraft components", as if he'd know the first thing about it. More likely London's getting a bit too warm for him.'

'Is he coming here?' Holly demanded.

'Yes,' Sapphie answered, 'he is . . . "as soon as I am able and my accommodation has been properly prepared"; you, Holly, being his accommodation, and possibly me too.'

'Why don't I just say you're not ready?' Herbert suggested.

'We have to face this sometime,' Sapphie answered. 'My thought is we get it done with sooner rather than later.'

'No, no, we must delay him!' Herbert insisted.

'Or I could just write myself and tell him to take a running jump,' Sapphie said. 'After all, I haven't done anything wrong.'

'No, no!' Herbert wailed. 'I'd be in terrible trouble, I'm sure, and Alexander. Thann's so vindictive! You don't know the man! He wouldn't give up on you, you'd just make him worse. He'd –'

'You may be right,' Sapphie cut in. 'So, thinking caps on, girls – what do we do when he comes down?'

'Why not suggest a walk on the moors, then strafe him?' Molly suggested. 'Alexander used to get hares that way . . .'

'Using a Gloster Gladiator to hunt hares is one thing,' Sapphie interrupted, 'but strafing government ministers is quite another, even junior ones. There'd be bound to be an inquiry. Now if we had a Messerschmidt . . . No, too complicated.'

'Couldn't we lead him into a bog?' Holly suggested. 'Like in the *Hound of the Baskervilles*?'

'I really don't think we need to murder the fellow at all,' Sapphie insisted. 'A photograph of him doing something thoroughly perverted to Holly would be all we needed to get him off our backs. There must be some limit to what he's prepared to sacrifice, and I'd have thought his career and his freedom together would be well beyond it.'

'I suppose so,' Holly admitted.

'Has to be,' Sapphie assured her. 'So we set something up, squeeze the bulb on him at the appropriate moment, and then it's all rosy. You two can get married and live happily ever after.'

'I suppose so,' Holly answered with a doubtful glance at Herbert Maray, 'but with Thann, I don't have to do anything dirty, do I?'

'Something, obviously,' Sapphie answered. 'We can hardly blackmail the fellow with a picture of you serving him tea, can we?'

Holly made a face.

'Just one thing,' Herbert put in. 'Wouldn't he be a bit suspicious if he sees Holly? I mean to say, she can, ah . . . hardly claim to be virgin the, ah . . . way she is.'

'True,' Sapphie admitted with a glance to Holly's now bulging abdomen. 'We'll deal with Thann after the birth.'

'And the wedding,' Holly pointed out.

20

Meadway Hall, Yorkshire – October 1940

Roberta stared in horror at the bull on the far side of the field gate. It was enormous, a great, sleek black and white thing, packed with muscle and with a maddened glint in its eye. Its horns had not been cut, and each rose to an impressive length to either side of its head. A massive, bulging bag of testicles hung down behind a cock sheath as thick as her arm, with a meaty red penis head protruding from the end.

'The Emperor of Meadway,' Lord Farthinghurst declared proudly. 'Magnificent, isn't he?'

Roberta didn't answer. She was naked, done up in her ludicrous cow paint, and shivering. A faint drizzle was blowing in on a north-east wind, and while their corner of the bull's field was well sheltered with a grove, much of it was wide open to the valley.

'In you go then, hurry along,' Farthinghurst said cheerfully and slapped her bottom, 'and remember to moo, especially when his pizzle goes in.'

'I won't,' Roberta managed.

'What?'

'I won't.'

'Why ever not?' he demanded, angry. 'You moo very well now, at least since I introduced you to the whalebone cane.'

'No . . . not moo. I won't go in, your Lordship. It's . . . it's dangerous!'

'Dangerous? Nonsense, girl! You're not scared of a bull, are you? You, a country girl born and bred!'

'I may be a country girl, but in Devon we don't have our girls mounted by bulls.'

'No? Devon's fine cattle country . . . big red fellows, seen them myself. Don't tell me old Jervis never put you to one for a bit of sport?'

'No, he did not!'

'Peculiar fellow. I would, with a fine girl like you, and I will. In you go, and no more nonsense.'

He slapped her bottom again, harder.

'I won't do it,' Roberta insisted.

'Get in there, damn you!' he ordered.

'No . . . Ow! Will you stop that a moment?'

'Get in the damn field then!'

'No!'

'You're a whore, damn you, you'll do as I order!'

'It'll kill me!' she protested.

'Nonsense, woman. You're a cow, remember, you should be looking forward to a good hard length of bull's beef, and they don't come longer or harder than the Emperor here. I mean to say, just look at that pizzle, and those balls, magnificent! You should be itching to get him into you!'

'I'm not a cow, I tell you, Lord Farthinghurst! It just wouldn't fit!'

'You can try, can't you? What's the matter with you, girl, no spunk? Mark you, you'll have plenty once the Emperor's done his business in your cunt, ha, ha . . . Extraordinary, the amount he makes, really extraordinary. Now come on, no croaking, in you go. You'll be as happy as Larry once he's up you, you'll see.'

'I'm truly sorry, your Lordship. I've done my best for you, and put up with all sorts of things I wouldn't normally, and things no man has ever asked of me before, but I'll not go in and kneel down for no bull. Now, if you've a mind for beastliness, and if it were a nice, gentle old hound, or –'

'That's absurd! Hounds don't fuck cows.'

'Bulls don't fuck women, normal –'

'Enough! In there this minute or I'll take my stick to your arse!'

'I won't!'

'You damn well will!'

He hefted the length of hawthorn he was using as a stick. Roberta took a step back. He swung the stick up. She pushed, to send him sprawling backwards into the mud, and fled.

21

Kerslake Manor, Devon – November 1940

Holly closed her eyes as the weight of her distended belly came into her hands. It was no longer possible for her to be strapped to the bench for milking, and she took it sitting but leaning forwards, with two of the village Matrons attending to her breasts while two girls held the pails. Eliza Grant and May Wonnacott were milking her, their strong, steady hands bringing blissful relief. Eliza's daughters, Anna and Sally, held the pails, both nude after having their own milk taken on the machines, and looking as flushed as Holly felt.

With the station staff required to give near continuous weather reports, they were alone, except for May's daughters, Sophie and Mary, who were seated on their milking frames, also stark naked. With the five girls in milk all naked, Holly felt relaxed, unashamed of her own nudity, and wondering if she would get a chance to play with herself once she was finished.

Her need was particularly strong because of an addition to the milking regime employed by the village girls. All four had been spanked, the sisters taking turns across each other's laps with their mothers watching indulgently, until all four fat white bottoms had been turned rosy red. Only then had they gone on to the frames, leaving their hot behinds stuck out in a line as they were milked, every one with a wet quim.

To Holly's question, Eliza had explained that it improved production. Jervis and Genevieve Maray had apparently often beaten the girls while they were on the frames, and more, to judge by Eliza's sudden change of subject. Holly had been left thinking of the spanking Sapphie had given her just the night before and wondering if she dared ask to have her own bottom smacked.

It hadn't been necessary. Anna had offered to do it, and Holly had found herself squatting over the milking bench with her bottom stuck out behind and her belly hanging down in front. Anna had spanked her by hand, slapping Holly's cheeks until she was warm and ready, much to the amusement of the four girls, whose mothers had stood by, looking on with an air of quiet under-standing.

Now, with her bottom hot and her milk pattering into the pails, it was hard to think of anything but her need. She was holding the weight of her pregnant belly for the sake of comfort, but also to give herself something to do with her hands other than masturbate. It was still hard, and as squirt after squirt of milk erupted from her straining nipples, she was seriously wondering if the Matron's mother hen attitude extended to allowing her to give herself an orgasm.

By the time the last drop had been squeezed from her, she was breathing deeply and it was impossible to hold back a low moan as the exquisite sensation finally stopped. She heard the clang of the pails being put down and shook her head in a desperate effort to get rid of her feelings. Eliza spoke.

'Why, the poor thing. Be a dear, Anna.'

'Yes, Mother,' Anna answered, and the next instant firm, powerful fingers had slipped beneath Holly's bottom to find her sex.

She gasped as Anna began to masturbate her, then again as both sisters fastened their mouths to her breasts, suckling her as she was rubbed. Seconds later she was coming, in a dizzying ecstasy made stronger still by the delighted giggles of May's daughters. She cried out as the first peak hit her, a second time as Anna's finger pushed firmly to her clit, and a third as a broad thumb found her anus. Then she was melting into their arms.

'That's better, I'll be bound,' Eliza said calmly. 'We'd better –'

She stopped abruptly as a new voice sounded, a voice she recognised.

'I'll bet it is! Nice to see you getting on so well, I must say.'

Holly turned in sudden shock. Sure enough, Alexander Gorringe stood at the door, as tall and straight and suave as ever, except that one leg was rigid and he was leaning heavily on a stick.

22

Babcary Manor, Somerset – November 1940

Holly braced herself as the Austin came to a halt on the carriage sweep. Within the house would be not only her true mother, Charlotte Lady Cary, but also Lord Toby Cary, Sapphie's mother Cicely, her half brothers and sisters and even Hazel's mother Kitty. The moment she had been dreading had come.

'Chin up!' Sapphie said blithely.

Holly didn't answer. She was thinking of all the lectures she'd been given; by her mother, by Cicely Yates, by Kitty Mullins. Now she had to face them all.

Sapphie was already striding towards the door, apparently eager to wade in to the fray. Holly followed, close to tears, one hand beneath her swollen belly. She ran over the good points in her mind as Sapphie rang the bell, that she was at least getting married to the man who had made her pregnant, that he came from a landed family, albeit one with a bizarre reputation, and that her pregnancy could be taken by someone of his knowledge as excusing the fact that she was quite obviously in milk.

The door was opened by the ancient butler, Spince, a man Holly had known all her life. He said nothing, but the gooseberry eyes in his wrinkled face were directed pointedly upwards, never once dropping below the level

217

of her cap. Sapphie gave the butler a friendly prod in the stomach with her riding crop as she strode past him.

'Good morning, Miss Yates. Good morning, Miss Bomefield-Mullins,' the butler intoned, ignoring the liberty.

'Morning, Spince, where's the Mater?' Sapphie asked.

'Mrs Yates is in the drawing room, Miss,' he answered. 'They are expecting you.'

'I bet they're not,' Sapphie answered him. 'Lead the way then.'

Spince closed the door and they followed him across the hall. As he opened the drawing room door Holly tried to hang back, only to be given a swift stroke of the whip across her behind and hustled inside by Sapphie. Behind her the door closed with a click.

Everybody in the room turned to look. Her own mother was nearest, in an armchair, mouth coming slowly open as she took in Holly's condition. Cicely Yates sat a little further away, on a settee beside her husband, Cyprian, who was in a suit of lavender-coloured twill. In the next chair was Lord Cary, staring. Kitty Mullins stood respectfully by one window, her hands on the shoulders of Holly's two half-sisters. Only her half-brother was absent. Lord Cary was the first to find his voice.

'Kitty, take the children upstairs, if you would be so kind.'

Kitty nodded and immediately began to steer her charges towards the door, both gaping with open, childish curiosity at Holly's belly. Sapphie perched herself on the arm of the settee, beside her mother. She had collected a cigar on her way across the room, and began to prepare it. Holly found her voice.

'Mother . . . everyone. I, ah . . . have an announcement to make.'

Nobody spoke. She went on.

'I . . . I am to be married . . . to, er . . . Mr Herbert Maray, of Kerslake Manor, Devon.'

'Oh, Holly!' her mother sighed. 'How could –'

'Hold on,' Sapphie put in. 'I don't really think that recriminations are in order.'

'Aren't they, by God?' Toby Cary exclaimed.

'No,' Sapphie stated firmly, 'and I'll tell you why not in just one moment . . .'

She had paused as she struck a match, and drew deep on her cigar before speaking again. Not even her mother interrupted her.

'Recriminations,' she stated, 'are all very satisfying, but in this case, they are hardly appropriate. For starters, Mater, you and Pater married altogether too soon before I was born. Then there's you, Charlotte, who we know about, and Kitty of course. A fine lot you are to talk.'

'Yes,' Cicely snapped, 'and it is precisely because of our own mistakes –'

'That you expected us to know better,' Sapphie interrupted her mother. 'Well we don't, or at least, Holly doesn't. Damn it, Hazel and I aren't preggers, are we? I'd say we've done rather better, on the whole. Oh, and I know the three of you used to get milked too.'

'Milked?' Cicely demanded.

'Oh, really, Mater. Do you suppose you can keep a secret like that? Great Uncle Francis was a friend of old man Maray, wasn't he, and he tricked the three of you into coming into milk yourselves. Isn't that true?'

'Yes,' Charlotte Cary admitted weakly.

'That was Archibald Maray, the father of Jervis Maray, who virtually turned the thing into an industry, and uncle to Herbert Maray, Holly's intended.'

'Oh, you don't mean . . .' Charlotte squeaked, her eyes flicking to Holly's chest, where the milk was beginning to leak through.

'I'm afraid so,' Sapphie answered. 'Hazel too, and a fair few others. Sorry, Holly, but it was bound to come out sooner or later. Best out in the open, really, and at least you understood what was going on.'

Holly could say nothing, but only stare as Sapphie casually spilled out all her deepest secrets, and those of others too.

'How ... how do you know all this?' Cicely demanded.

'Oh, I've been talking to all sorts of people in the last few months,' Sapphie explained, 'but mainly to Hazel, whose mother has been rather less tight-lipped than she might have been over the years. So, we'll have a nice, amicable wedding, shall we, and perhaps it would be nice if Charlotte openly acknowledged Holly as her daughter?'

Charlotte gave a dumb nod.

'Good,' Sapphie went on, 'and nice generous presents, please. Oh, and Lord Cary, I'd appreciate a word, alone, and I understand you own a good camera?'

'I'll be having words with Kitty Mullins!' Cicely snapped as she reached for the bell-pull.

'I suggest you spank her,' Sapphie suggested. 'It's what you always used to do, wasn't it? Or was it the other way around?'

Both Cicely and Charlotte had gone crimson. Sapphie chuckled.

23

Kerslake Manor, Devon –
December 1940

'We can dispense with protocol for once, I suppose,' Sapphie stated. 'After all, there is a war on. You can stay in the room, Fatso. You too, obviously, Alexander.'

'Thank you, Sapphie,' Herbert answered, his voice rich with gratitude.

He was red-faced and sweating, his eyes shining with both lust and desperation. A spasm of irritation passed across Alexander Gorringe's face at her words, but he held his peace. It was plain why. All around the drawing room, naked or semi-naked girls sat or sprawled at ease. Sapphie had invited all those village girls she felt might want to indulge themselves, and even managed to reassure the Matrons by pretending that both men had gone to Exeter on official business.

Seven village girls had arrived, making eleven women in all, who had been drinking steadily all afternoon. Sapphie was the only one fully dressed, immaculate in her WAAF uniform, complete with mid-blue trousers tucked into calf-length leather boots. She also carried her riding crop, a combination which had left Herbert Maray staring opened-mouthed. Molly MacCallion still had her jacket, blouse, tie and cap, but was naked from the waist down, the result of an impromptu spanking dished out by Sapphie purely in order to warm things up. It had worked, combined with generous helpings of Champagne and port from the cellar, leaving the girls giggling and Molly rubbing ruefully at a sore bottom.

After Molly's spanking, little more encouragement had been needed. Sapphie had suggested they make punch, and soon Cora, Hazel and Anna had been topless as they took turns to milk themselves into a bowl. Between them they had provided two quarts, and none had bothered to replace her top. With so many girls bare, it had not been long before those already showing began to demand that the others strip too. As the bride to be, Holly had been first, rolled on the floor and stripped nude as the others held her down. Lucy, Sophie and Mary had complied without fuss, rolling their dresses down to show off their breasts. Jenny had followed, but gone further, as had her sister, not to be outdone, and Alice was now nude but for her stockings and sat in Alexander's lap. Sally had been last, and like Holly she had been held down and her clothes pulled off, leaving her stark naked.

'But you'll have to work for it,' Sapphie continued. 'You can be butler, just the job for you. And you're to keep your clothes on. Nobody wants to see your horrible body.'

'Yes, Sapphie.'

'That's "Miss Sappho" to you, Fatso.'

'Yes, Miss Sapphie . . . Yes, Miss Sappho.'

'That's better. Now pour some more Champagne, then put some more bottles outside to cool.'

'Yes, Miss Sappho.'

She gave a chuckle of satisfaction as he went to fetch the bottle from the sideboard. Champagne was served, and they set to drinking, growing quickly merrier, and lewder. Before long another spanking had been dished out, this time to Sally, held kicking and squealing across her big sister's lap as the others clapped in time to the slaps of hand on bottom cheek. Sapphie joined in, applying her riding crop to the quivering buttocks as Sally was held down by her sister and Lucy Linnel.

Revenge followed, Sally hauling Lucy to the floor and dishing out a thorough walloping with her victim's dress up and the big knickers torn wide at the back. Lucy took it fighting and screeching, but still had her bottom turned red and the stub of a candle stuck up her hole for good measure.

Holly watched it all, giggling over the spankings and growing ever more aroused. She was sure her turn would come, as the bride to be, but as Sapphie ordered Anna to atone for punishing her sister, Holly began to feel left out. Anna had to be held, and was bent down in a chair, her dress pulled up and her knickers removed. Sapphie put six thick weals across the huge white bottom and made Anna thank her on threat of a dozen more. The thanks came in a resentful mumble, which sent most of the girls into fits of drunken laughter. Anna got up as she was released, rubbing her bottom, a gesture at once so pathetic and so sweet that Holly found herself opening her mouth.

'What about me?'

Sapphie turned to look down at her.

'Yes, what about you, Holly? What shall we do with our blushing bride? Shall we send her into church with a dozen whip cuts decorating her pretty bottom, shall we?'

'Make 'em hard if you do,' Alexander suggested. 'They have to last two weeks! Better Puffer and I fuck her, one in each end.'

'That wouldn't be right!' Lucy responded immediately. 'Not before her wedding! Why, she's to be in white!'

There was an immediate gale of laughter. Holly found herself blushing and put an instinctive hand to her belly, but also smiling now that she was the centre of attention.

'Be gentle with her,' Anna urged. 'Look at her condition, and that whip does sting.'

'She can lick us all, in turn,' Cora suggested.

'We should take her out in the yard and pee on her,' Hazel laughed.

'Better milk,' Sophie put in.

'Milk and pee and all!' Hazel crowed.

'No, no, too easy on her!' Alexander stated. 'She needs her arse whipped, and a stiff prick where it'll do the most good!'

'No,' Sapphie said firmly, 'she goes on the clysopomp, and she gets the whip only if she gives in.'

'Excellent!' Alexander called. 'On the clysopomp with her!'

'No!' Holly squeaked. 'Not that . . . that's not fair . . . that's . . .'

She stopped as her protests met a gale of laughter. They closed in on her, Hazel and Molly taking her arms. She was pulled from the room, resisting, yet unable to stop laughing, out into the hall and through the back. It was cold outside, but the air only made the swimming of her head worse and her will weaker. She was still struggling as they dragged her out to the shed, but not hard, and with her dread of what was to be done to her warring for a desire to get exactly that.

She was still wriggling and begging when they reached the shed. When she saw Molly hurrying behind with the butter dish and thought of how it felt to have her anus greased and popped with the nozzle her pleas grew more urgent, and more real. They were still ignored, and she was bundled into the shed, fighting half-heartedly until Hazel began to tickle her under the armpits. She dissolved into giggles immediately and her fate was sealed.

The men had followed, but the girls took little notice of them, pressing into the shed until it was packed full, with barely enough space behind the clysopomp to stand. Unable to stop laughing, Holly was forced down on to the seat until her pregnant belly was resting on the bench and her bottom stuck well out behind. Somebody took her legs, making quick work of the straps. Others took her arms, pulling them forwards until she was resting on her belly. Her wrists were fastened, not the usual way, but to leave her sitting. She was still helpless, her bottom still well thrust out, with her cheeks wide to make her anus vulnerable, perfect for both an enema and a beating.

'Fill the tank!' Sapphie ordered. 'Use milk.'

The girls obeyed immediately, crowding around the tank, each trying to get her breasts over it. They were laughing so hard that much of the milk was wasted on the floor or over each other's skin as they struggled to aim it into the reservoir. Plenty went in though, splashing on the glass and into the rapidly rising pool until the tank held a good two quarts.

'Plenty, I should say,' Sapphie declared. 'Right then, up goes the tube!'

The girls had stood back at the order. Their milk was still coming, dripping from engorged teats and running down over already wet boobs and bellies and legs. Anna went to the butter dish, to scoop out a thick pat with her fingers. Holly began to struggle again at the thought of having her anus greased, but an instant later the butter had been slapped between her cheeks and Anna's thick middle finger had invaded her rectum. She gasped, then sighed as the finger began to move about up her bottom, wriggling and pulling in and out a few times to ensure that her ring was sloppy and loose. There was more laughter at her helpless reaction to having her bottom fingered, and more than one slapped her to make her cheeks bounce. Anna's finger came out. Holly farted, then squeaked as the nozzle was pressed to her bottom hole. Her mouth came open as the greasy little ring stretched, popped and her rectum had been invaded once more.

'No, girls, don't . . .' she managed, a last plea and to no more avail than the others as Sapphie twisted the valve on.

Holly gasped as warm milk began to flow into her rectum. The pressure came immediately, and in no time she could feel herself starting to bulge. The girls stood back and Holly squeaked in fear as Sapphie raised the riding crop, then again, in pain, as it lashed down across her bottom.

'Ow! You said you wouldn't!' she squealed. 'You said if . . . Ow!'

'Ah, but you do have such a darling bottom,' Sapphie said. 'Oh, very well, hold it, and you'll be spared.'

Holly snatched her breath and hung her head, struggling to contain the already painful pressure in her gut. With her womb distended and her bladder full from the Champagne, her rectum had quickly started to bloat. She could feel her anus pushing out behind her, so that she was forced to tighten the little ring to keep the nozzle in. The effort set her gasping and wiggling her toes, then shaking her head from side to side in her urgency as the awful, uncontrolled feeling of having so much milk up her bottom rose and rose with the fear of Sapphie's whip . . .

The others could see every detail and were laughing in delight at her helpless struggles. She tightened her bottom, clamping both cheeks together in a desperate effort to keep her enema in, determined not to disgrace herself by spurting on the floor, determined to avoid the cruel whip cuts . . .

A glance to the tank showed that about half the milk had flowed up her bottom. It was still coming. She moaned in despair, kicking in her straps, her anus pouting despite her desperate efforts to hold in her load, her teeth gritted, her head thrown back, the tube of her gut twitching . . .

Suddenly it was unbearable. She screamed as she let go. The nozzle exploded from her rectum. Her enema

226

burst out behind her, arcing out to splash on the floor, even as her bladder went and a great gush of piddle splattered on to the bench beneath her. The girls were screaming in delight and disgust. Holly could do nothing, and her audience dissolved into gales of drunken laughter as they watched the full contents of her rectum spurt and splash on the floor behind her. She hung her head, sobbing in relief as it all came out, too far gone to care for the display she was making of herself. The mess puddled on the floor beneath her, pee and milk, then lumps as she gave in completely and pushed out what remained inside her. The girls went silent as it came, save for the occasional muffled titter to the plop and splash of Holly's turds. Finally the last piece was out, and she collapsed as the remaining liquid bubbled from her gaping anus.

'Tut, tut,' Sapphie said calmly, 'what a disgusting mess. Now what did we say happens to girls who mess themselves?'

'The whip,' Holly mumbled in between gasps.

'The whip,' Sapphie repeated and brought her riding crop hard down across Holly's bottom.

Holly squealed as it struck, and farted, loudly. Her ring was still pulsing as the whip was lifted once more, and suddenly she was babbling for mercy, with real feeling in her voice.

'You big baby,' Sapphie remarked. 'Into the dairy with her, girls, I've not finished with her yet.'

Immediately willing hands were at Holly's straps. She was released and helped up, supported from the shed to the dairy. There was no question of what was going to happen, no question of what she wanted. She went, unresisting. She was bent over. A sponge was applied to her bottom. She was laid on her back on the bench of a milking frame. Her thighs came open in invitation.

The girls crowded round, huge breasts hanging over her, laughing as they milked themselves over her swollen belly, until it was running down the sides. Holly began to rub it in, smoothing it over her skin. Her knees came up, one hand reached for her sex, and she was masturbating, surrendered to her need and indifferent to who saw. The girls went quiet, suddenly serious as they saw she wanted to come. Anna knelt down, offering one huge, dark nipple to Holly's mouth. Holly took it in, suckling eagerly. Hands found her knees, easing them gently apart. She glanced down, to find Jenny between her legs, eyes glazed with drink, plump face set in a happy smiled. Her hand was taken away, and Jenny's tongue replaced it.

As Jenny began to lick, other girls came closer. Bulging, milk-wet breasts squashed against Holly's face. More milk was squeezed out over her belly, her breasts and into Jenny's hair. Hazel began to suckle her, and Lucy, both kneeling low to get at her breasts. Still more came, until she was buried in soft, fat flesh, unable to see, or move, wriggling in her ecstasy as her quim was licked and her nipples sucked. Her belly was being licked too, girls lapping up their own milk and others'. Fingers were pushed into her quim, two, three, then a full fist, stretching her wide. Her bottom hole was penetrated, two fingers pushed easily up into the still slimy hole, and suddenly she was coming.

Her whole body contracted, then went into spasm. Milk spurted from her nipples into eager mouths. Her quim and anus clamped tight on the intruding hands. More milk filled her own mouth as Anna squeezed it out. For one long, glorious moment she was in a state of perfect bliss, squirming beneath the pile of milk-soaked girls with her body responding to every penetration and every touch, of mouth, vagina and anus, of breasts, nipples, belly and skin, until at the very peak of her orgasm it broke to a sudden wrenching feeling. She snatched her head from Anna's nipple, gasping in wordless panic before she found her voice.

'It's coming, it's coming, my baby's coming!'

'Oh nonsense, you silly thing,' Anna answered her. 'It's just your tummy button's popped out. Still, we'd best be careful. We were forgetting ourselves there, weren't we, girls?'

There was giggling agreement, and they began to disentangle themselves. At last Holly was able to see her own body. Sure enough, her tummy button had everted, to make a little fat sausage of flesh that stuck up from the top of her belly. She blew her breath out, lying back on the bench, only to start as Sapphie loomed over her, her slim figure and immaculate uniform in sharp contrast to the other girls' bare skin and fat breasts.

'My turn,' Sapphie announced.

Holly watched, trembling, as Sapphie's fingers went to the front of her uniform trousers. She was to be made to lick Sapphie, something far stronger, far more meaningful than licking Hazel, or Cora, or any of the other girls; something she wanted to be seen to do. The others had moved back, into a ring, some cuddling, some holding hands, all watching. Both men were there, Herbert behind Cora with his hands cupping her breasts, Alexander with his arms around Molly and Sophie. Holly's mouth came wide in submission, absolute and public, to her lover.

'I am yours, Sapphie,' she breathed. 'Do as you please.'

'That's my Holly, always eager,' Sapphie purred as her button came undone.

The blue trousers were pushed quickly down over Sapphie's slender hips, revealing tight silk knickers, cut high and with only the smallest trim. They followed and the golden puff of her pubic hair was on show in the V of her blouse. Holly gaped wider, her heart hammering with sudden need as Sapphie swung a leg up and over, to squat on Holly's head, legs braced apart, knickers taut under the bench.

The pouted lips of Sapphie's quim and the neat turn of her bum cheeks were just inches away from Holly's face. Above, the slender body rose, towering over Holly, to Sapphie's face, cool, serene and amused. Holly sighed and stuck her tongue out, ready for whatever she was to be made to do. The milk was still running slowly down over the dome of her belly and oozing from her teats. Her sex was still wet and ready, her bottom hole slack, her legs spread wide to show it all off, her body in a position of complete surrender.

Sapphie smiled and reached behind herself, to pull her bottom cheeks wide, spreading her anal butterfly and the tiny brown hole at the centre, also her virgin quim, the hymen stretched taut. Her anus pouted, showing a bright pink centre. Holly gaped wider still, wondering if Sapphie was determined to use her mouth as a toilet, and determined to take even that if it was what was wanted of her. Sapphie squatted, and suddenly Holly's tongue was on the wrinkled hole of her lover's anus, licking in wanton bliss, her nose pressed against the taut hymen, her eyes staring at the wrinkled pink folds of Sapphie's sex lips.

There were murmurs, of pleasure, of amusement, of shock, which seemed to come to Holly from a great distance. It didn't matter. She was where she should be, with her tongue up Sapphie's bottom, lapping up the earthy, female taste until her mouth was full of it and her head swimming with ecstasy. Sapphie sighed and wiggled her bottom into place. Her cheeks spread wider still over Holly's mouth, her anus opening to the eager tongue as she relaxed. Holly's licking grew more fervent still. Her own sex was twitching with need again, but she was sure nobody would dare attend to her.

Sapphie leaned forwards a touch and began to rub, squirming her sex in Holly's face. Suddenly Holly could barely breath. Her mouth was full of juicy, wet anal flesh, her face squashed beneath the firm little buttocks, her nose smothered in Sapphie's quim, the clit bumping over the bridge of her nose. Sapphie was using her face to masturbate on, and it felt wonderful. She heard Sapphie gasp in ecstasy and it was perfect, her lover using her face to come on, in front of an audience.

She was gasping for breath the moment Sapphie dismounted, but smiling happily as soon as her breathing quietened down. Everyone was still watching, some just smiling, more giggling behind their hands or bright eyed with arousal. Alexander's cock was out, erect in Molly's hand. He spoke.

'Well, I'm the best man, really I ought to fuck the bride! Don't you think so, Puffer, Sapphie?'

'Go ahead,' Sapphie said casually as she pulled her knickers and trousers up as one, 'be my guest.'

Holly felt an immediate sense of betrayal, but swallowed it, telling herself that she should be Sapphie's to give away. Alexander stepped forwards, grinning as he balanced his stiff leg. Suddenly Herbert spoke.

'Well, I'm not sure, really . . . if you should.'

'Fair enough,' Alexander declared happily. 'I'll have her up the bottom then!'

Herbert opened his mouth, but closed it as Cora squeezed his crotch. Alexander took Holly's ankles, to haul her legs up around her belly, spreading both quim and bottom for his attention. She gave a sigh as the thick stem of his cock came to rest on her sex, utterly surrendered to the penetration of her bottom hole.

'She looks open, but a spot of grease, I think, just the same,' he remarked. 'Where's the butter dish?'

'I left it outside,' Molly admitted.

'Oh, well, best use cunt-smear then – sorry, Puffer, old boy, just a dip to collect some cream . . .'

As he spoke his cock slid up Holly's vagina, deep in for a moment before being pulled out once more.

'Plenty!' he declared. 'She creams the way she milks, this one.'

231

He ended with a grunt as his cock-head pushed to Holly's anus. She felt her quim-cream squashed out between his helmet and the flesh of her ring and she was opening, her hole still slack after her enema. His cock-head went up, her anus tightened on the neck and he pulled back, making her hole pout.

'Tuppence more and up goes the donkey!' he said, and pushed.

Holly gasped as a good half of his cock was shoved into her rectum in one. Alexander laughed and pulled back a little. Most of his cock was now in her, and the pain of the rough push faded to pleasure as he began to work himself up more gently. Soon she was moaning in pleasure. Her hands went to her belly, feeling the swollen mound, then to her breasts, to squeeze gently, massaging herself as his cock moved in, deeper and deeper, pulling her anal ring in and out with each push.

Sapphie was looking down on her, cool and detached. Herbert was staring too, his cock now in Cora's hand. Sudden pity hit Holly and she opened her mouth. Cora smiled and led him forward by the cock, guiding his penis into Holly's mouth. Herbert groaned in pleasure as Holly began to suck, her head thrown back to take the thick cock in her throat, her body rocking to the motions of her buggery.

'Like a pig on a spit,' Alexander breathed. 'I'm going to make her ring clench too.'

A knuckle found Holly's sex and she was being masturbated. Herbert grunted in amusement and pushed his cock deeper into her mouth. Immediately she knew she was going to come. Her hands went to her boobs, squeezing them to start new milk. She began to rub it into her nipples, letting herself go, in wanton ecstasy as the motion of her buggery grew faster and the fat cock in her mouth was jammed deeper still.

Alexander rubbed harder, his knuckle moving on her clit in little circles. Her muscles began to twitch, her bottom cheeks tightened, her hands locked on her boobs and she was coming. So was Alexander, the instant her anus went into spasm, spurting the full load of his come deep in her rectum. He cried out, Herbert grunted and suddenly she was full of sperm at both ends, mouth and bottom. Milk squirted from her breasts as her hands tightened on them, to splash her neck and Herbert's cock as he rammed it home in her mouth, and her orgasm was fading.

Both men kept fucking, Alexander pulling out and immediately stuffing himself back up her slimy rectum, Herbert jamming his in until bubbles of sperm exploded from her nose. Unable to breathe, Holly went into a coughing fit, twisting her head off Herbert's cock to spew her mouthful of sperm on to the floor even as Alexander casually finished off up her bottom. She stayed down as he pulled out, her now sore anus closing with a wet noise behind his cock.

The girls helped her up, giggling over what had been done to her, infectious humour that quickly had her in embarrassed giggles. Sapphie ordered Hazel and Cora to mop up the mess they'd made, and the others made their way back to the yard, where Sapphie ordered them to clean up under the pump. Holly was helped in, and they were still laughing, even as the freezing water gushed over them. The others began to wash her, and themselves, at first with hands eager for plump flesh and wet crevices, but less so as the bitter cold began to penetrate their senses. They finished in haste and ran indoors, to find towels and wrap themselves up in front of the blazing fire in the drawing room.

The shock of washing outdoors brought an end to the party. Dusk was beginning to gather, and the village girls decided to leave, keen to get back across the moor before nightfall. Holly kissed each goodbye, giggling drunkenly and hugging them even as she made babbled apologies for her lewd behaviour.

With the last of the local girls gone, those left collapsed in the drawing room. Herbert served Champagne and they began to drink and talk, first in high delight over what had been done, then discussing their lives and at last growing maudlin as the war intruded. Holly, drunk and exhausted, made little contribution, but sat wondering how she would cope with marriage to Herbert when she was so deeply in love with Sapphie. It had begun to grow dark when the crunch of tyres on gravel interrupted their conversation.

'Who the hell's that?' Alexander demanded.

'Some more girls, maybe,' Herbert answered him, peering from the side of the curtain.

'In a car? Don't be . . .' Sapphie queried and stopped. Herbert had frozen, his face white.

'It's Reginald Thann!' he squeaked.

'Thann?' Sapphie demanded. 'I thought you'd put him off!'

'Well, I . . . that is . . .' Herbert started to bluster.'

'For goodness' sake!' Sapphie snapped. 'You are an imbecile, Fatso, a buffoon!'

'I'm sorry, I . . .'

'Be quiet! I need to think!'

'Couldn't . . . couldn't we, you know, have her play the slave for him, and just take the picture when it gets juicy?'

'Don't be absurd! Look at her! She's eight months pregnant, you moron!'

'Stick her in the Hotbox then,' Cora suggested, 'and put the rat cage on her head. That way she won't even be recognisable in the picture.'

'Sharp thinking, that girl!' Sapphie answered. 'Come on, Holly.'

Sapphie snatched for Holly's wrist, pulling her up. Holly came, still dizzy with the drink and the sex, stumbling repeatedly as she was dragged to the door. Sapphie let go as Hazel came to put an arm around

Holly's waist. Cora joined them and they left, Holly half-walking, half-carried between them. Behind her she heard Sapphie's rapid-fire orders, and Herbert's voice raised in plaintive query.

'But where are we supposed to get any rats?'

'Don't be afraid,' Hazel assured her as they stumbled out into the yard.

'I . . . I don't know . . .' Holly managed. 'What . . . what if he lets the rats go? What if . . .?'

'They won't get rats,' Cora assured her. 'Just a picture of him and the Hotbox with you inside will be enough.'

'But Herbert said . . .'

'Oh, you can't worry what Herbert says. He's going to be your husband, after all. Who takes notice of her husband?'

'Yes, but . . .'

They had reached the Hotbox. Hazel opened it and Holly allowed herself to be fixed into place, still protesting even as the clamps were fitted into place. As her neck was secured Sapphie appeared with the head cage.

'No, please,' Holly managed. 'Not that . . . Can't I just be like this? Isn't it enough?'

'You'd be recognisable in the picture,' Cora insisted. 'You don't want that, do you?'

'No, but . . .'

'Hurry up!' Sapphie urged. 'Molly's serving him Champagne, and she's still nude. He's impressed – Alexander's told him she's been made a slave by the Russian techniques. This will work, Holly, easy as pie.'

'What about you?' Hazel asked as the cage was fitted over Holly's head despite her muffled protests.

It was too small, designed for a much smaller woman, while the mass of her hair had caught at the back, pushing her face forwards against the wire of the inner door.

'I'll hide,' Sapphie answered Hazel. 'Where the hell does this strap go? Ah, yes.'

Holly found the wire mesh pressed harder still to her face as Sapphie tightened the leather strap behind her head. The tip of her nose and the flesh of her lips and cheeks had pushed through the mesh in little bulges, and she was barely able to open her mouth.

'Not like this!' she managed, no more than a mumble.

'Don't worry,' Sapphie assured her. 'Must run. Be calm, Holly.'

Sapphie ran off towards the dairy, leaving Holly with her fear rising sharply through the haze of alcohol in her head. She was trapped, absolutely unable to move, with bits of her face bulging through into the inner enclosure of the cage. If rats were put in, only the outer door needed to be opened and they would be able to get at her flesh.

'Be brave,' Hazel said as she closed the Hotbox lid.

Even as the darkness descended, Holly felt her panic rising up. It was worse than before, a hundred times worse. Not only her body was confined, but also her head, painfully compressed in a wire cage into which a man obsessed with her submission was about to introduce rats. They'd attack her, she was sure. He was bound to be too stupid to realise that she'd be hurt if the outer door was lifted, or he wouldn't care, or he'd want to . . .

Maybe her looks meant nothing to him. Maybe he'd be prepared to sacrifice her face to make her more dependent still, so hideously ugly that nobody else would want her . . .

She screamed, the sound bursting from her throat as panic and horror overwhelmed her. She began to fight in the box, struggling against the hard wood, her inability to escape only making her more frantic, more urgent, more terrified . . .

The lid opened.

Holly looked up, her heart hammering, her muscles jumping in raw terror. Someone was looking down at her, not a man, but a woman, thin, old, her face little more than a skull, and half hidden behind a veiled black bonnet. The woman's eyes burned into Holly's, without a shred of sympathy or sanity. The thin mouth curved up into a cruel smile and she spoke.

'A plaything, for me? How kind . . . Oh, where can Jervis be . . . Oh, where . . . silly me, he's dead.'

The expression on her face flickered to sorrow, to anger, to sorrow and back to cruel glee, a mad dance of emotions. Her arm came up in a single jerk, raising her gloved forearm. Holly screamed with the full power of her lungs.

The woman merely chuckled, then ducked down. Holly froze, her skin crawling. The woman was investigating the Hotbox. At any moment it would swing open. She would feel the cool air on her skin, then the steel tips of the horrible glove, on her breasts, on her belly . . .

Again she screamed. This time the crash of a door answered her, and voices, Alexander's then another, the man who had come before, Thann.

'She's close to fully trained. All . . .'

'Who the hell are you?'

The woman rose, turning towards the house with her face set in icy haughteur. She spoke.

'I might ask the same of you. Off with you, immediately!'

'Are you mad, woman?'

Fury showed in the woman's face. She stepped from the box, out of Holly's sight. Alexander called out in alarm, his warning cut off by a horrid, bubbling scream and Holly's world went black.

Holly came round to dim light and faces crowding around her. A bottle was pressed to her lips. She swallowed, felt the sting of brandy and started to cough. Immediately she was being propped up, her back patted, with a buzz of concerned voices all around her. Events came back as her head cleared. Fear welled up, only to sink as quickly. She found herself talking.

'Did you get the rats?'

She realised what a bizarre question it was even as she said it. Sapphie gave her a worried look. Someone behind her pressed a cool flannel to her forehead.

'How are you feeling?' Sapphie asked.

'Strange,' Holly managed. 'What happened? What about Thann? Who ... who was that woman? Is she gone?'

'That was Genevieve Maray,' Alexander answered her.

'You needn't worry about Thann,' Sapphie added. 'Or Genevieve. Now just relax. Hazel, keep an eye on her.'

Sapphie moved back, and the two men. Hazel took their place, putting a finger to her lips as Holly began to babble questions.

'Shh,' Hazel urged. 'You're fine, and baby's fine. We've locked the old woman in the shed with the clysopomp. Now just lie back and don't get in a take.'

Holly obeyed. Her head cleared slowly as Hazel tended to her, but was still full of questions. In the background she could hear others talking; Sapphie urgent and commanding, Herbert frightened, Alexander doubtful.

'Burn the Hotbox and the story becomes simple,' Sapphie was saying. 'He came to visit, went out to inspect the strip and she set on him.'

'Yes, but they'll ask questions!' Herbert bleated. 'They'll want to know what he was doing here, what she was doing here!'

'He's been here before,' Alexander pointed out. 'He is connected with the Ministry, and he is my uncle. As for her coming here, where else would you expect her to go? It is her house, you know, technically. And it's hardly our fault she got out of the bin, is it?'

'He's right,' Sapphie insisted. 'We just need to stick to our story and keep mum. She caught him across the face, he trod in the butter, fell backwards and brained himself on the wall.'

'And how are you going to explain the butter dish . . .'

Holly collapsed back into the pillows, too drained to take in more than one thing from the conversation. Reginald Thann was dead.

24

Kerslake Village, Devon –
December 1940

Holly looked up to the steeple of Kerslake Church, then abruptly down as her wedding dress tightened over her swollen belly. Despite her best efforts, and those of several other girls, with advice from yet more, it was blatantly obvious she was pregnant. Her belly stuck out as a round, hard hump, impossible to hide, while her breasts had swollen to make two huge, fleshy balloons, from both of which milk leaked continuously.

It was hideously embarrassing. At least with the station staff and the village girls swollen breasts and milk stains were the norm, if not swollen bellies. The vicar at Kerslake had been a different matter, and had only been persuaded to perform the ceremony by the promise of herself and Herbert contributing to parish life in the future. The interview, and her subsequent attendances at church had been agonising, especially the banns. As future wife to the future Squire, she was naturally the focus of attention, and the condition she was in had come to form a topic of gossip more popular even than the war. People had been coming for miles to catch a glimpse of her. If anything, it had been worse than telling her mother.

Now, even with the invited guests inside the church, the graveyard and the streets to each side were full of people, some pretending to be doing something else, most staring openly. Beneath her veil, her face was scarlet with blushes. To make matters worse, Sapphie had insisted that their father give her away, Cyprian Yates, whose bouffant hair and affected mannerisms were drawing almost as many sniggers and whispered comments as Holly's condition.

It wasn't Sapphie's only decision. After Reginald Thann's death she had held the rest of them together, always calm and always confident. The facts had been accepted without further investigation, and Genevieve Maray locked up more securely than before. For once Holly had felt grateful for the war. She still felt nervous and insecure, and often the image of Genevieve's face had come to haunt her in her sleep. Like the others, she had given not the slightest resistance to Sapphie's assumption of control. Even the village Matrons approved.

She had begun to feel resentful, though, and now understood Hazel's lifelong attitude to Sapphie. To surrender sexually was bliss, but Sapphie took it beyond that, to full control. Yet it was so easy just to give in, to surrender her responsibility absolutely. It had, she realised, always been that way, whether it was being in the straps on a milking machine or the clysopomp so that she could be taken advantage of, or under Sapphie's orders as cocks were pushed into her mouth and up her bottom at the same time. To temper surrender with resentment was easy, to rebel impossible.

Even her future life had been organised. Marriage would make no difference, and at Kerslake she would live as subordinate in her work and little more than a slave in her private time. When and if the war ended in victory, Sapphie would remain with her, in charge, with Hazel as maid.

Sapphie had organised just about every detail of the wedding, riding roughshod over the opinions of Holly,

Herbert, both families and anybody else who became involved. Only when she had been unable to provide had others been allowed to step in, as with the silk for the dress, provided by Alexander Gorringe. The actual sewing had been done by May and her daughters, as closely supervised by Sapphie as duty allowed.

Cyprian turned to her, smiling, and motioned towards the church, only to stop. A latecomer was hurrying in beneath the lichgate, a woman in an extravagant crimson gown ten years out of date and several sizes too small, with a bonnet to match, but apparently no hair beneath it.

'Good heavens,' Cyprian remarked as the woman disappeared into the church.

'A Miss Slater,' Holly said, with a glance to the confection of mauve silk her father wore as a cravat. 'We had best go in.'

Cyprian offered his arm. Holly took it and allowed herself to be walked slowly forward, down the gravel path and into the church itself. Molly and Hazel fell into step behind her. The Wedding March struck up, and for the thousandth time she found herself wondering what she was doing. Life had been so simple, and now she was heavily pregnant, in milk and getting married to the man responsible for both.

Herbert was stood before the vicar, looking fatter than ever in his tails. Alexander was beside him, in full uniform, his damaged leg barely noticeable beneath his trousers. Holly stifled a sigh at the contrast between the two and tried to think of how it had always been Herbert she wanted, at least when it came to being ravished while tied helpless and ready for cock.

She reached his side. The vicar gave her a welcoming smile and the ceremony began. As Herbert stumbled his way through the responses, she found herself glancing back. Sapphie was looking at her, steely-eyed. The vicar had reached her part.

'I do,' she answered sullenly.

She was Mrs Maray, but she was Sapphie's slave.

The service over, they returned to the Manor in the Austin, with the guests trailing behind along the lane. Holly accepted Herbert's fondling of her leg as his right, just as she knew she would accept Sapphie's authority. Both were going to enjoy her body, thoroughly. With Herbert there was a balance. He would be good to her, if not faithful, and use her only when she gave in to him. Sapphie was different. Sapphie would do as she pleased.

Deep down she knew it was what she wanted, and by the time they reached the Manor she had decided it was right. Sapphie would always be above her, dominant, decisive, completely in control, untouchable save as she herself ordained, a goddess. That way at least Holly could keep her pride, knowing that the woman she worshipped was worthy of that respect, that she never yielded her dignity.

She was smiling happily as she climbed from the car. In the short journey from the church she had come to accept her true nature. Suddenly life was simple again. She went through the greetings in a state of rosy euphoria, as she had always imagined her wedding day. True, her feelings were not for the man by her side, but in marrying him she had found her place, security and the love she had never dared hope she would be able to express, for Sapphie, her own half-sister.

As soon as she had greeted the last of the guests, she sought Sapphie out, finding her in the drawing room, talking to Alexander Gorringe.

'Who is the seedy-looking man with his daughter, talking to Molly?' Sapphie was asking.

'That?' Alexander replied. 'But of course you've never met him. Bob Tweedie, and that's not his daughter, that's Vera, his best girl.'

'Bob Tweedie, the pimp?' Sapphie demanded.

'That's the fellow.'

'You invited a pimp and his tart?'

'Yes, but be fair,' Alexander answered her. 'He's a spiv too. Where d'you think the silk for Holly's dress came from?'

'I might have guessed,' Sapphie snapped. 'Well, he's being altogether too familiar with Molly.'

'Don't worry. They know each other. She was one of his, Cora too.'

'Molly and Cora? Tweedie's tarts? So that's how you got them to join in with your dirty little scheme. You'd better watch your step in future, Gorringe.'

Alexander Gorringe began to stutter. Holly smiled to see that even he was awed by Sapphie, only for her mouth to come slowly open as the significance of what he had said sank in. Even as she struggled for the right words to express herself he spoke again, defensively.

'Be fair, Sapphie, we aren't all born with a silver spoon in our mouths. Molly was offered employment as a maid and got kicked out. Cora was over here as cook to some Yankee family and got dumped when they took on somebody else. Both of them would have starved if it weren't for Tweedie. It's a necessary service, anyway. Look at Roberta.'

'Roberta?'

'Roberta Slater, big woman in the crimson dress and the enormous hat.'

Sapphie turned in indignation to where Roberta had joined Eliza and Ned Grant. Holly caught the conversation.

'Roberta?' Eliza asked. 'Whatever has happened to your hair?'

'It was shaved off,' Roberta answered sullenly, 'and you were right, Mrs Grant, and I owe you an apology. I should never have gone.'

'Least said, soonest mended,' Eliza answered, 'and a lesson learned, no doubt.'

'Yes,' Roberta admitted with feeling. 'Now I've need of a word with Mr Gorringe, excusing me.'

She turned to them, her face set in determination.

'And what can I do for you, Roberta?' Alexander asked.

'You can give me what I'm owed,' Roberta answered, 'begging your pardon, Miss Holly ... Mrs Maray, I should say, and congratulations ...'

'How dare you?' Sapphie interrupted in a hiss. 'This is a wedding reception.'

'That's as may be,' Roberta answered, 'but I'm in no mind to wait. Abused, that's what I've been, by that Lord Farthinghurst. Mad he is, no more sense than old Genevieve, and near on as cruel.'

'Well, you got paid, didn't you?' Alexander put in. 'I don't see what you're so browned off about.'

'I got paid, yes, sir, but not near enough, not for that.'

'This is no place for your sordid discussion!' Sapphie hissed. 'You will leave immediately, Roberta.'

'I'll leave when I've what's due to me, and the half above,' Roberta answered.

'Get out!' Sapphie snapped. 'How dare you come in here, a common prostitute –'

'That I may be,' Roberta answered, 'but I'm no worse than you, for all your airs and graces, Miss Yates.'

'How dare you?'

'I dare, 'cause I've heard, from Lucy Linnel –'

'Get out, this instant!'

'How Genevieve Maray started – that was, same as you –'

'Out!'

Sapphie snatched at Roberta's arm. Roberta jerked away, her face red with anger. Again Sapphie snatched, only to be caught by the wrist. Roberta twisted. Sapphie yelled in wordless outrage. Roberta dropped heavily into a chair. Sapphie was dragged down, helpless against Roberta's weight and strength, but still yelling, twice as loud as before as she realised what was about to happen to her.

'No!' she screamed. 'You cannot! You cannot! Let go! I order you to let me go!'

'No,' Roberta answered. 'You're due a spanking, and a spanking's what you're getting, you wilful, spoilt little brat.'

Sapphie went wild, lashing out with her free hand, kicking with desperate energy, screaming with fury at the impossible indignity about to be inflicted on her. Roberta's face set in stolid determination as she clung on, barely flinching as Sapphie's nails raked her leg.

'You cannot do this!' Sapphie screamed. 'You cannot!'

'I can, seems so,' Roberta answered and set about stripping her victim.

Holly could only stare in open-mouthed horror as Roberta took a firm grip on the hem of Sapphie's immaculate uniform skirt and pulled.

'No!' Sapphie screamed.

The skirt tore.

'Stop, I order you to stop!'

The skirt seams split wide. Sapphie's stockinged legs came on show.

'No! Put me down this instant!'

The ruins of the skirt were jerked high. Two slices of creamy thigh flesh and a bulging, silk-covered bottom were revealed. Holly was not the only one watching, they all were. Alexander Gorringe was grinning, so was Herbert. Molly and Hazel were hiding giggles behind their hands. Eliza Grant seemed indifferent, Ned delighted. Even Sapphie's own mother wore a quiet smile as she watched her daughter prepared for spanking.

'Help me!' Sapphie squealed as a big hand closed on the seat of her knickers. 'Mother!'

Cicely shook her head. Roberta began to pull.

'No!' Sapphie wailed. 'No! I forbid it! No! Not that!'

The top of her bottom crease came on show.

'Not my knickers! No! No! No!'

Sapphie's pleas broke to a long, wordless scream as her precious garment was stripped down and her little round bottom exposed, her cheeks quivering with her emotion. The instant it was bare she went wild again, worse than before, a mindless, crazed tantrum, flailing wildly with her single free arm, shaking her head, kicking her legs. Her cap fell off, her shoes flew high, one, then the other, to crash onto the sideboard. Roberta calmly pulled the little silk knickers down and off. Sapphie's screams became ear splitting as her virgin cunt was put on view.

'Now, now,' Roberta chided, 'kick like that and you'll only go showing your rude bits. Best to take it like the lady you claim to be. Now, let's have that bottom up a little higher, shall we?'

Roberta kicked her knee up. Sapphie's bottom spread, to show off the little brown dimple of her anus and the dun-coloured marking around it.

'Why, what a funny little bum-button you have,' Roberta remarked. 'Just like a butterfly.'

Sapphie went berserk, thrashing, kicking, scratching, biting, screaming and cursing. Roberta waited until Sapphie's struggles had begun to die down, and then quite calmly began to spank the little bare bottom stuck up so helplessly across her muscular leg. With the first slap Sapphie burst into tears.

Holly let out a deep sigh. Roberta was right. Sapphie was no goddess, just a wilful, spoilt little brat.

NEXUS BACKLIST

This information is correct at time of printing. For up-to-date information, please visit our website at www.nexus-books.co.uk

All books are priced at £5.99 unless another price is given.

Nexus books with a contemporary setting

ACCIDENTS WILL HAPPEN	Lucy Golden ISBN 0 352 33596 3	☐
ANGEL	Lindsay Gordon ISBN 0 352 33590 4	☐
BARE BEHIND £6.99	Penny Birch ISBN 0 352 33721 4	☐
BEAST	Wendy Swanscombe ISBN 0 352 33649 8	☐
THE BLACK FLAME	Lisette Ashton ISBN 0 352 33668 4	☐
BROUGHT TO HEEL	Arabella Knight ISBN 0 352 33508 4	☐
CAGED!	Yolanda Celbridge ISBN 0 352 33650 1	☐
CANDY IN CAPTIVITY	Arabella Knight ISBN 0 352 33495 9	☐
CAPTIVES OF THE PRIVATE HOUSE	Esme Ombreux ISBN 0 352 33619 6	☐
CHERI CHASTISED £6.99	Yolanda Celbridge ISBN 0 352 33707 9	☐
DANCE OF SUBMISSION	Lisette Ashton ISBN 0 352 33450 9	☐
DIRTY LAUNDRY £6.99	Penny Birch ISBN 0 352 33680 3	☐
DISCIPLINED SKIN	Wendy Swanscombe ISBN 0 352 33541 6	☐

- - - - - - ✂ -

Please send me the books I have ticked above.

Name   ....

Address   ....

....

....

.... Post code..................

Send to: **Cash Sales, Nexus Books, Thames Wharf Studios, Rainville Road, London W6 9HA**

US customers: for prices and details of how to order books for delivery by mail, call 1-800-343-4499.

Please enclose a cheque or postal order, made payable to **Nexus Books Ltd**, to the value of the books you have ordered plus postage and packing costs as follows:
UK and BFPO – £1.00 for the first book, 50p for each subsequent book.
Overseas (including Republic of Ireland) – £2.00 for the first book, £1.00 for each subsequent book.

If you would prefer to pay by VISA, ACCESS/MASTERCARD, AMEX, DINERS CLUB or SWITCH, please write your card number and expiry date here:

....

Please allow up to 28 days for delivery.

Signature ....

Our privacy policy

We will not disclose information you supply us to any other parties. We will not disclose any information which identifies you personally to any person without your express consent.

From time to time we may send out information about Nexus books and special offers. Please tick here if you do *not* wish to receive Nexus information.   ☐

- - - - - - ✂ -